ANGRY WATER

Kirk House Publishers

An Outdoor Adventure

ANGRY WATER

ALLEN THEISEN

Angry Water: An Outdoor Adventure
Copyright © 2023 by Allen Theisen

Paperback ISBN: 978-1-959681-05-2
eBook ISBN: 978-1-959681-06-9
Hardcover: 978-1-959681-07-6

Library of Congress Number: 2022923709

Artistry Credit: Brittany Rose-Vianney Huebl
Cover Image: Book Brush
Cover and Interior Design by Ann Aubitz
Published by Kirk House Publishers

Kirk House Publishers
1250 E 115th Street
Burnsville, MN 55337
612-781-2815
Kirkhousepublishers.com

MAPS

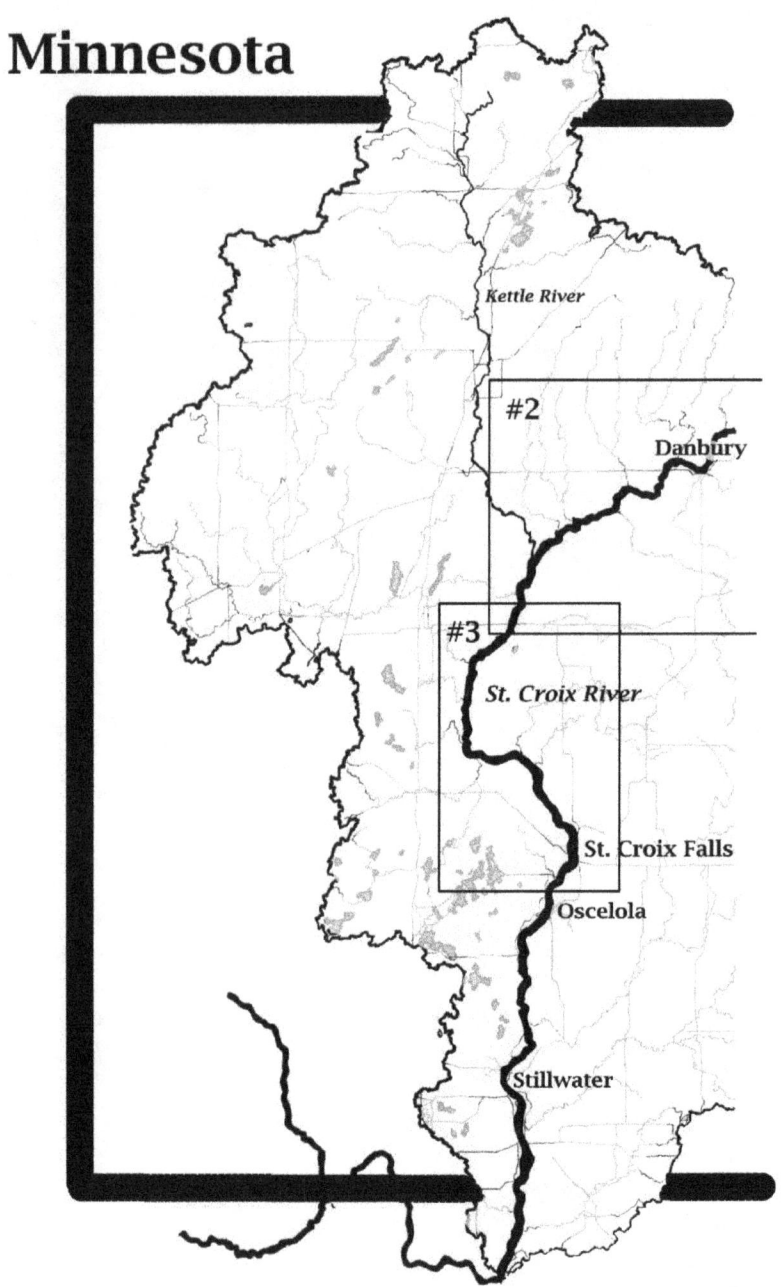

Minnesota

Kettle River

#2

Danbury

#3

St. Croix River

St. Croix Falls

Oscelola

Stillwater

Wisconsin

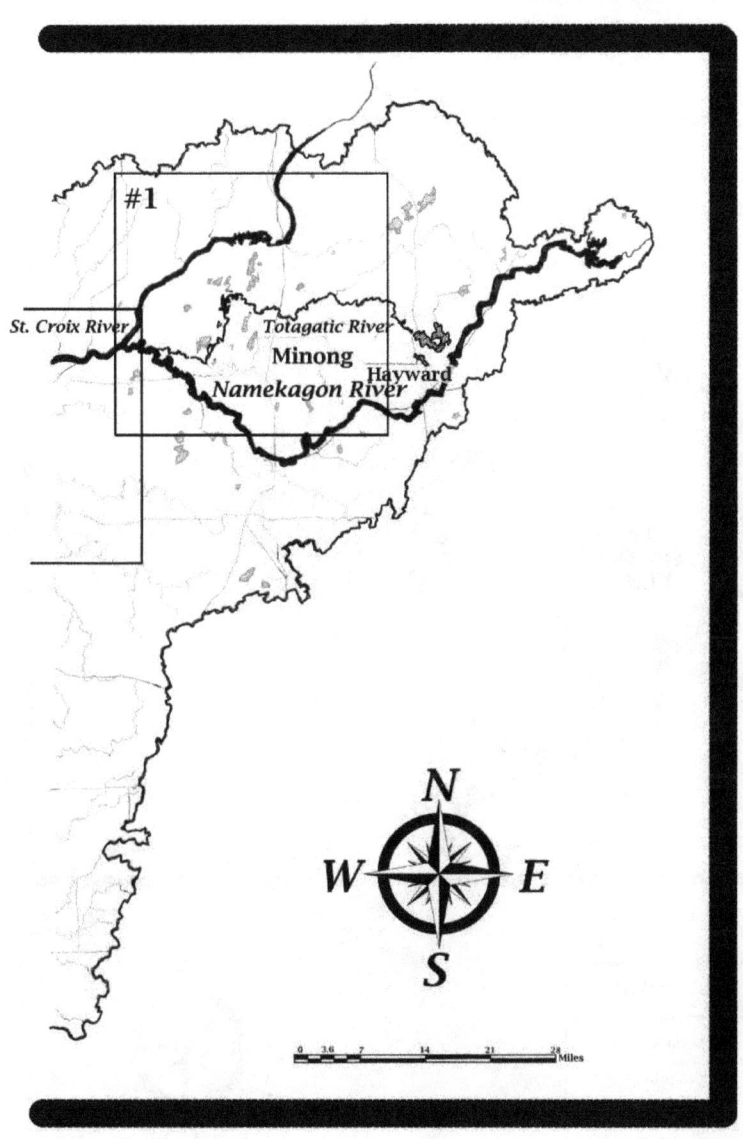

#1- Drop in point to the St. Croix River

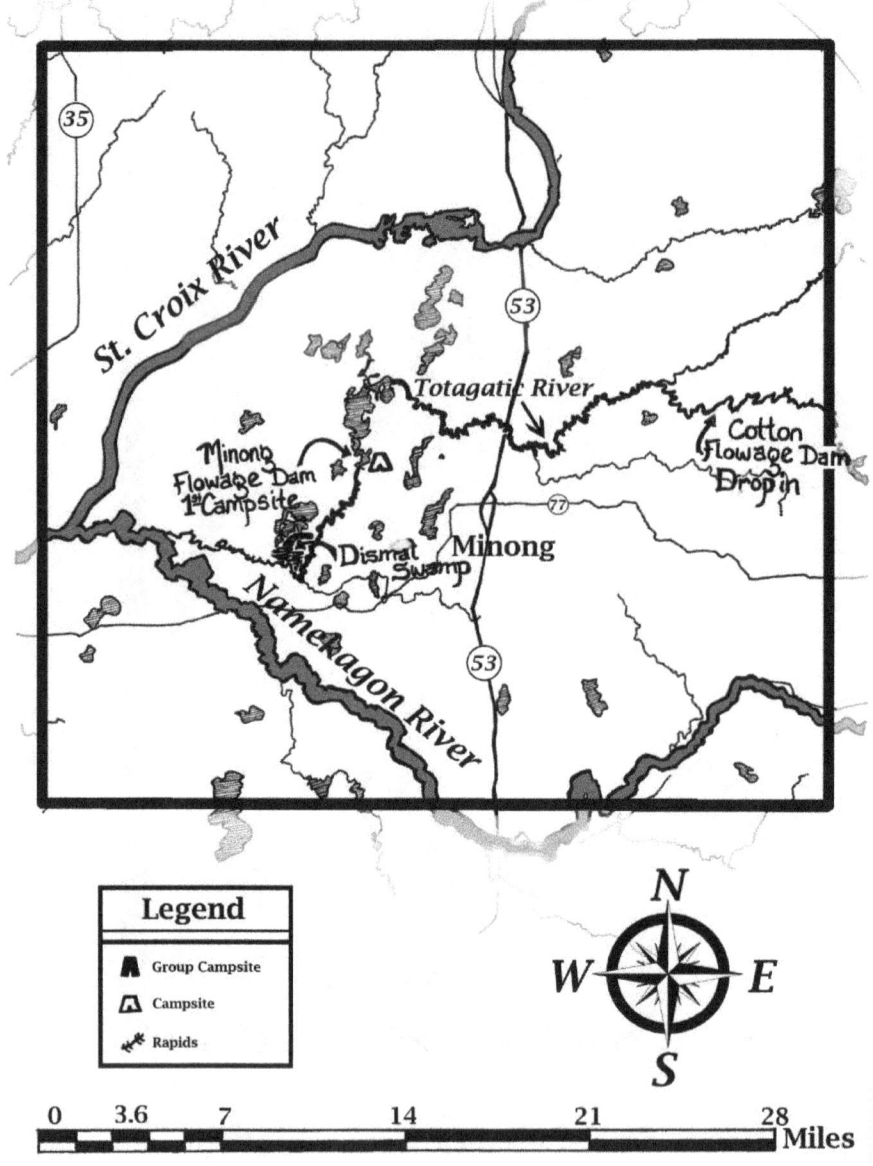

#2- Riverside Landing to Hwy 70 Bridge

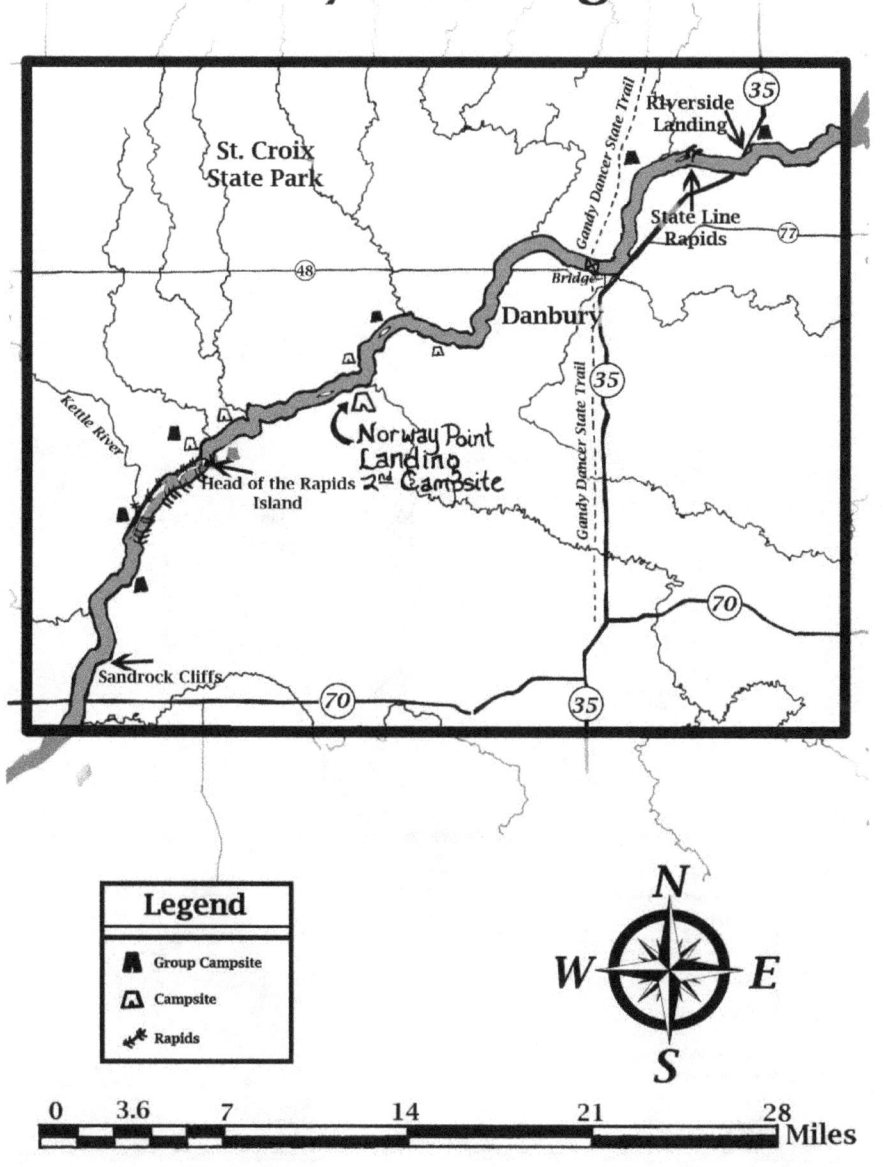

St. Croix State Park

Riverside Landing

Gandy Dancer State Trail

State Line Rapids

Bridge

Danbury

Kettle River

Norway Point Landing 2nd Campsite

Head of the Rapids Island

Gandy Dancer State Trail

Sandrock Cliffs

Legend

▲ Group Campsite

◮ Campsite

🪷 Rapids

N
W   E
S

| 0 | 3.6 | 7 | 14 | 21 | 28 Miles |

#3-Hwy 70 Bridge to St. Croix Falls

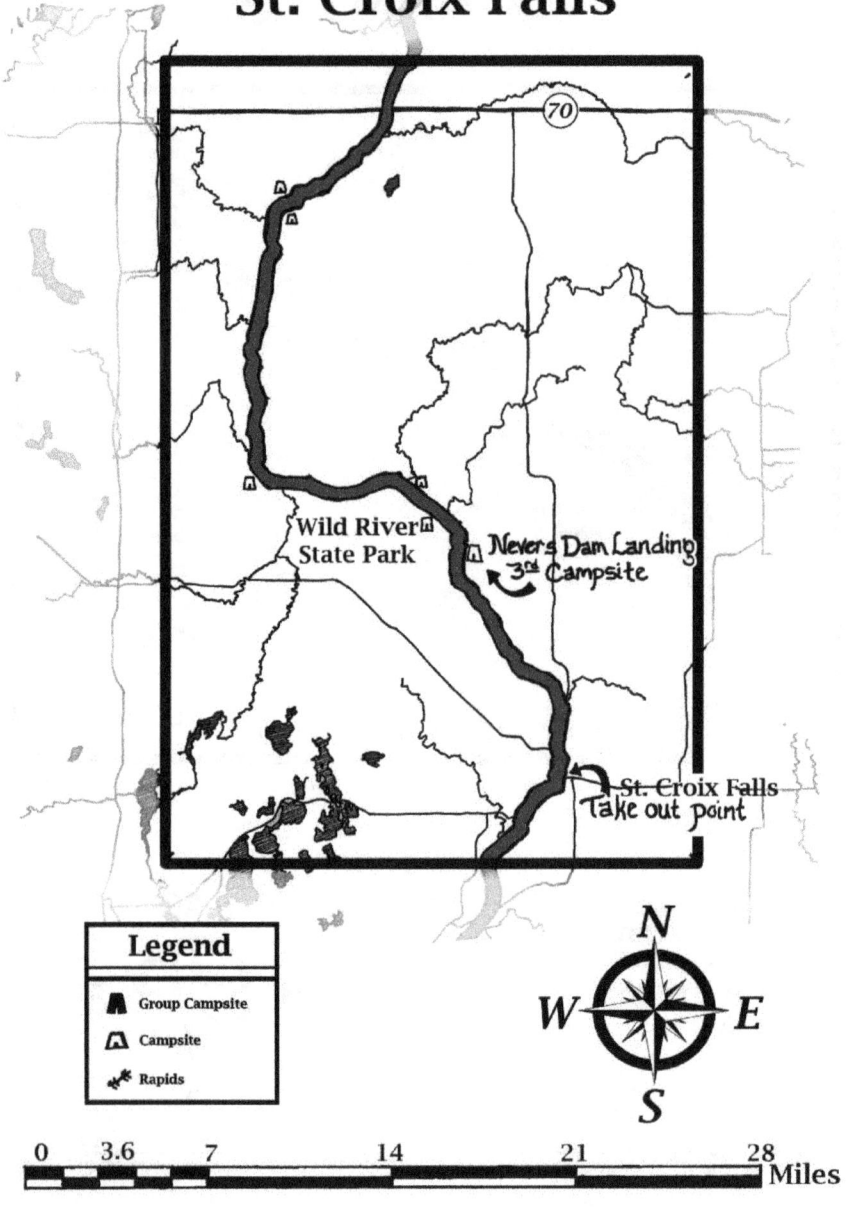

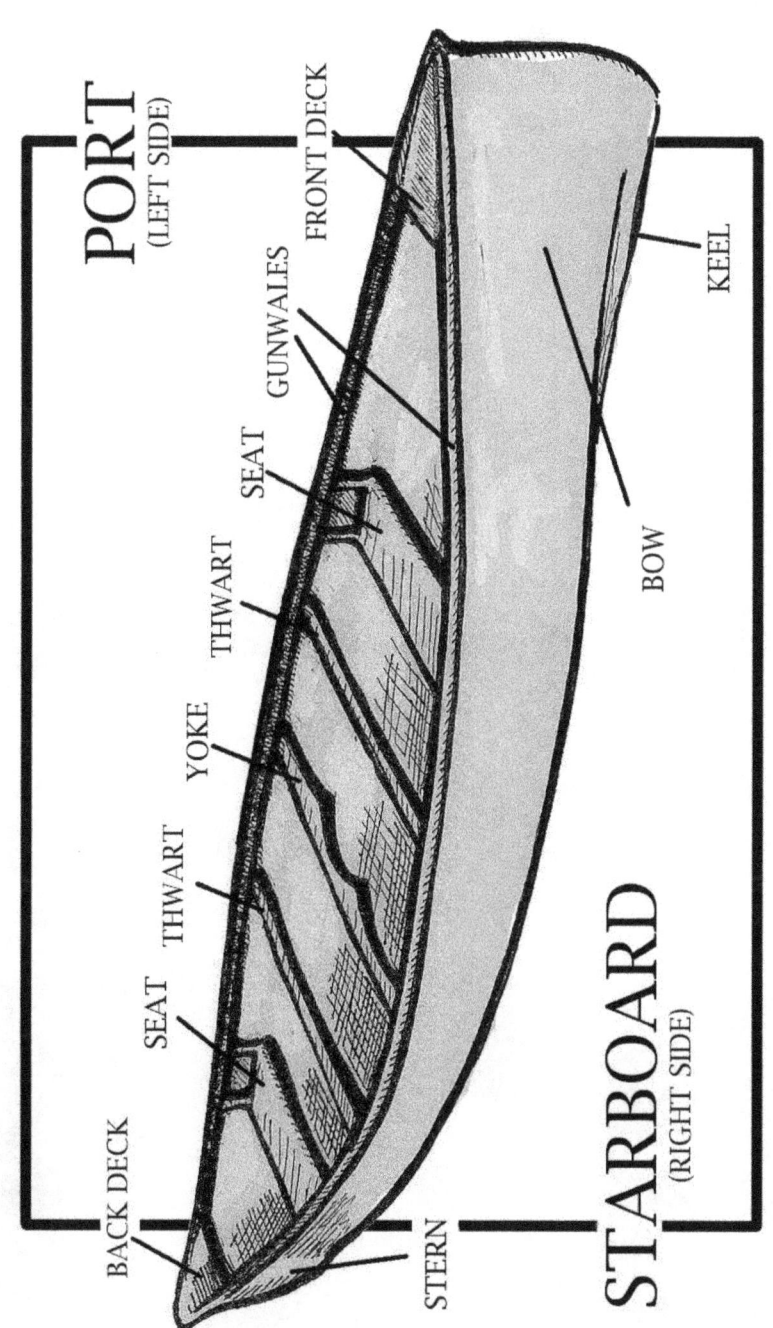

PORT
(LEFT SIDE)

STARBOARD
(RIGHT SIDE)

FRONT DECK

GUNWALES

SEAT

THWART

YOKE

THWART

SEAT

BACK DECK

STERN

BOW

KEEL

1

It Begins Again

The raging torrent of froth and waves churned below where John stood. Branches torn from riverbank trees poured over the dam. Deadfall dragged from the upstream shallows followed the branches, slamming into the raging water below. Logs and sticks bobbed in the wave action farther out as the water began to settle. A half mile out, the channel widened and water flowed over the riverbanks, trapping the debris against the forest edge.

John could see three canoes caught against the debris wall. The young men in two of the canoes cut and slashed at the debris, trying to break through the deadwood stopping them. He could hear them yelling, "Where are you! Hang on, we're coming!"

The empty third canoe twisted and bobbed in the water when half-submerged deadwood slammed into its side. He had to help them, but how could he reach them? John pulled out his phone and dialed 911. Two seconds after hitting send, *Beep-Beep-Beep*. No signal!

He cupped his hands around his mouth, inhaled deeply, and yelled, "I'll find help! Keep looking!" The water's roar muffled his voice so much that no one could comprehend his words.

John snapped his head left and right, looking for means to reach his friends. The remote shoreline held no docks, no boats, and no one else was in sight. Right before turning back toward the water, he caught a glimpse of something moving in the woods to his right. He snapped his head around again, but whatever his peripheral vision picked up had disappeared. The hair on the back of his neck stood up as he hyperfocused on the woods where he'd seen movement. The upright shadowy figure that had caught his eye could not have vanished that quickly. A broad cedar tree shielded the background a short distance into the woods—a perfect hiding place for whoever he saw.

He started toward the tree, intending to get help from whoever might be hiding behind it. Two steps into his pursuit, he felt a heavy shove on his back. John slid down the rocky bank and plunged into the raging water. When his head went under, the sound of churning, bubbling water filled his ears. Branches brushed by his legs and arms as they flailed in the heavy current. It seemed like forever before he surfaced, and when he did, John spit the river water from his mouth and gulped a huge breath of air.

Looking back to where he'd been standing, he swore he saw a person disappearing into the underbrush. Taking powerful swim strokes, John fought to reach the river's bank, dodging debris with every stretch of his arm. He paused to let a tangled mass of brush sweep past. As he started again, remnant branches caught his pant leg and dragged him downstream. He realized the strong current threatened to pull him under again, so he spun in the water, looking for something to help him. A few strokes away, an old log bobbed in the water. It slowly rotated in the river's eddies. Reaching the log, he swung both arms over the top, grabbing knobs left from branches long broken away.

The three canoes were still some distance away. John closed his eyes and tried reasoning through his options to reach his friends. He probably wouldn't float directly to their location. Unfortunately, swimming in the fast water wasn't an option. The tree line meant shallow water. He could wade from wherever he landed, but the log reaching the tree line was a problem too. It weighed hundreds of pounds and would crush him if he was between the shoreline and log.

John opened his eyes to gauge the log's twisting motion and discovered he was moving away from the canoes. In a panic, he kicked his legs, hoping to affect the log's direction. It changed, but not as expected. Instead of moving downstream, he and the log floated upstream. Ten seconds later, he seemed to float across the current. After another few seconds, downstream again. John pulled himself higher onto the log, hoping to gain a better perspective on what was happening. Horror filled his mind at what he saw. The log was caught in a backwater current moving in a circular motion. The rushing water over the dam created a back current along the near shore. A whirlpool!

Each trip around the whirlpool brought the log closer to the center. John dared not let go of the log because he couldn't fight the current. He could see smaller branches sucked down at the whirlpool's center. Each trip around the center was speeding up. He didn't have much time.

He called out to his friends in the canoes. "Help!"

They were too far away to reach him before the log spun into the center. The log spun faster, tearing at John's grip. One hand slipped from the smooth tree's surface. A second later, the other gave way. He cried out again. "No! No!" The water pulled him under.

John's eyes flew open and he gasped for air. Bright sunlight from the window outlined a small figure standing in front of him. He slid the recliner up and forward, changing the sun's angle in his eyes. It was his son, Robby.

"Were you having a bad dream, Dad?" Robby seemed afraid to approach John, almost as if the dream's bad vibe would rub off on him. "You were yelling in your sleep."

Every year before they left, the same type of dream came to John. When he woke very early that morning, it still hadn't occurred and he believed the annual nightmare cycle was broken. Just after lunch, he felt sleep calling him, so he lay back in his recliner to catch a catnap. That's when it happened again.

"I'm sorry if I scared you, Robby. Yes, it was a bad dream, but I'm fine now." John reached out his arms and Robby came to him, hugging his midsection.

When Robby let go, he spun in his dad's arms to survey the equipment strewn across the living room. A single folding chair sat in the middle of the living room. The coffee table and ottoman were pushed back against one wall. Piles of gear surrounded the recliner. To the left sat pots, pans, cooking utensils, and a small bottle of dish soap. To the right, a tent and a coil of paracord lay on top of tarps. Two freshly varnished paddles leaned against the wall near the front door. Sleeping bags and pillows sat on the couch, waiting to be stuffed into the Duluth pack that lay alongside them. The last pile was the miscellaneous camping equipment sitting near the packs at the living room entrance. Robby spotted a hatchet and pulled away from John to pick it up.

"Careful with that hatchet, Robby. If the sheath comes off, the sharp edge could cut you."

"I will, Dad." Robby ran his fingers over the image of the two people canoeing on a lake. "How long will you and Mom be gone?"

"We'll be gone five days this year."

"I don't want to stay here with Grandpa and Grandma. Can I come with you?"

"When you're old enough to paddle on your own and carry a big pack, you can go on this trip. Besides, Gramps and Grams haven't seen you since Christmas. The last time you stayed with them you talked for days about how they spoiled you. You helped them feed all of their chickens, cows, and pigs. They took you to Mall of America and you came home with a big bag of Grandma's cookies."

"I'm big enough." Robby walked over and grabbed the shoulder straps of the food pack and lifted. The pack didn't budge. Robby's arms were barely thicker than the straps and they definitely weren't as wide. He strained with both arms, then looked over at his father. "Dad, help me put this on."

John walked over and gripped the thick loop sewn into the top of the pack. Campers typically tied a rope to the loop to hoist the pack into a tree so bears couldn't reach it. John lifted and Robby slid his arms through the straps. He grasped each strap with his hands just before John let go. Robby stumbled backward two steps. His arms flung wide, and his feet left the ground as gravity overpowered the young boy. His shirt slid halfway up his body as he did a half somersault over the bag. His trapped arms stretched and then pulled him back onto the bag.

Even though John knew what would happen, he couldn't hide his laughter. "You look like a turtle flipped over onto its back. Do you need some help?"

"No!" Robby replied as he slid his arms out of the straps and rolled over onto the floor. He pulled down his shirt and looked up at his dad with a disappointed face. "How old will I be when I'm strong enough to lift that?"

"I'd say probably fourteen. Seven years from now."

"I know, Dad. I can do math. But how come you and Mom go canoeing every year?"

"Good question. See that book lying over on the coffee table? Hand it to me and come sit on my lap." Robby walked over to the table and picked up the book. On the cover was a close shot of four guys next to three beached canoes on the edge of a narrow river. In the background was a torrent of water rushing over a dam. The camera picked up sunlight glistening off the mist, creating iridescent rainbows behind the canoeists.

John let his son absorb the front cover's details and then said, "Your mom made this book before she left for college. You recognize these guys, don't you?"

"Yah, that's you and the tall skinny one is Uncle Al. The short guy with big curly hair is Paul. I like him. He's fun. The last one is Tom and you call him Animal."

"That's right. You have a good memory. This book has photos from a trip we took before you were born."

"Wow! That's a lot of water." Robby pointed to the churning river in the background, and then he turned to his dad with a puzzled look on his face. "Wait a minute. Who took the picture?"

"Well, there was one more guy on this trip." John opened the cover to reveal a young man in an ROTC uniform. "This is Bob. He took this picture. We went on this trip because he was leaving to become a pilot. That takes a long time and we would miss him while he was gone. He is the reason we go camping every year."

Robby turned and looked at his dad. "Why? I don't understand."

John shut the album again and pointed at the cover photo. "The day Bob took this picture, we drove up north…"

2

On the Road

John saw the sign marking the road and let off from the gas. His Ford F250 had no trouble pulling the trailer full of gear, but he didn't want to jar the three canoes they had tied down to the makeshift rack.

His copilot Al was staring at the blue dot on his phone showing their location. They had been friends since elementary school and grew up not far from each other in Stillwater, Minnesota. They spent so much time together during summer vacations that some people thought they were brothers. As boys, they were both tall and skinny. Even though John had brown hair and Al's was blond, their hair looked similar because their parents took them to the same barber. Sharing so much time together similarly shaped their sense of humor. They joked between themselves as they spent countless hours together, but thoroughly enjoyed tag-teaming and poking fun at their friends. They knew each other's quirks and sometimes finished each other's sentences.

"Yup, that's the right road," Al said, showing John the phone. "Sometimes these township roads have more than one name. The map app does fine with state and county roads, but I don't always trust it when I'm in rural northern Wisconsin."

John downshifted to help slow the truck. When he'd bought it a few years back, the truck came with a full topper that sealed the truck bed with a space high enough so someone could walk bent over or sit in a low-slung chair. Earlier that morning, three reclining lawn chairs were thrown beneath the topper to hold the rest of the crew. Paul lay comfortably because of his smaller stature, but the quarters were cramped for Tom and Bob. Bob was the muscular heavyweight for the school wrestling team, and the flimsy lawn chair creaked under his weight. Tom had it no better. He was slightly smaller than Bob, with wider shoulders that touched the outside supports of the chair back. All three were stretched out flat, staying beneath the rear window line. They were running out of patience and wanted out of the slightly illegal surroundings.

A few miles back, the truck drove by a Wisconsin highway patrol waiting at a stop sign, its blinker on. As the crew passed the side road, John slid open the back window and yelled, "Cop! Make yourselves small."

Downshifting helped, but they were still coming up to the turn faster than John liked. The gear and trailer weight forced him to really lean on the brakes, and he heard a cooler slide in the back of the truck. "You guys okay back there?"

"Yah, we're fine," Paul said. "Tom took his feet off the cooler when we picked up the cop. We just weren't expecting to drop out of warp so quickly. Is the cop still there? I'm ready to sit up."

John finished the turn onto the country road and watched in his mirror as the highway patrol sped past. "He went straight. You guys can relax."

"That was close," Paul said. "How much longer? I'm ready to get out of this rolling bunker."

Al laid his forearm on the center console and twisted his body so he could see the three guys in the truck bed. "Relax and quit your whining. We only have another fifteen to twenty minutes." Then he added with a touch of sarcasm, "I'd love to trade with you, but John needs help finding the drop-in point."

Four of the guys were accustomed to one-to-two week trips in Minnesota's Boundary Waters Canoe Area, locally known as the BWCA. Those trips involved a six-hour drive from Stillwater, Minnesota. This trip was only about two and a half hours to the river systems in northwest Wisconsin. Their planned five-day canoe trip was going to be a short camping excursion before the Memorial Day weekend.

The shorter trip was perfect for Bob. It was his first trip experiencing real North Country camping. He had camped with his family in their RV and paddled the St. Croix Valley just north of Stillwater, but he'd never ventured farther north in the time he lived in the area. This trip was a good baptism for him, and his friends kidded him about being the new guy. They promised not to overload him with too big a dose of Mother Nature's ruggedness.

They had already dropped a second car at the take-out spot in St. Croix Falls, and they made good time on the state highways. The turn meant slowed progress because of the twisting and turning township roads. The narrower roads followed old property lines more than they intended to connect destinations. Northwest Wisconsin was funny that way. Property owners held a lot of influence back when settlers were taming the landscape. They forced road building to follow the edge of property lines rather than building the shortest possible route. Once things were in place, they rarely changed, right down to road names like Kimble Lake Road and Smith Bridge Trail. Few remembered the people whose names first appeared on the landmarks over a century ago, but the names hung on into the new millennia.

John smiled and thought back to earlier that day. He had volunteered his pickup and trailer to take the guys and gear up to the starting point. This gave him a guaranteed spot in the front seat. Early that morning, he sent Al a maps link for the trip and said, "Here. You navigate. We've canoed this area before, but we've never run this river. Finding a start point on these small country roads is tricky."

"I don't think the new guy will say anything, but Tom and Paul are going to have a problem with this," Al said. "They know what it's like to ride in the back of a pickup to the BWCA with only the topper's small side windows for fresh air. I know it's only a hundred twenty miles up to Gordon, Wisconsin, but your old F250 really bounces around on rough road."

John had planned Al as the navigator all along but hadn't anticipated a fight for the front seat. He thought for a moment, then said, "I'll fix that." He jogged into the house.

John was a practical guy, always thinking about how to keep things running smoothly, and he knew how to read people. He knew Al was right. Any one of the four could follow a dot on a maps app, but he knew that Tom, Paul, and Bob were navigationally challenged without a phone. They were only a few minutes from leaving, and John knew that none of them wanted to sit in a lawn chair for two hours. They would only get grouchy if someone forced them out of the front seat. His solution was simple, and all four of his friends would buy into it.

John came back with four party toothpicks and said to Al, "Let's pull the guys together to decide who rides shotgun. We'll draw straws and the short one sits up front."

Al looked at the toothpicks in John's outstretched hand. He had two blue, one red, and one yellow tooth pick. Al asked, "How will this get you your navigator?"

John snapped the end off the yellow toothpick and said, "Simple. You pick the short yellow one. Just to make sure everybody thinks this is on the up-and-up, Tom will pick first and you second. We all know Tom will pick the red one."

Tom was seriously into weightlifting and was full of extra testosterone because of it. He firmly believed the color red activated extra adrenaline when he was lifting, so he always wore something red.

Mostly he wore Stillwater's red and black school colors. He also had an ample supply of red sweatbands and red socks. There was also rumor that he owned a red jock strap.

John clenched the toothpicks in his fist and called out, "Hey guys, gather up. Short straw rides shotgun." He walked over to Tom and held out his arm. Like clockwork, Tom picked the red toothpick. Al picked the yellow and John got his navigator.

The township road ditches were nothing like the rural road ditches around Stillwater. Sparse grass was not mowed and ATV tracks exposed the sandy soil where fat tires kicked out dirt at the corners. ATVs weren't allowed in road ditches around their hometown. Even though Stillwater was considered the birthplace of Minnesota and the gateway to the wild and scenic St. Croix River watershed, it was almost considered a St. Paul suburb. Driving northward, John and Al watched through the Ford F250 windshield as the valley's hardwoods gave way to aspen and pine. The Stillwater Valley's cliffs changed to farm fields, then to northern forest. The ATV tracks were a sure sign they had left the city behind them.

"Only a half dozen miles until we turn off this township road." Al slid his fingers across the phone's screen to resize the map. He leaned over onto the center console and showed John the last leg of the trip.

"Yah, but the road looks like a corkscrew, and it turns to dirt at the last turnoff. That should be a lot of fun for the guys in the back of the truck. The dirt roads up here are never well maintained."

Al glanced back through the sliding topper window as he sat up again. Tom had a soda in his hand, and it made him realize how thirsty he was. The whole group was up early, loading gear and canoes. Al had worked up a sweat finishing the work. His water bottle was packed in the trailer, but getting it meant stopping to pull it out. That wasn't going to happen. Once they were on the road, everyone wanted to get from point A to point B as quickly as possible. The maddening part was that John never sped when his truck was loaded down with people and gear.

To compensate for the slow, steady pace, Al knew that he rarely stopped.

He slid the rear window open. "Hey, the navigator needs a caffeine fix. Is there extra Dew for me?"

"Yah, plenty. I loaded a twelve-pack into a cooler before we left and these guys are drinking water." Tom dug his hand into the cooler, rattled the ice, and pulled out a can. "Here you go."

Al popped the top and tipped the ice-cold can back until it was empty. "Ahhhh. That hit the spot."

Small challenge games and pranks were a staple between the guys. They were woven into the fabric of the group by the wrestling coach during their freshman season. The coach introduced challenge games to push the team's competitiveness. The athletes introduced pranks and practical jokes to lighten the mood when the pressure was high. After four years, any situation that smelled remotely like competition turned into a game. Tom jumped on the opportunity with Al.

"That was a pretty poor excuse for downing a Dew." Tom tipped his head back and drained his newly opened can in about two-thirds the time. It was his second. "Think you can beat that?" He reached into the cooler, grabbed another can, and tossed it onto the truck's front seat.

"I have no doubt." Al grabbed the can, popped it open, and chugged down the soda, roughly matching Tom's time. When he was done, he crushed the can and tossed it into the truck bed. "Game on! Let's do it again."

Paul enjoyed working behind the scenes of practical jokes. It meant he wouldn't be the brunt of any joke and could watch the theatrics unfold. He already had both hands in the cooler, pulling out two more Dews. "Let's see who's really the fastest." He tossed one into the front seat and handed Tom his third can. "On three, drain them."

In the front seat, John poked Al's leg and put out his hand. It had been a while since they pulled something on Tom. Al just smiled, popped open the can, and handed it to John. Paul yelled, "Three!"

Tom tilted his can back. With his back against the window, he couldn't see John emptying Al's third can. Paul and Bob cheered on both guys, clearly seeing what was going on. Tom finished the can, crushed it, and threw it against the tailgate. They congratulated Tom, distracting him just long enough to let John finish the soda and hand the empty back to Al.

"Wait. I wasn't ready," Al complained. "I thought Paul was counting to three. Let's do it again."

"I'm already ahead two to zero," Tom celebrated. "I'm just too fast and there aren't enough cans left to catch me. You might as well give up."

"Wait a minute. It's actually one to one." Al egged him on. "Let's go, tough guy." He reached his hand through the sliding window and Paul filled it again. He popped the top and signaled a *cheers* through the opening. While Paul counted to three, Al handed off the full can to John for an early start. Al faced away from the rear window and faked the full tilt back. "Done!" He shouted, a full second in front of Tom. Out of eyesight, John handed back the empty can and Al tossed it into the truck bed.

Tom grabbed the can and shook it to see if it was empty. He shook his head in disbelief, then paused. All of a sudden, Tom grabbed the lawn chair arms and froze in place. Both Paul and Bob looked puzzled when Tom winced in pain. When he grabbed his stomach, they both panicked and slid away from him as fast as they could. Then it came. "BURRRRP!"

"Wow, great tone quality, Tom." Al reached his hand through the sliding window. "I'm ahead two to one. Want to try evening the score? Give me another one, Paul."

Tom was beginning to look a little Mountain Dew green, but his competitive nature wouldn't let him drop the challenge. "More like two to one in my favor." He grabbed his fifth can from the cooler and opened it. Al turned sideways so Tom could clearly see what was about to happen. He also wanted to see if Tom could finish another can.

Paul started the count, "One, two, Three!"

Their heads swung back and sweet liquid flowed. Glancing sideways as he swallowed, Al saw Tom pull the can down. He smiled a second later when Tom raised it again to his lips.

"Done!" he called back to Tom.

Tom pulled the half-empty can away from his face. "So am I. I can't finish this." Al raised his arms in a victory celebration. All five laughed. Tom won those challenges more often than not, but this time the joke was on him. He lay back on his chair and curled into a ball to nurse his aching stomach.

John pulled them back to reality when he said, "I think we're getting close."

Al picked up his phone as the truck rounded a 15 MPH curve. He activated the screen, then looked out the front window. "There's the turn for the dirt road."

John slowed the truck again and smirked a little as an idea came into his head. "Let's give the boys in the back a little warm-up for the last five miles to the drop-in point." He downshifted, slowed the truck to a crawl, then turned the corner. As the rear tires left the tar road, John drove the gas pedal to the floor for a couple seconds. The rear tires broke loose on the gravel and slid the truck sideways. The three lawn chairs in the back slid against the truck bed and a simultaneous "HEY!!" could be heard over the laughing in the front seat.

The little driving stunt kicked up a cloud of dust around the truck before John had the chance to pull away. The boys in the back began coughing and quickly closed the topper's windows to stop the dust from pouring in. They braced themselves for the washboard road ahead.

Both sides of the dirt road had very little ditch. The Tamarack trees grew over the road and showed bright green sprouts of new growth. The wet spring filled the boggy forest floor with water, feeding the trees ample moisture in the early season. About a mile before the landing, the trees dropped back on the left side of the truck and the forest opened up to a water-filled swamp.

John yelled, "Wow! Look at that."

A cow moose and two calves stood in the swampy shallows less than fifty yards from the road. Al banged on the back window and pointed left for the three guys in the back. Paul, Bob, and Tom crowded around the topper window, admiring a scene rarely seen anymore this far south. Before they left that morning, Paul talked about past trips and how many moose he saw when he was younger. He also commented how he hadn't seen moose south of Duluth since he was a kid. The ticks, wolves, and warming climate all but eliminated them south of Lake Superior. John slowed the truck to a roll while all four guys tried snapping photos with their phones. Seeing a moose with two calves was a good sign, and they wanted to capture the moment.

The road widened to what could only be called a dirt cul-de-sac. The edge pushed back the woods on each side to a fence line, leaving just enough room for a plow truck to clear snow in the winter. A hinged gate was centered on the far side of the cul-de-sac. The tornado razor wire at the top, along with the chain and padlock on the gate, meant that the truck was going no further. The sign on the fence read "*Totagatic River State Wildlife Management Area, Dam Access, Restricted Area.*" John stopped the truck and trailer at the gate on the far side of the cul-de-sac.

"Hey, are we there?" Tom yelled from the back.

"Yah. I think so, but…." Before Al could finish, Tom burst out of the back and sprinted toward the forest edge.

"I really got to pee! John's dirt road driving almost broke my bladder." The amazing power of suggestion suddenly had Paul crossing his legs. He jumped out of the truck bed and followed Tom. By the time Paul stopped and unzipped his pants, John and Al felt the overwhelming pressure at their belt line. With all of the Mountain Dew in their system, they left the truck doors open and waddled over to join the other two.

Bob saw a great opportunity to record the first major event of the trip. He grabbed his phone and snapped a shot of the four guys facing into the woods. "Now that's a memorable moment. Kind of reminds me of my dad's old vinyl records. I think he has an album called *Who's Next*. The album cover shows a huge concrete pillar in the middle of nowhere and the band peeing on it. Really edgy for the early seventies. This will be a great social media post when we get back. I'll pair it with one of the album's songs. It'll be great."

"Your warped sense of creativity never ends," Paul yelled back.

John, Al, and Paul finished their business and walked back next to the trailer. With the boredom of the long drive behind them, they could start enjoying the North Country they liked so much. The rivers they chose ran through state forests and were designated as part of the St. Croix National Scenic Riverway. This meant that much of the area was wild and untouched by industry.

John tilted his head back, stuck his nose in the air, inhaled, and said, "Smell that? Smells like Up North."

The other three took a deep inhale and Al said, "Yah, I love the north woods smell. The pines and aspens are a great change from the stench of the city. There's no exhaust smell and no freeway noise."

Tom finished his business last. As he retied his pants and followed the other three back to the truck, Paul commented, "I see why it took you the longest—you drank at least three cans more than anyone else."

Tom stopped walking, stared at his friends, and put both hands on his hips. "What do you mean Paul? Al and I were going one for one."

"Ummm.... Dope!" Paul ducked his head forward as if Tom were throwing rocks and shuffled quickly past the other three guys. Reaching the truck, he hopped in the passenger side and locked the doors. Tom was right behind him and grabbed the door handle. He pulled so hard the truck rocked, and when the door didn't give, Tom let go and slapped the window with the palm of his hand.

Paul sneered and stuck out his tongue. Then he brought his face right up to the glass, gave his biggest smile, and said, "I didn't know Al was going to pass half of his Mountain Dew to John."

Tom knew he was duped. He spun around, glared at Al, and started toward him.

"Oh crap!" Al's eyes turned as big as saucers and he turned to run. He and Tom rarely sparred on the wrestling mat because Tom had twenty pounds on him. He knew Tom wasn't really mad, but that didn't change the quantum of pain Tom wanted to inflict in retribution for the bruised ego.

When Tom caught the back of Al's shirt, Al spun and grabbed Tom's wrist. With the wrestler's death grip, Tom couldn't free his hand. He reached up and grabbed the back of Al's neck with the free hand, forced the imprisoned arm around back of Al and threw his weight into him. On the way to the ground, Al released Tom's wrist and locked his arms around Tom's red trunks. He planted a foot and pivoted all of Tom's weight so that Tom hit the ground first.

Tom had seen every move in his Greko-Roman wrestling career and practiced countermoves endlessly. As Al's weight came down on him, Tom continued rolling and grabbed a head and arm on the way over. Al ended up on his back, with Tom squarely across his chest, squeezing the breath out of him.

Al slapped the ground with his hand and squeaked, "I give! Tap out!" Tom let him go and sprung to his feet. He flexed a bodybuilding pose and growled, "Now we're even."

Al opened his mouth to say something but thought better of it. Tom always wanted revenge when he was cheated, and pushing back only meant more pain. Besides, Paul let the secret slip. Al glared at him as Paul dropped from the truck's passenger seat onto the ground. He thought to himself, *Your time will come my friend.*

Tom let his muscles relax from the pose and started brushing sand off his shirt. Now that his bladder was empty and payback given out, he finally paid some attention to the surroundings. He twisted his head and scanned the dirt cul-de-sac. When he turned away from his noisy friends at the truck, he heard a background sound he recognized from past canoeing trips. He turned, took a few steps, and cocked his head to find which direction the sound was coming from. Within a few seconds, he broke into a jog and yelled back to the group, "Speaking of freeway noise, do you hear that dull roar? There's a trail over here. I think it leads to the river."

All four of Tom's friends stopped what they were doing and looked Tom's direction. Paul, John, and Al broke into a run, following Tom toward the wooded trail.

Bob yelled, "What about the truck?"

"Leave it," John yelled back. "Who's going to touch it? We're in the middle of nowhere."

Bob looked at the truck, turned, and watched the last guy disappear into the woods. Not spending much time in the wilderness, Bob suddenly felt uneasy. Other than the river, it was eerily quiet. He started toward the truck cab, thinking he should at least close the passenger door. He froze when he heard a twig snap in the woods beyond the fence.

Who could that be, he thought. *John said we were in the middle of nowhere. I should ask what was that rather than who.* His heart raced. *Maybe it's the moose we saw back up the road. Man those things are big! Wait a minute. That was over a mile away. The moose couldn't have run that far in such a short time. Maybe it was just a branch dropping off from a tree, or maybe not.* The hair stood up on the back of his neck. *Maybe a bear!* The split second before he broke into a sprint, he pictured a hungry bear walking out of the woods seeing him as its next meal.

The trail dropped down a hill that was littered with sharp-edged blue trap rock. Anyone wearing sandals or walking in bare feet would definitely come away with cuts. Some of the trap rock lay loose in a small gully created by the rains. Someone carrying heavy gear or a canoe would find unstable conditions walking down the trail. A medium-sized tree had fallen in their path, further complicating what would be the only route to the river. The knee-high step was not difficult itself, but the extra wash created a hole on the downhill side of the trunk. They would need to divert off from the trail to go around the hole.

The group caught up with Tom at the end of the trail. He was standing at water's edge looking upstream at the dam. The river was a small tributary in the whole Upper St. Croix River flowage, but with all the rain, the water flowing over the fifteen-foot high dam was deafening. There was an outcropping of large trap rock on either side of the dam that created a twenty-yard-wide funnel of churning white water. The sun created rainbows in the mist lifting off from the falling water, and the coolness could still be felt thirty yards downstream from the dam. The water lost its rolling motion before it reached the spot in front of the group, but the current still had eddies from the upstream turbulence.

Paul had seen a lot of white water and canoed some fast rivers. The shocked look on his face said a lot about the group's drop-in location. "Holy crap that current is moving!! When we were planning the trip, I remember somebody saying; *'The small river shouldn't be a problem. The water's plenty high.'*" Then in an accusing tone, Paul asked, "Who chose this river anyway?"

All four guys turned and looked at Tom.

3

Three Weeks Earlier

Paul and Bob left the school's library. Over their shoulders, each of them carried backpacks loaded with forty pounds of notes, electronics, and their laptops. They just finished over two hours of studying for senior year finals and needed a change of pace to clear their heads. They pushed through the crowded hallway toward their lockers to dump their backpacks before heading to the athletic center's locker room. There wasn't space in the athletic lockers to store that kind of bulk while they lifted weights.

Bob led the way as they weaved through the main hallway. He was sharply dressed in his Air Force ROTC uniform, and his six-foot three-inch frame was like a bulldozer pushing through the crowds stopped in the middle of the hall. Groups of girls laughed and hugged while they signed each other's yearbooks, knowing that college would begin prying at the bonds formed during their high school years. Occasionally they passed four or five guys steeling glances at the groups, daring each other to interrupt the frenzy to get some attention. As Paul followed his friend, letting his big frame plow through the crowd, he took in the excitement and apprehension. In a very short time, all of their lives would change as they crossed one of life's milestones: graduation.

"What a madhouse! You can just feel the electricity. In another week, this whole school will be a ghost town," he said to Bob.

"Yah, in some ways, I'm going to miss this chaos. The Air Force Academy will be completely different." Bob pushed open the fire doors that led to the athletic center and locker room. "I get why everyone is so anxious. I'm there too. You and I have spent a lot of time hanging out. We shared a lot of classes and we joined the wrestling team together. At the end of May, that all changes when I follow in my dad's footsteps and head for Colorado Springs."

Bob's family was military. Every few years his dad would transfer to a new base and he would move to a new school. Every time this happened, he would start with a new group of friends. It wasn't all bad. Every other kid at the base's school was doing the same thing. He saw a lot of the world and he now had friends spread across the United States. He knew if he kept in contact with them, he could travel to any city later in life and probably find somebody local he knew from his younger years.

At the beginning of his ninth grade year, Bob's dad retired from his civil engineering job in the Air Force and the family moved to Stillwater, Minnesota. His dad used his connections with someone he knew at the 133rd airlift wing in St. Paul and found a job at Holman Field. The air field sat in the Mississippi River's flood plain. It was a perfect place for a civil engineer to practice his skills, protecting the airport from the river's spring torrents. His mom was army and she was also not far from retiring. She shifted to the National Guard to finish her commitment to Uncle Sam and was assigned to the armory in Stillwater.

Bob met Paul the first day of school during a male hormone event that defines pecking order in the hallways. Three sophomores had a smallish freshman boy cornered and were taunting him just for fun. Paul stepped in to help, but the three older guys laughed at his short, stocky frame and started pushing him around as well. Bob watched the tense situation from his locker, and when two of the sophomores pinned Paul against the wall, his protect and serve military upbringing kicked in. He grabbed the arm of one sophomore and pulled him off Paul. When the kid pushed back, Bob expertly flipped him onto the floor and placed a foot across his neck. With one of the sophomores gone, Paul reacted with lightning speed. He tripped the second kid and landed on top of him. The third sophomore and the smallish freshman stepped back, stunned at what had happened.

The heroic hallway event earned Paul and Bob a personal meeting with the vice principal. While they waited outside his office, Paul said to Bob, "That was awesome how you tossed that kid onto the floor. How did you do that?"

"We moved a lot when my dad and mom were active duty. They told me that joining a club was the quickest way to find friends, so I got into Jiu-Jitsu in fourth grade and worked my way up to a brown belt."

"Thanks for helping out. Those guys bully people just for kicks. I couldn't let them torture that kid. They would pick on him all year. By the way, my name's Paul."

"Mine's Bob. I saw what you did to help out. Just figured you could use some backup."

"Well, I know just what to do with you two." It was the vice principal. He had been standing in his office doorway listening to their conversation. "Grab a seat in my office and let's talk about how fighting doesn't solve problems." The vice principal gave them credit for stopping the bullying but also told them that fighting on school property broke the rules, regardless of the reason. Suspension was the typical punishment, but since both Paul and Bob grappled with the sophomores rather than using their fists, he gave them a choice. They could join the wrestling team or face the suspension. Both of them thought telling their parents about joining a sport was far easier than telling them they were suspended.

Paul followed his friend through the fire doors. The athletic center's hallway was lined with team photos and trophy cases rather than lockers so it was almost free of people. He walked up alongside Bob thinking about how he would miss his friend. "A military commitment is huge.

One day you're living the life with all of us and the next day you're in boot camp. It's a shame for you to just leave without saying goodbye. We should throw a going-away party."

"Thanks, but no thanks. You guys have been great to me since I came here my freshman year, but a party would cost a lot of money and would only last one night. Besides, it would leave us with a big clean-up job if the party was too big."

"Seriously, we should do something special for you before you leave," Paul continued. "How about if we just keep it small? Maybe just invite the guys from the wrestling team."

"That's still a lot of people. You would have to invite the whole team. Some would bring their girlfriends, and the cheerleaders would feel hurt if they weren't invited. A one-night thing just seems to fall short."

Paul pulled open the locker room door and the sour smell of sweat slapped them both. "Wow! Smells like the cleaning crew took off the last week of school." He pinched his nose with two fingers and continued with a nasal voice, "Come on Bob. What's more memorable than a HUGE party?"

They walked past the coaches' office toward the corner that led to the locker bays. Turning left, the long walkway stretched past alternately colored sets of gym lockers. The heavy contrast of the school's colors, bright red then deep black, always seemed to stir something inside Bob when he rounded that corner. The Air Force's dress blue with the sharp contrast of rank insignia did the same thing for him. He was looking forward to wearing his cadet uniform.

Bob turned to look at Paul. "Nah, pass. I would see everyone for a couple hours, say hi, repeat the same Air Force story fifty times, and maybe shed a quick tear. Ten years from now, I wouldn't remember who all came to the party." They turned into the third bay and sat down on the plain wood bench. "In June and July, I'm going to spend five and a half weeks in Colorado going through basic cadet training. All of the cadets will spend the hottest part of the year abused by the upper classmen. We'll probably live in a barracks that smells a lot like this locker room. I won't know a soul when I get there, but I bet we'll be really tight when we graduate. I'm pretty certain that I won't forget those weeks. Too bad there isn't anything similar here because that would be memorable."

Tom, one of their wrestling teammates, was sitting in front of a red locker two bench lengths away. He caught the end of their conversation. "Looking sharp in those dress blues, Bob. I'm going to miss kicking your butt on the mat." Bob was the team's anchor, always wrestling last as the heavyweight. Tom wrestled one weight class below him. While the two never competed for a varsity roster spot, the coach always paired them as sparing partners. Bob's Jiu-Jitsu finesse was completely different than Tom's brute-force approach. They taught each other a lot about strength and technique.

"Thanks Tom." Bob picked a towel off the floor and threw it at Tom. "I seem to remember it the other way around."

"Paul's right. We have to do something for a sendoff, but I agree about the party thing. That would be too much like graduation parties."

They dressed and left for the weight room. The three of them stretched their arms and shoulders while they walked. The clanking free weight noise grew as they went, then the whir of resistance machines filled in as background noise as they turned the corner. The long window wall between the corner and the weight room door was a building feature meant to impress athletes. Bright white light poured out of the overlit weight room into the dim hallway. Beyond the windows, the curved black shapes of free weights contrasted the stark white lines formed by the support and resistance equipment. The glossy white walls were dotted with mirrors that created bizarre viewing angles. The other half of the room was an open theater with a soft red mat covering the floor, stretch bars mounted to the walls, and the school's pony logo painted directly across from the windows. The equipment was busy. A few gymnasts practiced tumbling routines, preparing for summer camp. Al and John were stretching in one corner of the mat. They just finished a workout, trying to keep some of their strength and flexibility from their senior year wrestling season.

A smile grew on Tom's face as they neared the door. "I love weightlifting. This new weight room is one of the best I've seen."

"Aren't you doing some bodybuilding competitions this summer?" Paul asked.

"Yah, but the first event is at the end of June. I could use a break that blends something aerobic into my routine. That would let my muscles recover before I hit the weights hard in June."

Paul stopped at the edge of the red mat and turned to face Tom and Bob. He was looking at the floor and they could tell he was thinking. When he lifted his head, his eyes lit up and his lips parted, exposing bright white teeth behind his curly mustache. "I have a great idea. What do you think about a river trip?" When Tom and Bob gave him a blank stare, he continued. "Think about it! A small group of us camping, running some rapids, and enjoying nature. Tom, we've seen some great wildlife on the river and at least one good story comes out of every trip."

A puzzled look came across Bob's face. "How would that turn into something to remember?"

"Are you kidding?" Paul turned and yelled, "Hey John, Al! Wanna do a river trip?" Paul waved them over.

Stillwater was the dividing point between the Upper and Lower St. Croix River. Below the lift bridge, the river opened up and extended south some thirty-five miles through Lake St. Croix before pouring over the Prescott Wisconsin dam and merging with the Mississippi. Above the bridge began the no-wake-zone. From Stillwater twenty-five miles north to the St. Croix Falls dam, there were hundreds of islands, sand bars, and backwaters dotting the much narrower river.

Growing up in the St. Croix Valley had its influence on leisure time. Paul, John, Al, and Tom spent countless hours on the St. Croix as boys.

Instead of pick-up basketball on outdoor courts or heading to the skate park after supper, they spent their time on or near the river. At first it was canoeing and camping with their families on the docile part of the river where large boats couldn't navigate the changing depths. They spent some time with their scout troop at Andersen Scout Camp, located on the river just north of Stillwater. As they aged, they took father and son trips north of the St. Croix Falls dam for more rugged camping and more challenging canoeing. Finally, as high schoolers, they used the river as a haven to get away from adult supervision.

This was not the case for Bob. He had only spent four years in Stillwater and only began canoeing with his friends after his sophomore year. While he joined friends on day trips or overnights just north of Stillwater, he had never ventured north of St. Croix Falls.

Al and John joined the group and Paul asked them, "How many stories do you guys have from the river trips you've taken?"

"Too many to count," Al replied.

"More than one from every trip," John added. "And, we've done trips since we were kids."

"See what I mean, Bob? You're looking for something memorable that doesn't involve a lot of people and lasts longer than a one-night party. A river trip has excitement and the chance to make some great stories. It would be like a mini boot camp with friends."

"I don't' want to start boot camp any earlier than I have to."

"It's not what you think, Bob," Tom said. "We don't do pushups, but we do paddle canoes for a couple days. That's the hard part. The fun part includes the camping, running rapids, seeing wildlife, and experiencing the unpredictable outdoors."

Bob's eyes widened. "What do you mean by unpredictable outdoors?"

Tom looked up toward the empty ceiling space, recalling a memory. "I remember the last trip giving us a nighttime fright. Paul and I canoed the Namekagon River last September. Mother Nature blessed us with rain three out of the five days we were on the water. On the last day, it rained all afternoon and into the evening. We made supper wearing our rain gear, and then I said, *'Let's let Mother Nature wash the dishes. Just leave them on the campsite picnic table.'* We climbed into the tent at sundown, leaving all of the dishes out in the open. Big mistake. About three a.m. *'clank, crash.'* Both Paul and I sat straight up. I swear we both looked at each other and said, *'Bear?'* We sat in the dark and listened while the meal continued outside. Forks and knives moved. Plates slid across the table and onto the ground. Neither one of us made a sound because we didn't want to become part of the meal.

"All of a sudden *'clunk.'* The pot tipped over. A lot of high-pitched chatter followed. Then we knew. Paul said, *'Raccoons are cleaning the dishes, not a bear.'* He reached over and picked up the flashlight, got out of his sleeping bag, and quietly opened the tent zipper. On the table, we could see the outline of two raccoons in the dark. When he turned on the light, we saw four beady eyes staring back at us. The raccoons scattered when we yelled and unzipped the tent screen. They were gone by the time we put on our shoes and climbed out of the tent."

Bob chuckled and said, "That doesn't sound like fun."

"At the time it wasn't. We had to get up, stow all of the meal gear in the food pack, and rehang the pack. We didn't want the raccoons to come back. Now the whole thing is a great camping story."

Paul jumped back in and said, "This will be great! There are a ton of campsites and landings for ninety miles between the St. Croix headwaters and St. Croix Falls. There's also a half dozen smaller rivers dumping into the St. Croix. We could pick anything that fits your taste. What do you think Bob? All of you guys in?"

"I'm in," Tom said. "It's great aerobic exercise for a break and I'm taking the summer off to do competitions before college. My time is my own."

John smiled and said, "I'm always up for a river trip, but I need to check my work schedule. I'll let you know if I can get the time off."

"I'm supposed to start working on my uncle's concrete crews right after school ends," Al added. "It's been raining a lot and they can't pour outdoors if it's raining. I'll call him and see what's up."

"I guess I'm in," Bob said. "I hear you guys tell stories about all the trips you've taken. You talk about the camping, the rapids, raccoons in the camp sites, bears, and other stuff. I've always wished I could go."

"Here's your chance," Paul said to Bob. "We have a week of school left, then two weeks before you head to Colorado Springs. Let's meet on Saturday to plan the trip."

"My place is open," John volunteered. "My parents are gone for the weekend and we can take as much time as we need."

They agreed on eleven o'clock and then split, going their separate ways for a workout or a shower.

4

The Trip Plan

John's house sat close to the bluff on Stillwater's North Hill. His front window framed a perfect picture of downtown Stillwater and the lift bridge crossing into Wisconsin. Where the grass dropped away at the bluff's edge, the view opened up to a three-mile stretch of the St. Croix River flowing past the historic downtown. On sunny summer days, the water glistened and the river was busy with pleasure boats. On cool fall mornings, the fog rolled into the valley and hid the view with a gray blanket that reflected the deep orange sunrises. The weeks through April and May, the valley transitioned from a sea of woody brown with small blotches of evergreen to a plush deep forest green. It was the perfect backdrop to plan a river trip.

John, Paul, Al, and Tom took frequent trips on the Upper St. Croix and Namekagon rivers. You could drop in anywhere for just a day, or you could pack full canoes for a ten-day trip from the rivers' headwaters. Few towns dotted the hundreds of river-way miles, creating a remote and scenic sojourn for anyone looking to get back to nature. They were the go-to destinations for the group's quick getaway trips. Introducing Bob to the rivers was the best going-away gift they could imagine. Anytime Bob returned home, the rivers would be there waiting to take away life's hectic pace.

John saw their pizza delivery come up the walk. The driver glanced back over her shoulder to look at the valley, then turned to take in the whole view. She stood there a good ten seconds before John got up and opened the front door. He recognized her from school, although she looked a little different with her blond ponytail sticking out through the back of her hat. She worked for the school newspaper, covering the home sporting events. He remembered the first time seeing her with a camera in the gymnasium stands at a home wrestling meet. Warming up at the edge of the mat, just before going out to face his opponent, he glanced into the stands and saw her snapping photos of him. When she pulled the camera away from her face, he stared, admiring how her high cheekbones and strong jaw complemented her bright green eyes. When they locked eyes, her face drew back into a smile that would put the Mona Lisa to shame. John gave her a quick smile and turned away, thinking, *I don't need that kind of distraction before a match.* As a junior, she photographed all of last winter's home matches for the paper. John had talked to her a couple of times after matches and knew her name was Anne. During the season, he had hoped to get to know her, but things stayed casually cool. Now here she was on his front doorstep.

"Picturesque, isn't it?" he called out from the porch.

"Yah! It must be rough living with a view like this. I'm sure glad I got this delivery."

John fantasized that she was talking about finding him rather than the discovering the view. "Oh, it's just part of the whole river valley. You kind of get used to it, but it's always beautiful. Even better today," he added. "I haven't talked with you since the season ended. How are your spring classes?"

She blushed but recovered quickly, "They're keeping very busy. Along with the school newspaper and work, I don't have time for anything else. Hey, would you mind if I come back sometime and take photos from your front yard? I'm planning to study photojournalism when I go to college and I'm collecting a portfolio of the river valley as an admission project."

"No, not at all," John said as he thought about the chance to see her again. "I just started working early shifts over at the grocery store, now that school is out. I'm usually around most afternoons. Stop by anytime."

"I'll take you up on that. Thanks. Here are your four pizzas."

He gave her the money collected from the guys earlier and threw in a little extra as a large tip, hopping she'd remember his generosity. He stood in the doorway and watched her walk back to her car. She smiled and waved as she got in. He smiled back and nodded, hoping she would return soon.

The guys inside rushed away from the window as John came back into the living room with a big smile on his face.

"Sweet delivery," Tom cat-called from the couch. "Did you get her number?"

John felt the weight of his four friends staring at him and realized he came back into the room starry-eyed. His face turned a little red, but he recovered and said to Tom, "Nah, I did better than that. She's coming back to take pictures of the valley from my front yard."

All four guys reacted to John's opportunity with the gorgeous pizza delivery girl. There were surprise and shock comments like "Wow!" and "All right!" because they rarely remembered John dating during school.

Tom hoped to goad him a little more by saying, "Try not to get into the photo when she comes back. You'll ruin the view."

John desperately wanted to shift attention away from the exchange with Anne. He ignored Tom's second comment and set down the pizzas. "Come on. Let's eat. We have a lot of planning to do."

Paul threw open a top pizza box and grabbed two pieces of the garbage pizza. He folded them at the cut and bit into what he called a Supreme Pizza Sandwich. Bob pulled the pepperoni box from underneath. The smell of aged pepperoni filled his nostrils when he opened the top, and rich, meaty grease dripped from the slice when he pulled it from the box.

"I'm glad all of you can make the trip," Bob said just before biting into the slice. It was a miracle that all five of their schedules synced before the Memorial Day weekend. The short timeframe made it a challenge for the group to juggle plans already in place following school's end.

The easy one was Bob. He just needed a couple days to pack for Colorado Springs. Tom's time was his own, with only weight training on his schedule. It was kind of his *'Golden Summer'* for him to enjoy, but he needed to keep pumping iron.

John worked part time at Stillwater's Cub Foods home store. He started there during his sophomore year, so he had a little seniority over the incoming people starting just after school ended. The store manager wanted him to train in some of the new people before the Memorial weekend rush, but John convinced him that he needed some time off.

Al worked as a laborer on his uncle's concrete crews during summers, and May was usually the month things ramped up. Fortunately, the late spring pattern of rainy weather slowed the startup. His uncle told him he should check back after Memorial Day and plan to work overtime because the crews would need to make up for lost ground.

Paul was headed for summer school at the University of North Dakota in Grand Forks. He volunteered to help with the fall freshman orientation program. His outgoing *'personality plus'* approach to life was perfect for soothing nervous and lost freshmen, but the program required him to live on campus over the summer for volunteer training. The work was a perfect match to fulfill the pilot training program's volunteer requirement as well. Paul could get the requirement out of the way so it didn't take time away from studies when he started the university's rigorous aviation degree.

"This is a great idea, Paul," Al said as he pulled his second piece of garbage pizza from the box. Both he and Paul loved garbage pizza and Al wanted his share before Paul finished his pizza sandwich. Taking in half the slice in one bite, he thought about the odd number of guys sitting in the room. "Was there anyone else interested in the trip? Five isn't a real good number for two-person canoes."

"Nope, sorry. I asked around," Paul said. "Everybody else is busy."

With his many years of canoeing experience, John had seen a lot of ways to solve outdoor travel problems. He jumped in and said, "Not a problem. We use three canoes and pack heavy gear in the front seat of the third boat. The food pack and tents can weigh down the front so the person in back can steer."

"What about keeping up with the other two canoes?" Tom asked.

"Not a big deal because we are doing rivers rather than lakes. We are not in a hurry and the current will push the heavier canoe along," John said.

Al jumped into the discussion, thinking about past trips. "That works for most of a trip, but I remember a few tough obstacles. The lower Namekagon River is like a gravel pit right before it dumps into the St. Croix. It's not dangerous, but we've had to drag canoes through its shallow level-one rapids. No one can avoid it and nobody wants to drag a loaded canoe alone." Al continued. "And, what about the St. Croix River south of Grantsburg? The river opens up for about twenty miles and the current really slows down. That's a long paddle to keep up with the two-person canoes."

"I think we'll be okay," John replied. "The water's high right now, so we should go right over any shallow areas. We won't even know some of the small rapids are there. We can trade off halfway through the long stretch of open river if someone's arms give out."

Tom was thinking about the itinerary. "By the way, how far are we going and which rivers should we take? I was just on the Namekagon last fall. I'd like to see some different scenery."

"I was thinking five days when we started talking about the trip. We wanted to do something fun that would give Bob the weekend to spend with his family before he ships out," Paul said.

John walked into the other room and came back with his large waterproof river maps. Bob and Al moved the empty pizza boxes and slid the coffee table out of the way. John opened a couple of maps, laid them on the floor, and all five crowed around. "Let's see. If we want five days, that eliminates the upper St. Croix from its headwaters. It's too short. The Namekagon would be perfect. It's a hundred eighty miles from the headwaters to St. Croix Falls. We could drop in and pull out anywhere."

Tom was trying to read the room, watching the group kneeling around the maps. He knew everyone except Bob had run the entire Namekagon at least twice. The river was a hidden gem. The Wisconsin DNR listed it as one of the top destinations in the state with many easy access points and wild remote areas between. It had a lot to offer, and you could see something new on every trip. It was the easy go-to, but Tom was a little bored with it and didn't want to just pick the route because it was easy. He stood, walked over, and peered down through the four heads below him. "It's a really great river, but I really want to do something different."

"What do you suggest?" Al asked.

Tom leaned in a little closer and scanned the maps. They had already eliminated the St. Croix's first segment above its confluence with the Namekagon River. He knew there were a lot of other smaller rivers in the area. It was a matter of finding something large enough for canoes and long enough for a five-day trip. Then he spotted something interesting.

"Have any of you done this river?" He reached out and pointed to a stretch of map that fell between the St. Croix headwaters and the Namekagon flowage. Everyone got up on all fours and followed his finger. Tom traced out a snake-like pattern that followed a smaller river, the Totagatic.

Bob said, "I haven't heard of that river, but I don't care where we go as long as we all have a good time."

Al pulled out his phone and searched the river name. "It says here that the Totagatic is eighty miles long and dumps into the Namekagon River. The name is Ojibwe and it means *River of Boggy River Way*."

Paul bent close to the map. He had trouble seeing small print, even with his glasses on. "The name probably comes from this area labeled the Dismal Swamp. Look how it snakes through all of these state forest areas and there are only two roads crossing along the whole stretch of river."

Tom knew he needed to sell his idea, so he jumped back into the conversation to boost momentum. "Now if that doesn't sound exciting, I don't know what does. Anyone else up for a new challenge?" His four friends pulled back from the maps, thinking about the route. "Come on guys, look! The river is right in the middle of an area we've canoed before, but we really haven't seen these state forests. It dumps into the Namekagon River right before the St. Croix. That still gives us the chance to hit the State Line Rapids near Danbury and the big rapids on the St. Croix near the Kettle River."

"Says here that the river should only be traveled during times of higher water and traveled by kayak or experienced canoeists," Al commented, still looking at his phone.

"Shouldn't be a problem," said John. "We're all experienced and the water's plenty high. It's rained for two solid weeks and the St. Croix River is over the barrier wall in downtown Stillwater. Guess where all that water came from? Up here." He swept his hands across all four of his maps. "I just worry about a smaller twisting river."

"Why?" Tom asked.

"It's just a lot of back and forth, and the map doesn't show any rapids. It might be really boring."

Bob looked concerned. "I don't know about all of the high water. Doesn't that make these rivers a lot more dangerous?"

Tom elbowed him and said, "Come on Bob, you use to swim in the ocean when you lived in California. Now that's a lot of water! Besides, it's a lot less dangerous than flying jets."

Bob picked up a piece of pepperoni and flicked it at Tom. "Good points, but—"

Tom cut him off. "Come on guys. We don't have all day. Is this the one or not?" Tom was now on his knees with his arms stretched out to the other guys in the circle. His face poured out anticipation as he asked, "All in favor?"

There was a short apprehensive pause and then each one of them said, "Aye."

They spent the rest of the afternoon planning the trip. The 131 total mileage broke down into a forty-four-mile start on the Totagatic River, a short six miles on the Namekagon River, then the last eighty-one miles on the St. Croix River. The pull-out point was the dam in St. Croix Falls. They inserted a buffer campsite at the old Nevers Dam site. Its location was on the Wisconsin side of the river, nine miles above the pull-out location. This gave them the chance to vary their itinerary if needed. They figured the group would be on the river for four to five days.

They also planned how to reach the start point and pull-out point without an independent driver. They knew none of their friends wanted to spend most of a day driving them to the middle of nowhere. Their parents couldn't shuttle them on such short notice because the trip occurred during the workweek. They decided to drive two vehicles to the take-out point and pile everyone into one vehicle for the trip to the start point.

They used a creative solution to transport gear, canoes, and five guys. John had driven an old Ford F150 his sophomore year. It was his first vehicle and he really grew attached to it. He hated to see it go, but the old Ford had too many issues to keep it on the road. To help John with his separation anxiety, his dad took the cab off, pressed the frame together, and welded a hitch on the front. This made a heavy-duty trailer John could use to nostalgically haul anything his heart desired. His junior year, John picked up a newer F250 with a rear topper. He used the newer truck to haul gear for camping trips, move his friends and family, and occasionally for an emergency camping tent when the weather wasn't cooperating.

This trip, the newer pickup would pull the old pickup bed his dad made. John specially fabricated a removable rack system to carry at least four canoes over the trailer's bed. This left the middle open to pack in gear. The extra passengers had to ride in the F250's topper-covered bed. Just so it wouldn't be entirely uncomfortable, Paul volunteered three fold-up lawn chairs. They were the style where you could stretch your legs out or lay back and take a nap. They sat low enough to let someone sit in the truck bed without banging their head. At best, they would act as uncomfortable lounge chairs. Lastly, the group added snack-filled coolers as makeshift coffee tables. The trip north would take about two and a half hours. The cramped quarters and semicomfortable chairs would act as a good warm-up for the five days in canoe seats.

The last thing the group dealt with were trip rules. None of them believed a long list of rules was needed if they focused on a few simple things. First and most important was pitching in. Canoeing and camping had a lot of idle brain time dipping a paddle in the water or sitting around the fire. During camp setup, meal time, or camp takedown, there were a lot of tasks. It didn't matter who volunteered for what, but everyone needed to participate.

Cooking meals involved the whole group. Some trips, one volunteer cooked every meal. Other trips, the chore rotated. All five agreed they would decide at camp each day who would cook the meals. This also automatically rotated who cleaned mealtime dishes, and since the cook never cleaned up, someone always volunteered to make meals.

They covered the important trip details in about two hours and everyone stood as the session ended. When Tom pulled out his phone to check messages, it prompted Paul to ask an all-important question. "Who's bringing their phone or is this a *'No Electronics'* trip?"

There was a short, stunned silence as Paul's question sunk in. They finished the planning session and hadn't discussed the touchy subject of electronics.

The guys were active Boy Scouts three to five years earlier. During outings, their scoutmaster often mandated *'No Electronics.'* The leaders believed more social interaction strengthened the troop's bond and forced the boys to work through problems rather than hiding behind their battery-powered entertainment. The scouts thought it was a plot to turn them all into cavemen. Now they understood that the deprivation allowed them to get the most from an outing.

Everyone owned a phone and some felt like they lost their left arm if it wasn't with them. Al was one of them. His gadget-guy personality liked all of the handy apps available at the touch of a finger. "I'm bringing mine," he said.

"It wouldn't hurt to bring them this trip," Tom added. "Sometimes phones are nothing more than a glorified camera because there's no service, but we should have service for most of the second half of the trip."

"Who has a working solar charger?" Al asked. He'd bought an inexpensive charger the previous summer, but it stopped working on the first canoe trip. He'd laid the solar panels on his gear while paddling across a lake. Water drops from his paddle seeped into the charger and shorted it out.

When they all looked at each other and no one answered, John hesitantly volunteered, "I can grab mine and bring it along."

Paul hated to bring electronics on camping trips because he believed in disconnecting from technology once in a while. He wasn't exactly an outdoor purist, but he was closer than his four friends. He knew that more electronics on the trip meant less time enjoying Mother Nature. Rather than pointing this out as he had in the past, he took another approach.

"Let's think about this," Paul said. "Phones spend a lot of time in plastic bags, and since we are running rapids and dealing with high water, they will stay tucked away in packs most of the time. That means solar charging them is difficult. Experience says we use them very little on these trips because we are so afraid of getting them wet."

"Hold on," Bob complained. "This is kind of my Air Force send off, and I'd like to have some pictures to remind me of the trip. Although, I really don't want to use my brand new phone just as a camera and risk losing it in a river."

"I have my GoPro in the car," Al said. "I can slip it into the waterproof case and bring a couple of different mounts. An extra battery should help us finish the trip if we don't use it continuously in video mode. It can take hundreds of pictures with two batteries."

John was thinking about trip logistics and asked, "How about river maps? We've all downloaded them for reference. We can access them anytime during the trip."

Tom frowned and snarled. "I quit taking phone maps with me unless I'm navigating. If I download them, my phone is like a little kid sitting in the back seat on a long trip. It keeps calling to me *'Are we there yet?'* When it does, I pull out my phone and check our location. It gives me the feeling that the trip is longer than it really is. I hate that. Maybe I can leave mine behind."

"I'm bringing mine," Al barked.

"Me too," said Bob. "John?"

"I haven't decided yet, but I know I'm bringing the large maps. They're always easier for the navigator than dealing with a phone."

Paul looked a little irritated but gave in and said, "Looks like it's going to be a blended trip. I'm leaving mine in the truck."

That ended the planning and they all left John's house to begin packing.

◆ ◆ ◆

Gear arrived at John's house the whole next week. Al and Paul brought over their canoes. Like John, they'd had them for years. All three canoes were seventeen-foot Alumicraft, made for long trips on lakes with space for gear and room to stretch out legs. They worked great paddling across open bodies of water, helping the canoeists maintain straight lines. On rivers, they worked okay as long as you didn't expect to maneuver too quickly. They were also built like battleships. Each boat had scars from years of use. The paint and decals were scratched and the undersides had long lines etched into the aluminum where rock and boat had met in the past. The front of Al's canoe was dented from a collision with a log floating in the water. He'd thought about knocking out the dent but left it because it fell behind the riveted panel that held the flotation chamber in the front of the canoe. Now it was just an honor badge, reminding him of the nighttime excursion when it happened.

Sunday evening before departure, John was in his garage sorting through the gear. His Bluetooth speaker was playing background music while he worked. He had his back to the open overhead door and paused when he heard the sound of gravel underfoot. He turned to see Anne walking up the steep driveway. She was wearing cargo shorts and hiking boots that showed off her tan, muscular legs. She also had two small camera bags slung over her shoulder. *Wow! She looks great*, thought John. *Definitely the outdoor type. T-shirt sleeves rolled up over the shoulders. Look at those toned muscular arms and long hair pulled back into a loose ponytail. It's a lot different than the jeans and sweatshirts she wore at the wrestling matches last winter. Much nicer!* He hadn't dated much through high school because he was kept busy with wrestling, working, doing homework, and hanging out with his friends.

Now that school was finished, he definitely had time to date. Walking up the driveway was someone who could fill that void. "Hey Anne. How-ya doing?"

"Hey back. Are you going on a trip?" Anne walked past the canoes and the old pickup trailer. She scanned the equipment strewn across the garage floor and commented to John, "This is some serious effort. It looks like you're packing for the wilderness."

"We are. We head out for five days tomorrow morning. Looks like you're working on your photojournalism career."

"Yeah, I'm heading for the Boom Site. I'm planning to take some bluff photos along the river. The trees are just leafing out and the sunlight creates some neat patterns on the forest floor. Since it was on the way, thought I'd stop by and see if I could take a few shots of the valley from your yard. Where are you guys going?"

John smiled and thought, *I wonder if she just stopped back to take scenic photos or if she has something else in mind?* He laid the camp saw in the pile with the rope and axe, then responded to her questions, "Yah, shoot away. We're heading to Northwestern Wisconsin, planning to canoe three rivers in one trip."

Anne pulled out her Nikon and hung the strap around her neck. She swept the lens across the valley's horizon, snapping photos as she moved. "Sounds like a lot of fun. Who's all going?"

"Five of us from the wrestling team. Me, Al, Paul, Bob, and Tom."

Anne's face brightened with interest. "Wow! I bet there would be some great outdoor shots on a trip like that." While she was speaking, she glanced back across the yard. She saw three two-person canoes and she quickly did the math, comparing canoe seats to bodies. "Wait a minute. That's five people for three canoes." She paused and then said with a little anticipation in her voice, "Those things don't steer well without help in the front." She hadn't expected that to come out like it did and she had a little adrenaline surge as she had a conflicting thought, *I wish I could fill the empty space, but it's an all-guys trip.*

John pretended to look for something in one of the gear bags, thinking about what he'd just heard. *Did she just hint about filling the open seat? This would be a great chance to get to know Anne better. The guys might be open to it, but I would take a little ribbing.* Then he said, "The steering won't cause too much trouble. We'll balance the canoe with heavy gear in the front to help the lone person paddle. We tried to find a sixth person, but everybody was busy. Have you seen that part of Wisconsin from the water? National Geographic could shoot a great documentary about the area. Great wildlife. Great scenery. You could spend days collecting pictures for your project."

Wow! I think he really wants me to go on the trip, she thought. "No. I haven't canoed north of St. Croix Falls. Maybe I'll plan to visit that area with a friend later this summer."

John still debated whether to ask Anne on the trip. *If I ask her and she says yes, that would mean slimming down the gear to fit the sixth person and running out to buy more food. Also, there's the awkward fact that five guys and one female on a camping trip doesn't paint a healthy picture of anybody's reputation.* He didn't want to miss this opportunity. Then he came up with a different idea he'd hoped would fly. "Too bad we didn't know about your photography thing two weeks ago. Do you think you could quickly find an interested friend?"

Anne looked shocked. *He just asked me to join them, but they leave tomorrow morning* "Wait, what?" Anne pursed her lips and shook her head. "John, how would I find someone in a day's notice? Not to mention pulling together food and gear." Then she smiled and chuckled. "Besides, I wouldn't want to spend five days camping with five guys. You know, all the burping, farting, and bad humor."

John laughed as well. "You must know my friends. Seriously though, what do you think about this idea? Our last campsite is at a place called Nevers Dam. If you can find a friend, you can meet us there and catch us at the end of the trip. You can take pictures of the guys coming off the river, and you can join us for the last nine miles on the water, taking more photos the next day. It's a beautiful stretch of river."

Her expression brightened as she thought, *This might work. I'd have to juggle my work schedule, find a friend, and convince my parents, but there's a chance.* Then she asked, "I could do that?"

"It's a free river."

"How will I know when to show up?"

"We leave tomorrow morning and should reach Nevers Dam sometime Thursday." John hadn't decided whether he was taking his phone. If Anne could join them, he would definitely need to reach her. "I can call or text you from somewhere upriver. We're bound to have service near one of the highways that cross the St. Croix." John's heart was pounding. He had just found a great way to ask Anne for her number. This was the moment of truth. If she bit on the idea, there was a chance something good was happening between them.

"That could work," Anne said. "I'll plan to take Thursday off from work. Let me check on a few things and get back to you. I think I have enough photos here. I gotta go before I lose my light. What's your number? I'll text you and we'll connect later in the week."

John gave her his biggest smile as he rattled off his number. She typed it into her phone and texted a quick ping.

"There you go. See you soon." She turned and walked down the driveway. Halfway to the street, she stopped and pulled up her camera again. She turned and snapped off a few photos of John working in the trip's prep scene, then continued on.

John called after her as she walked away, "Air out your tent and sleeping bag. Hope to see you Thursday." After she hopped into her car, John created her contact in his phone. He pulled up his list of ringtones and assigned the wolf whistle to Anne's name, hoping to hear it soon.

5

Anne

Anne was excited about the one-day trip on the upper St. Croix River. She hadn't canoed or camped on the river north of St. Croix Falls, but a year earlier she and her family spent a week at a lake cabin near the St. Croix's headwaters. As she drove to the Boom Site north of town, she began comparing the Boom Site to what she remembered about the woodlands further north. Both areas were beautiful. There were a few majestic trees in the woods along the river at the Boom Site that created a great place for short walks, but the area was close to town and used extensively. Up north, forest trails went for miles and you could walk for hours without seeing another person. The wildlife at the Boom Site had only a taste of what could be found in northwest Wisconsin. The Boom Site's high bluffs offered people the opportunity to see some birds not usually seen in open forests. Unfortunately, the bluffs and the frequent visitors also curbed the diversity of animals she had seen up north. Simply put, northwest Wisconsin had a more abundant and diverse ecology and she wanted to see more of it.

She was also excited about getting to know John. She had spent a lot of time photographing the home wrestling meets last winter and got to know most of the guys on the team. They were an intense bunch before every match, focusing on how they could beat their opponents.

After the matches, they turned into a laid-back bunch of guys who were just fun to be around. She and John shared conversations during the wrestling season, but those talks were always part of the frenzy occurring before or after a wrestling meet. John's reputation was good. He worked hard at school and held the same job for almost three years. His group of friends were close and they had been together for years. This meant that he understood relationships. Unfortunately, that was all she knew about John. She hoped to get to know him more and believed that could happen if they could talk one-on-one during this trip. The difficulty was that a lot of pieces had to fall into place before she could go.

Anne made her way down the long steps from the Boom Site parking area into the walled valley between the bluffs. Her mind was racing as she snapped photos. To go on this short trip, she had to solve some difficult problems—some she'd never tackled before. She had been on mixed overnight camping trips, but all of them were at church camp or were chaperoned by parents. This trip included five graduating senior guys and no chaperones. John earned bonus points for suggesting she find a friend to join her. It showed he was concerned about her and believed she felt uncomfortable joining the group overnight. This concern helped, but it was only a small token to begin solving the overall challenges. Could she get away later in the week? Would her parents allow her to go? Which of her friends could go with her?

The terrain north of the steps gradually roughened and eventually became a goat path, ending at a steep bluff a couple miles upriver. Anne really hadn't noticed that the trail began narrowing. When she did, she was a mile from the parking area and snapped only a half dozen pictures. Her mind wasn't really photography-focused today. The trip's biggest obstacle involved her mom. If she didn't buy into this trip, any other planning was a waste of time. It was Sunday afternoon and Anne really wanted to meet the group up river on Thursday. Realizing what needed to be done, she snapped the cover on her lens, turned, and jogged back downriver. The conversation with her mom needed to happen today.

◆ ◆ ◆

It was dusk when Anne pulled into the driveway. Her head was still spinning with excitement about the trip and worry about the upcoming talk with her mom. She grabbed her gear from the back seat, ideas ticking off in her head on how she could start the conversation.

"Mom, I'm home!" Anne yelled as she walked in the back door. The dog bounded over from her kennel in the corner, tail wagging, and looking for some attention. Anne reached down and scratched the dog's chin. "Good girl. Did you miss me, Molly?"

"How was the photoshoot?" Anne's mom Sherry called from the other room. "Anything spectacular show up for your portfolio?"

"Nah, I only shot a half dozen pictures." Anne dropped her gear on the kitchen table, then walked into the pantry and grabbed a power bar. Molly followed her back to the table, tail swinging in anticipation. When Anne pulled out a snack, something usually went to the dog.

Sherry walked into the kitchen and over to the refrigerator. She glanced at Anne sitting at the table. "What happened? You were gone for a couple hours. Have problems with your camera?"

Anne broke off a piece of the bar and held it out next to her hip. Molly's front paws left the floor and landed on Anne's leg. The dog grabbed the snack and swallowed it whole, tail a blur of motion. Idle conversation was a great icebreaker, but Anne was looking for an opportunity to talk about the trip. Earlier, she thought about just sneaking away and saying that she was staying at a friend's house, but she remembered lying to her mom when she was younger. It had never worked then and she understood why. Lies always had holes in them. To cover the holes, you needed to grow the lie. Eventually, the lie becomes so big that you can't get out of it. This would be the biggest lie she ever told, and her mom had a knack for seeing through untruth. Finally, she took a big breath and just jumped into it.

"Mom, you remember that guy John I told you about, the one that lives on the North Hill bluffs? He's going on an upper St. Croix River canoe trip. He invited me to show up on the trip's last night and, then canoe the last day." Sherry was bent over looking into the fridge. She stood up from behind the open door and twisted her head toward Anne. If the door wasn't open between them, Sherry's jaw may have dropped all the way to the floor. "Before you say anything, Mom, please hear me out."

While she was driving back home from the Boom Site, Anne had rehearsed the reasons to go on the trip. She didn't know how many she could list before her mom cut in, but she started anyway. "I told John about my plan for a photojournalism degree and my college entrance portfolio. He suggested this would be a great chance to take some great photos because they are canoeing the upper St. Croix River. I would meet them on the last evening, photograph their canoeing and camping, and then catch the scenic upper river way the next day."

"Them? How many people are going on this trip?" Sherry caught that there were more than just the two of them. One point for Mom.

"Well, there are actually five guys from the wrestling team, but that's a good thing."

"Five guys! How are five guys and one young woman a good thing?"

"Oh, I'm not planning to go alone. I'm taking a friend but haven't yet figured out who. Our neighbor, Al, is one of the guys. Remember how he has been like a big brother to me? He looked out for me and his younger sister Sandy when we were all at church camp two summers ago."

"That helps a little, but I'm not convinced this is a good idea."

Anne understood the power of a question during negotiations and this is what the discussion was. Her mom wasn't yelling, and she came over and sat across from her. So she asked, "What else would it take to convince you to trust me on this? I've taken hundreds of photos around town, and this is the first chance I've had to include something from another area."

"It isn't trusting you that worries me. I do have trust. You understand what's going on and you have been raised well. I worry more about five young men influencing my daughter." Sherry paused, smiled, then said, "I have to tell you that I have met John. He greets me at the grocery store and we talk school and wrestling. He knows you are my daughter. He's sweet and considerate, but I still don't know him as well as I know Al. Maybe if more of your friends were going, I might hear a little more."

"Come on Mom. This is kind of a short-notice photo opportunity. I'm sure I can find one other person on short notice, but I don't think I can find more than that. Isn't that enough? "

"Well no. I have a lot of other questions. Who else is going? Where is the campsite? How will you get there, and who picks you up? What else can you tell me?"

When Sherry started asking about the trip details, Anne found that she really hadn't found out much about the trip. "John just mentioned it this morning and I came to you before doing any real planning. I don't know how to answer all the questions you have. Let me call John. He can fill in a lot of blanks."

Then Sherry's features softened and she looked right at Anne. "This is a big ask, Anne, and I know you're old enough to handle something like this. I really appreciate talking about it. How about if I call our neighbors and see what they know about the trip. I'm still not convinced you can go, but talking to them may raise my comfort level."

Anne sat up a little and cracked a smile. Maybe there was some hope. "Thanks Mom. That would be great. I'll call John first thing tomorrow and find out more details."

"Since it's getting late, I'll also call the neighbors first thing in the morning. Okay?"

"Sounds good, Mom." Anne grabbed her bags and got up from the table.

Departure Morning

The morning of departure, John's garage floor was littered with tents, rope, cooking gear, and packs. Sitting next to the food pack, Al and John were taking meal inventory and packing the food inside the garbage bag–lined pack. Paul and Tom checked the camp gear for all the necessary tools. Each tent needed a tarp as a barrier between the ground and the tent floor to keep moisture off their sleeping bags. Multiple ropes and paracord were needed to hang food packs and erect rain flies. They also checked for unnecessary duplicate gear. Nobody wanted to handle or carry extra gear if it wasn't essential.

It was shortly after seven in the morning. The group planned to go through the gear and pack everything into the trailer. They would back out of the driveway around nine, arrive at the start point by noon, and spend a half day on the river.

"Where's the cook stove and lantern?" Paul asked. "I want to make sure they are full of fuel before we leave. That will eliminate one extra can of white gas."

"Wow! There's a lot of stuff here," Bob said as he walked up with his sleeping bag. "How are we going to get it all into the canoes?"

Tom tossed Paul the funnel to fill the stove and said, "It's like Tetris. Everything has its place, and we use every bit of space. By the way, Bob, you're gonna want that sleeping bag in a garbage bag just in case you tip over. There's nothing like spending the night in a soggy sleeping bag."

Bob went wide-eyed in disbelief, "Wadda-ya mean tip over. I'm not planning to do any serious leaning while I'm in the boat." He had a healthy respect for the tippy nature of canoes and believed he had a good handle on what to do.

Tom smiled and said, "Oh, you'll see. There are a couple rapids that are tough for these boats. One wrong move and you're sideways on a rock. Then the water pushes on the canoe from upstream and just rolls you over."

"I guess I'll just stay away from the rocks."

"Sure, that'll work," Tom said with a hint of sarcasm.

"Is that the food pack," Bob asked, looking over at John and Al sorting through the big Duluth pack. "It's huge!"

"Yah. This is what's going to feed us for five days," Al said. "It has the cooking gear and the food. We're about done here. You want to load this into the trailer, Bob?"

Bob walked over and grabbed the shoulder strap and lifted. "Holy Crap! This thing must weigh eighty pounds. Who's going to carry it?"

"Nobody really," John said behind a giggle. "It sits in the canoe until we unload for the day. The only exception is our one portage around the dam at the start of day two."

"Figures," Bob responded. "An early portage means that the pack is still fairly full. How long is the portage?"

Al walked over and grabbed one of the straps to help Bob lift the pack over the side and into the trailer bed. "I think we can handle it. It's ten rods. That's a little over fifty yards, Mr. New Guy."

While they were loading the pack, John's phone let out a wolf whistle. He smiled and pulled it out of his pocket. Al and Bob looked at each other, a little puzzled and a lot curious. They saw the expression on John's face and couldn't remember ever seeing John smile when his phone rang.

"Hello."

"Hey John, who is that?" Al yelled. John just turned, waved his arm at the guys, and left them to finish loading the trailer. He walked over to the porch where he could talk privately.

"John, this is Anne. I know you're busy packing, but I wanted to let you know that I'm working out some details for the trip, but I think I can go." Anne knew that the details might still stop her from meeting John on the river, but she had over three days to work on them. She hoped that the over confidence wasn't a jinx.

"Great! Can I help with any of those details?"

"As a matter of fact, you can…..."

Anne and John talked for the next half hour. She told him about the conversation with her mom and how she needed more details about the trip. John filled in the details and they talked about how she could fold into the group on the last day. She had to figure out how to move a canoe and gear to the Nevers Dam campsite, but there was room on the trailer to bring everything back. Food wouldn't be a problem, but John suggested that she bring along a little something to share. The guys would appreciate something that wouldn't necessarily keep well on a weeklong trip. She could decide what that might be.

Just as they were about to hang up, Anne asked John for some help with her mom. "I have a little problem to solve before I can meet you on Thursday. Mom needs some reassurance that you guys are okay to hang out with. She's okay with Al because he's our neighbor and she knows you from grocery shopping. What can you give me on the other guys?"

"I've known most of these guys more than six years and all of our parents know each other. That's probably the best reference I can give you. Your mom can talk to any of the parents if she wants to. I've only known Bob about three years. He's the reason we're going on the trip.

You've probably seen him walking the school halls in his ROTC uniform. He's heading for the Air Force Academy in about a week. He wants to be a pilot and doesn't want to do anything to screw that up, so your parents don't need to worry about him. You might call him a rule follower, but the guy has a great personality and makes friends easily. I know your mom would like him."

"Thanks. That helps. She'll talk with your parents and hopefully that will be enough. I'll let you know when you call on Thursday morning."

"Sounds like a plan. I've gotta go. The guys are almost done loading the trailer. Talk to you Thursday." They hung up and John walked back to his gear. With his back to the group, he pulled out a Ziplock bag, sealed his phone in it, and dropped it into his day pack. He hadn't told them whether he was taking his phone. Even though no one knew who he was talking to, it was a guarantee the guys would heckle him about bringing it to talk to Anne. Hopefully the guys didn't see him stash it. He would need it later and didn't want to leave it in the truck.

John lifted his pack and turned to walk it over to the trailer. He took a step and looked up to see his four friends staring at him. He froze and thought, *Oh-Oh! They look like a pack of wolves ready to pounce.*

Al spoke first, using a tone that sounded like he was taunting a younger sibling. "You were sure happy to get that call. Seems you knew who it was when it rang. Let me guess. Wolf whistle ring tone. Gotta be female. Maybe our homecoming queen?" The four laughed, continuing to look at John. Something was up and they wanted to know what. He was cornered.

John's mind began fabricating a story about the phone call. He'd agonized all morning about how to tell the guys that Anne and a friend were joining them, and now he had to cover his butt. Then he thought differently. This was a case when truth was stranger than fiction. They would never expect to hear what was really happening.

The four of them were still staring at John, all with mocking grins. John just smiled back at them and said, "You're funny, but not far off." He received the surprise looks he was hoping for. "I have some good news. Two ladies will join us the last day of the trip."

"Wait, what? Who? Really?" came the comments from the group.

"Yah, I'm serious. You know the pizza delivery last week? That was Anne from the school newspaper. Remember her? She wrote about the wrestling team last winter. She stopped back here yesterday with her camera gear, on her way out to take pictures of the valley. She's creating a college entrance portfolio. We talked about the trip and she mentioned how shots of the Upper St. Croix and active canoeing photos would really add to the collection." John was stretching the photography reasoning a bit and holding back on the real reason he hoped she was coming. "She and a friend will meet us at Nevers Dam, camp overnight, and canoe the last day."

"You dog!" Al put his hands on his hips and smiled slyly. "I know her. She's my neighbor. She's also the one who took team photos this season. Who is coming with her?"

"She hasn't said."

"I don't know about babes on this camping trip," remarked Paul. "This was supposed to be a sendoff for Bob. They might cramp our style."

Bob disagreed, "There's nothing wrong with adding a couple babes to the end of this trip. They'll definitely improve the scenery after spending a couple days and nights with you guys."

Tom couldn't resist jumping into the fray, "And what's wrong with my company? Don't you like the smell of bug dope and musk? I know you love it when I talk weightlifting all day long."

Bob picked up a bungee cord and tossed it at Tom. "You know what I mean. I'd take female company over yours anytime. John, back me up here. You set up this deal with the babes."

"Hey guys, it's a free river," John said. "Besides, it's just for one night and half of a day on the slowest part of the trip. The extra company will break the boredom. It's almost nine. Let's load the canoes and get out of here."

The change in focus ended the debate and everyone moved to load the trailer. Tom grabbed the yoke in the middle of one of the aluminum canoes and flipped it up over his head.

"Tom, you're an animal," Paul called out. "Let me help you with that."

"I got it." Every muscle in Tom's back and arms flexed as he hoisted the canoe onto the top rack. He had his shirt off and all the guys watched in envy as he lifted. It wasn't so much that each of them couldn't lift a seventy-pound canoe on their own. It was the fact that the spring's bodybuilding had filled out and sculpted Tom's physique. A month earlier, Tom had participated in his first competition. He'd worked hard to build muscle and lean his body. He even had his body professionally shaved to show muscle definition. He was still ripped, but now all the jet-black body hair was growing back. Tom really did look like an animal.

"I'm not too proud," Paul needled. "Bob can you give me a hand with this one? We'll let Animal load the last one too." Tom grinned and growled as he lifted and tossed the last canoe on the lower rack.

The three of them had just finished tying down the canoes when John called them over to see who would ride shotgun. After Al won the spot, they piled into the two vehicles and headed north toward St. Croix Falls.

7

Anne Closes the Deal

Anne hit the red button on her mobile phone, ending the call with John. She had set her alarm to make sure she caught him before he left town and made the call from her room before breakfast to make sure her mom couldn't hear the conversation. Anne didn't want to give her mom any reasons to cancel the trip, if any reasons were discussed. She now had the details needed to meet the group on the river.

During the summer, eight-thirty was a little earlier than she liked to get up, but Anne had a lot to do before the trip could happen. This morning, she needed to dig out the camping gear for an overnight trip. Her sleeping bag hadn't been used since last fall on an overnight at a friend's house. The tent hadn't been used since late last summer, and both needed some air to take away the musty closet smell.

Finding a canoe was another problem. Anytime she and her friends went out north of Stillwater, they rented an Alumicraft from a downtown vendor. The seventeen-foot, all-aluminum canoes were like battleships. They could take a beating from rocks, trees, and careless teenagers and still last long enough to pass to the next generation. The problem was cost. Renting for a day was reasonable, but once overnight crept into the picture, the vendor charged more than Anne felt it was worth. It was not that she didn't have enough money from her pizza delivery tips to pay for the rental; it was the fact that those tips were supposed to go into her college fund and not toward indulgence. Justifying the cost by saying she would take pictures for her portfolio seemed reasonable, but she would only go there if there were no other options.

She and her dad used the family canoe occasionally. That was always a special treat because it was a work of art. Her dad spent nearly five years building the wooden canoe in the garage. He started on it before kits were readily available, so it was essentially built from scratch. When she was in elementary school, her dad would take her to small lumber yards and sawmills looking for just the right materials. He would sort through piles of white cedar wood to find straight pieces with very few knots. At the time, she was bored with trips, but now she understood why they were important. Cedar was very rot resistant, and clear cedar was hard to come by. He needed both qualities to keep the canoe watertight and to give it a long life. By the time she reached the end of middle school, the canoe was assembled, and her dad started the finishing process. Anne would help him hand sand the cedar and sometimes light sand between varnish coats. It was a lot of work. She doubted her dad would let her use it on this trip. Maybe one of her friends knew someone who could lend her a canoe.

Anne also had more detailed answers to her mom's questions about the trip. She could point out Nevers Dam as the starting location, just north of St. Croix Falls, Wisconsin. They would camp there overnight and start downriver the next morning. There were no rapids on the stretch of river, so there was little worry about capsizing, and St. Croix Falls was a short couple of hours away. The logistics wouldn't totally convince her that the trip was a good idea, but they would raise the comfort level.

Anne kicked the blankets off her body, rolled over, and swung her legs across the bed's edge. The cold maple floor against her feet distracted her from the trip planning, and she fished her slippers out from under the bed. She sat there thinking about the transportation problem while she stretched her arms high over her head. There was one remaining slot on John's trailer rack, so returning home was already taken care of. Getting to Nevers Dam still needed planning. The best solution would have someone drop her and a friend at the dam so they wouldn't need to retrieve a car. The vehicle didn't need to carry a lot of gear, but it needed to handle a canoe. That meant the vehicle should have either a top rack to carry the canoe or a trailer hitch. *Great,* she thought. *I might have to find a trailer too.*

She needed to grab a little food. Their refrigerator and pantry probably had enough for two meals and something to snack on while paddling. That would all fit in one cooler. John mentioned occasional problems with raccoons or bears, so Anne thought about a food pack she could hang, then remembered that their family had a locking cooler out in the garage. It would keep out any wildlife and serve the purpose for carrying one day's food supply.

She and a friend wouldn't need much gear. The guys would have most of the odd necessities because they packed for multiple days. They needed a tent and sleeping bag for the overnight and some extra clothes. Add in a water bottle, her camera gear, and that should be it.

Next, Anne needed to find someone go with her. The trip was really short notice, and many of her close friends already had plans or were working. She brought up contacts on her phone and started to thumb through them as she stood up. The change in position shifted pressure onto her bladder, so she walked down the hall to the bathroom.

She came across a few names to call before she closed the bathroom door. As Anne turned toward the toilet, she glanced out the small window that faced their backyard. Through the transparent curtains, she saw their neighbor Sandy walking a dog in her fenced yard behind their house.

Mom mentioned her yesterday, and if Sandy is willing, Mom's comfort level really jumps, Anne thought, deciding Sandy was the quickest and best option. *I need to get to her before Mom talks to the neighbors. If Sandy hears about the trip from the parents, she'll be my chaperone rather than a friend coming along on a river trip. If Sandy says yes, we can develop a story about what gentlemen the guys are.*

Anne quickly finished her business and jogged back to her room. She threw on some clean workout clothes and went downstairs. Anne passed her mom in the kitchen as she went out the back door.

"Want some breakfast, Anne?"

"Yes, but in a minute, Mom. I want to take the dog out first. Come on Molly! Let's go outside."

Sandy's dog heard the pair walk down the back steps, and it briefly barked. Sandy hushed the yellow lab as Anne came across her yard to the chain-link fence.

"Morning, Sandy. How's the new dog?"

Sandy picked up a stick, tossed it toward the back fence for the dog, and walked over to Anne. "Oh, not too bad, but these early mornings are a little rough on me. If I don't walk the dog first thing in the morning, I usually have to clean up the kitchen floor. I found this out the first morning I slept in. My socks soaked up a puddle next to the refrigerator."

"She'll eventually grow out of it. How old is she?"

"Almost a year. I hope it happens soon. I work in the afternoons and evenings, and I'd like to sleep in during summer break."

Anne panicked a little. That probably meant Sandy couldn't go on the short trip. "Where are you working this summer?"

"Next week I start serving ice cream and making malts at Leo's Café downtown. Summers have been really busy for them since the old lift bridge opened as a St. Croix River bike and pedestrian crossing this year. They've had trouble keeping up with all of the tourists."

Breathing a sigh of relief, Anne said, "Speaking of the St. Croix, when did Al leave for his trip?"

"Pretty early. I think he was up before six. How did you know he was going on a trip?"

"I delivered pizza to his friend John's place when the group was planning the trip. Doesn't he have a great place to live? His front window is like a picture frame looking out onto the valley. You can see the lift bridge and most of downtown's main street."

"I kind of know where it is. Somewhere up on the North Hill bluffs. Of course, any view from up there is fantastic. Since you're on the school newspaper, I'm betting you've taken some photos from the bluffs."

That was the cue Anne was looking for. "As a matter of fact, I stopped back to John's house yesterday to take a few pictures. I'm working on a college entrance portfolio and he invited me to take photos from his front yard. When I pulled up, he was packing up gear in the driveway. While I shot pictures, we started talking about how beautiful the river is. Next thing I know we're talking about how the upper St. Croix would make a great photo opportunity and he suggests that I join him and his buddies on the last leg of the trip."

"Are you planning to go? Where would you meet them?"

"He suggested meeting them at a place called Nevers Dam on the last night of the trip. I'd stay overnight and canoe the last nine miles with them."

"Wow! Your mom's okay with that?"

Anne rolled her eyes at the thought of convincing her mom. "I'm working on that, and I have other problems to solve today. This whole thing has a short fuse. I have to pull out gear, find a canoe, and rearrange my work schedule. My biggest problem is finding a second person for the trip. I'm planning to meet the guys on Thursday evening. Whoever I ask really has to have a flexible schedule, a comfort level in a canoe, and the green light to go."

Sandy stood there for a second thinking about what Anne just said. *I was really jealous when Al said he was going canoeing and I really want to go up river a few times this summer. I usually go camping somewhere every summer, but I have nothing planned this year because of my summer job at Leo's Café. This might be a chance to squeeze something in before starting work.*

"Find anyone yet?" Sandy asked Anne.

"Funny you should ask. I'm not going on a trip like this without another female, and my mom is really hung up on the fact that she doesn't know three of the guys. She mentioned your name yesterday when I told her about the trip because she knows Al would look out for you. I know we haven't done much together since church camp a few years ago, but would you like to go?"

Sandy smiled and said, "Maybe. I wouldn't go alone with five guys either, but here's the question. You're going just to take pictures?"

"Well, not entirely. I'm a little interested in John. I've talked with him during the wrestling season, and he seems really nice. This is a good excuse to find out more about him. You know, like seeing a guy with his friends in the wild. Sometimes guys can be real animals."

"Good plan. Your parents are okay with this, as long as I'm going along?"

"Maybe. My mom's gonna call your parents later this morning to talk about the guys. I think it's because your brother's on the trip. He would know if there are there any skeletons in their closets."

"Al and I are pretty close, as siblings go. He sometimes tells me about things they do as a team, like practical jokes and stuff."

"How about the new guy? He's only been around since freshman year. Know anything about him?"

"I know a little. His name is Bob and he's the reason they took this trip. I think Al mentioned that he's leaving for Air Force boot camp after Memorial Day. Bob is in ROTC and really wants to become pilot. He's a pretty straight-up guy and wouldn't do anything to screw up a future military career."

"That's perfect. Do you know anything about the last two, Tom and Paul?"

"Probably nothing more than you do, Anne. I see them in the halls at school and talked to them a little during the wrestling season. I think Al mentioned that Tom is competing in bodybuilding, but that's about it."

"So what do you think? We haven't done anything as neighbors for quite a while and this could be a chance to catch up. Would you like to go up river?"

Sandy paused a few seconds and watched the dogs sniff across the back fence line. She liked camping on the river. Her brother wasn't who she would choose to camp with, but he was already part of the package. She and Anne had grown up together. When they were younger, the two of them would spend entire days playing in the yards or at each other's houses. When they reached high school, they developed interests with new friends that took them different directions. That separation hadn't caused any harm, but it built an unfamiliar gap between them. She kind of missed the old friendship they had.

Sandy smiled and said, "I'm interested. Since your mom is calling my parents this morning, let me check with them and see if it's okay. Maybe I can help them convince your mom."

Anne reached across the fence and gave Sandy a big hug. "Thanks Sandy. I really appreciate this. Just in case it works out, can we talk about what we need?"

They spent the next twenty minutes talking about camping gear and the phone call between their parents. Sandy's family easily had enough gear to outfit her on a short overnight trip. Al had taken most of the equipment needed for a weeklong camping excursion, but all of that gear would be there when they met the guys at Nevers Dam. Al had also taken the family canoe. That meant they still had no river transportation.

The two of them debated whether Sandy should prompt her mom about the trip or if she should let the idea develop as part of their parent's phone call. In the end, they figured the topic would come up naturally because Anne's mom was watching the two of them talking in the yard. There was only one reason why Anne would get up early, go into the back yard, and talk with Sandy. They also agreed that the best tactic placed Sandy in the room when the phone call took place. However, Sandy was not willing to wait around all day for Anne's mom to call.

"Tell you what," Anne said. "My mom's in the kitchen now, but she's heading out for some appointment midmorning. Why don't you head inside and text me if one of your parents are around. If so, I'll ask Mom to call."

"Sounds good." Sandy whistled for her dog and walked back to her house.

When Anne walked in the back door, there was a plate on the table with a glass of orange juice next to it. Her mom walked to the microwave and pushed the +30. "You two talked long enough that your breakfast got cold. Do you think your trip plan is developed enough to share?"

Anne picked up the glass and took a big gulp of juice. "It's a lot further than it was yesterday. I can fill in the where, when, and how details, but I'm betting that there's still doubt in your mind about the company."

"Yes there is. It's hard to reach a good comfort level when I don't know a few of the young men on the trip. I'm sure you and Sandy talked about all five of the guys while you were in the yard. What else can you tell me?"

Anne's mom brought breakfast over to the table and sat down. While Anne ate, she shared what logistics she knew and told her about Bob's Air Force aspirations. They talked about John's friendly character at the store and how Anne's mom enjoyed their conversations. They also talked about the good sibling relationship Sandy and Al had. That led to Anne describing how Al was kind of a big brother to her, watching out for her when they were younger and helping her in the one math class they shared. Tom's bodybuilding didn't impress Mom. She frowned a little and shook her head but conceded that it was something that required dedication and focus.

Anne was just about finished with breakfast when the phone next to her plate buzzed. She touched the screen and read *"Mom's around right now."*

"Mom, why don't you call our neighbors." Anne held up her phone and showed her the text. "Sandy say's her mom is around."

"All right, all right. You're really working this one hard." Anne's mom got up and walked over to her purse. She reached in, pulled out her phone, and found the contact she needed. When she pushed send, she walked into the next room, leaving Anne to finish her breakfast in the kitchen.

Much as Anne wanted to get up and follow her mother, she sat tight. Appearing too anxious might tip the scales against the trip's photography premise and make her seem eager to see John. Her mom was pretty sharp, and Anne was certain she already knew some kind of relationship was developing. It was best to let this phone call happen and hope Sandy could help her on the other end of the call.

Anne listened hard but only caught bits and pieces of the ten-minute conversation. When her mother said goodbye, she walked back into the kitchen and sat down.

"Well, our neighbor has nothing but good things to say about the four young men. Al has invited his friends over to their house several times in the past few years. Sandy's mom says they are a high-energy group and a lot of fun to be around. They are respectful and engaging to the point where they have helped the family with several projects. They even helped Paul's family clean up some major storm damage late last summer. Regardless of Sandy's coaching in the background, I think I have a good sense of what these guys are like. I know Al and John, but it's just a shame I haven't met the last three young men. That would probably seal the deal."

"It sounds like you also talked about Sandy joining me on the trip."

"Yes, her mom is okay with it if I'm okay with it."

Anne smiled and said, "Well then, I have an idea how you can meet the last three guys. We need a ride to Nevers Dam. If you're willing to take us there, we can introduce you to the entire group."

"You would be okay with that? Are you sure I won't say something embarrassing to your friends?"

Anne smirked and said, "You probably will, but it's a price I'm willing to pay."

"If you have everything loaded and ready to go Thursday morning, I'll drive you. All I want to do is hop into the driver's seat and point the car north. Can you handle that?"

"Yes Mom. Thanks."

By late Monday afternoon, Anne and Sandy had collected the small amount of gear they needed. They stored it in the garage next to the car for easy loading Wednesday evening. When Anne received John's call on Thursday, they could just hop into the car and drive north.

There was still one major problem Anne needed to solve. She hadn't found a canoe. Several of her friends owned canoes, but all of them were stored at a cabin or in the back of a self-storage garage somewhere. Each time she brought equipment into the garage, Anne would glance at the wooden canoe hanging from the garage rafters. It had been more than a year since the handcrafted boat had seen water. Dust had collected along the sides, but the varnished finish still reflected the sunlight shining through the open garage door. It looked more and more like she would need to spend the money to rent a canoe since using the wooden work of art was probably out of the question.

An alarm chimed on Anne's phone. She pulled it out of her back pocket and saw it was her four o'clock work reminder. The dinner rush hour was starting at the pizza place and she had to be at work before c.

She also saw there was a new voicemail, but it would have to wait until she made it to work. She could pick up the message during the downtime between deliveries.

Anne rushed upstairs to change clothes for her six-hour shift. As she pulled back her hair, looking in the bathroom mirror, it occurred to her that she actually hadn't asked her dad for the canoe. She thought to herself. *Why should I be afraid to ask? The worst he could say is no.* She made up her mind that it was worth the chance, but she wanted to ask face to face so her dad would see how important the trip was to her. That meant getting up very early again tomorrow. Dad arrived home from work around five and would jump into bed sometime before she finished work. He left for work around six a.m., hours before she usually got up. She set her phone alarm for five thirty a.m. and headed to work.

Day 1 – Totagatic River

The early afternoon sun highlighted the small dam. The rusty flow over the top was broken up by floating drops reflecting the sunlight. It resembled a magazine cover, dream of the rugged outdoors. The weather had turned from three weeks of spring rain to pre-summer, cloudless, and almost eighty degrees. The three who spent an hour riding under the topper were refreshed by the torrent produced by the dam.

The guys stared at Tom, waiting for him to react to Paul's accusing question about who chose the river. They were used to the slower, less flooded version of the Upper St. Croix flowage. None of them had tackled such intense water, and they all looked worried.

Tom looked from his friends to the dam, and then to the current rushing by their launch point. Turning his head back toward his four friends, he said, "Come on, this is what we live for!" Tom glanced at the water, then continued, almost stuttering. "It's a new challenge, an unknown opponent, and an obstacle to overcome. How is this any different than wrestling at the state tournament, or graduating high school, or joining the Air Force?"

Tom stood there, his hands out with a look of unease on his face, trying to overcome his anxiety. His four friends were pondering what he said. He knew they were cautious, but he also knew they liked to push their limits.

Al's adrenaline surged watching the water flow over the dam. A couple of small branches floated past them. In less than thirty seconds, they were around the first bend in the river. The maps showed the Totagatic River twisting and turning through the forest, but maps rarely went to the detail you saw in person. The river channel was a narrow twenty yards wide with the trees leaning over the river, clinging to the bank where half of their roots hung bare in the rushing water. The bend just downstream almost seemed like a sharp ninety-degree turn with the bank acting like a curb, forcing the water around the corner. He had canoed fast water through rapids on an open river but had never taken his long lake canoes on swift water with sharp bends. The adrenaline surge helped him make up his mind. "Let's get the gear and boats," he said. "I can't wait to tackle this river."

Tom was already jogging up the trail and yelled to the group, "On my way."

The four started walking up the trail to the truck. They could hear the bang of aluminum against the trailer racks. A minute later, they heard Tom's classic weightlifting yell.

"What is he lifting up there?" Paul asked. "It sounds like he's finishing one of his three hundred-pound bench press workouts."

They had their answer when Tom came into view through the trees. His stutter stepping down the steep incline was accented by the 140-pound load on his shoulders. He had loaded the food pack on his back and then picked up a canoe and rested it across his shoulders. The four of them backed off the trail and into the woods just before Tom sped past them, going down the hill.

"Somebody want to give me a hand putting this down? There's not much room between the bottom of the hill and the water's edge."

Al ran after him and said, "If you keep picking up speed, you won't need to worry about that. You'll end up in the water." He grabbed the back of the canoe just to slow him down.

Tom stopped when he reached the narrow strip of bank at the river's edge. The canoe's nose hung over the water and Tom had to rotate his body to tip the nose down onto solid ground. Al stepped under the canoe with Tom and lifted it off his back so he could drop the food pack. Normally, there was an edge where the water eroded the soil away, but the flooding river was over the bank. This forced Tom and Al to slide the front end into the water and leave the back half resting on the narrow strip of dirt between the rushing water and the woods. Things were a little tippy as Tom crawled out front to place the food pack. Al sat on the rear deck plate to steady it for Tom. The last thing they wanted was a cool dip in the water before they got started.

Soon all three canoes were nosed into the water and gear piled on the bank. With the bows sticking out into the water and the current angling the boats downstream, the canoes resembled three long silver sardines layered into a can. Al and Tom stayed with the canoes and began loading them. Al shifted from one canoe to the other, sitting on the rear deck and handing Tom equipment. The process was slow. When Tom stepped from the middle of one canoe to another, the second canoe would roll sideways in the water. Al had to grab the second stern to steady his movement between the boats. Thirty minutes later, all three canoes were packed, tarps tucked over the top, and ready to slide off the bank.

"One last thing to do before we shove off," Paul said. He remembered the moaning and indecision at the end of the planning session when they talked about leaving their phones behind and it made him grin. "Who's going to break the connection to civilization?" Paul pulled out his phone and then held out his hand to collect any others.

"I'm in." Tom pulled his phone out of his cargo shorts and handed it to Paul. "I don't want that map app calling my name every time I want to know where we are."

John was hoping the topic was forgotten and planned to never mention it until they pushed off the river bank.

"How-bout you, lover boy?" Paul asked.

All John could think was, *Let the heckling begin.* "I'm keeping mine. Al? Bob?"

Al put a hand over the phone in his pocket. "I gotta have mine. Who else is going to use the map app for navigation? I'm the best at it. Besides, I'll use it for other stuff."

"I'm taking mine too," Bob said. "Photos, lots of photos."

"Are you sure?" Paul asked. "Last chance to improve the experience." All three shook their heads.

When Paul returned, Bob was directing the other three guys in what looked like a movie scene. "I want to get a shot of this before we leave." Bob was looking at his screen and shuffling along the narrow riverbank to get the best shot. "Paul, can you sit in the back of the last canoe? I want to get all of you in the shot with the dam in the background." Bob backed far enough away to get the four guys and three canoes into the picture. "This will be a great shot." After taking three photos, he shoved his phone in his shirt pocket and picked up his paddle. "Can you push us off, John?" He stepped around Paul and crawled across the gear to the front of the canoe.

John pushed them off and stepped into the rear of the single-man canoe that was counterweighted with the food pack and the tents. Paul and Bob were just rounding the first bend as Tom gave John's canoe a shove.

This was the first trip of the year for both Tom and Al, but neither one of them felt rusty from the long winter. Al looked at Tom and asked, "Rock-paper-scissors for the back?"

"Okay," Tom said. "One, two, three. Rock!"

"Ha! Paper, got-ya," Al laughed.

Al's celebration was cut short by a flurry of yells from the first canoe. Something was wrong, but neither Tom nor Al could figure out what was said over the dam's roar. They quickly pushed off and let the current naturally carry them across the river, aiming for the far bank at the first bend.

John was just about to disappear down river when he turned back and yelled, "Go to the inside! Go to the inside!" He was paddling like crazy, trying to course-correct the front end of his canoe. Tom and Al were in the middle of the narrow river, moving quickly toward the bend. They were trying to navigate toward the inner bank when their position finally revealed the downstream view. Shortly after the bend, a good size pine tree hung half in the water with its branches trapping debris.

"Paddle! Paddle hard!" Al yelled to Tom. Al jammed his paddle into the water in an effort to rudder the front of the canoe to the right. Tom dug in his paddle to help Al steer. Their effort pointed the canoe right, but they needed to paddle hard to clear the tree. They both stroked hard to move the boat forward, but not fast enough to overcome the current coming off from the nose of the bend. The swift water swept the canoe across the narrow river, then sideways against the branches. The pine boughs forced both Tom and Al to lean upstream. Within a few seconds, they abandoned the canoe into the cold May water. This capsized the canoe and swept them around the end of the branches, clearing the tree. The river carried them toward the opposite bank. Everything but their day packs were laced into the canoe under a tarp, so both guys hung onto the canoe and grabbed the grassy bank when they reached the other side. Along the edge, the water was only chest deep, so they were able to right the canoe and tip out as much water as possible. Each of them managed to grab their waterproof day packs and not let go of their paddles. Within three minutes, they were both back in the canoe.

"You okay?" Tom asked.

"Yah, but that water was cold."

"The workout we're going to get will take care of that. If we stop paddling, this river's going to sweep us from bank to bank wherever there is a sharp bend. Remember the map? It showed a lot of them."

Moving toward the next bend Al said, "I wonder how the others are? They cleared that tree and I don't see them."

"I know just where they are… Downstream." Tom laughed.

"Alright smart guy! Keep up that kind of humor and I'll sweep you into another branch."

◆ ◆ ◆

Paul glanced at the pine needles scattered on the gear in front of him. "We were lucky back there, Bob. I decided to hug the inside bank and that gave us space to miss most of the branches on that downed pine tree. I hope the others cleared it."

"I'm thinking we need to keep hugging the inside bank just to give us time to react to what's up ahead," Bob replied.

They were coming up on the fourth river bend and Paul perfectly lined up the canoe to cut the inside corner. Bob paddled hard when they cleared the bend and Paul stuck his paddle in the water to rudder. After the canoe swung sideways, they paddled hard to keep the current from sweeping them to the far bank. It was the perfect maneuver to beat the river's best efforts to swamp them.

"Paul! What do we do about that?" Bob pointed his paddle to a wall of leaves and branches crossing the channel in front of them. The high water had worn the bank under a tree on each side of the river. When the soil could no longer hold their weight, they fell together across the channel like two sumo wrestlers, each trying to push the other back into the forest. The lower branches formed a barrier trapping debris that created a channel-wide blockade. Paul scanned the wall of green and brown for an opening. There was none. He quickly scanned the river banks to see if they could beach their canoe and go around the tangle over land, but they were too close to change course. Paul pointed the canoe toward the clearest path in the tangle, hoping they could push the branches aside and move through. Bob ducked and deflected foliage with his paddle when they hit the trees. "Ow! There's just too much brush!" Bob screamed.

Seconds later the bow thumped against a large underwater branch and stopped the canoe. The current swept the back of the canoe around into the trees and a sharp branch poked Paul out of the canoe.

"Bob, help!" Paul's head went under the water.

◆ ◆ ◆

John was two sharp bends in front of Tom and Al when he noticed how the river narrowed to less than twenty yards wide. With no front man in the canoe, it was extremely hard for him to round the sharp corners and not sweep against the opposite bank. He didn't have the option to rudder because there was no power paddler in front. It was either paddle or allow the river to have its way. He was in for a long workout.

As he rounded another bend, he saw the first canoe swept sideways against a wall of debris. Bob was climbing across the top of their canoe toward the rear. Paul was nowhere to be seen.

"Where's Paul?" John called.

"He's under the canoe!" Bob yelled as he reached the back of the boat. John was coming fast, and there was nothing Bob could do to stop him. He needed to help his friend, so he ignored the coming canoe and peered into the water. Seeing nothing, Bob plopped onto his belly across the canoe's back deck and thrust his arm into the water, fishing around for Paul. After a few seconds, he made contact and pulled Paul's head out of the water. His friend coughed and flailed for the side of the boat.

"I got you! I got you!" Bob said as he pulled him close to the gunwale. Paul grabbed the side and took a deep breath.

Meanwhile, John's canoe plowed into the trees just in front of the already trapped canoe. There was no stopping his momentum and he hoped to move through the trees at the same spot Paul and Bob chose. Instead, he hit the same log and his back end swung around toward Paul. John dug his paddle into the water for a couple of hard strokes. That moved his canoe forward a couple of feet, leaving just enough space at the back of the first canoe for Paul to hang in the water without being crushed.

"Where are my glasses?" Paul called to the others, still breathing hard and straining to hang onto the canoe.

Bob got up on all fours and looked around their canoe. "They're not here in the bottom. You were underwater for almost thirty seconds. I bet the current swept them right off your face."

"I think I lost them when I hit the trees. I'm blind as a bat without them. Looks like I'm done steering for the trip."

John crawled across the top of the canoes and said, "Let's get you out of the water before Tom and Al get here. They're going to hit us somewhere and you wouldn't make a good bumper." He and Bob grabbed the back of Paul's clothes and pulled him onto the middle of the canoe.

Paul was catching his breath when he said to Bob, "Thanks. When I went under the water, the current swept me against the underwater branches. I tried to surface but bumped my head against the canoe bottom. I panicked and didn't know what to do. I might have died if you hadn't pulled me up."

"No problem, Paul, but if you would have drowned, I definitely would have a lifelong memory."

"Thanks. I'd rather be around to tell the story."

John interrupted. "We're not done yet boys. Here come Al and Tom. They're going to ram right into this mess." He glanced left and right, then yelled, "Bring it in right behind Paul and Bob! That has the fewest branches and you might stay upright."

"Everyone okay?" Tom yelled.

"We are now," Bob called back.

Al and Tom back paddled, slowing their speed as they reached the blockade. Al guided their canoe behind where Paul had been in the water and slowly let the back end drift into the tangle. He made sure their back end swung away from the other two canoes so they could freely shift all three boats.

John and Tom pulled out the camp saws and began cutting branches while the other three steadied the canoes. They needed an opening large enough to thread the canoes downstream through the debris wall. John was out of his canoe, standing on an underwater branch. His left hand clung to part of the tree while he sawed downstream branches with his right. Tom cut branches away from the opening and tossed them to the side. Finally, a large branch dropped into the water and floated away, leaving space to cross the debris wall.

John called out to Tom, "Hey, can you give me a hand? If we pull this first canoe over the tree, that will leave space to freely shift the other two canoes."

Tom placed one foot in Bob and Paul's canoe, then stepped onto the sunken branch with the other. He and John grabbed the gunwales of John's canoe and slid it through the opening.

"Don't let go!" Tom said as the last of the canoe slid by them. Both of them grabbed the rear deck to stop its progress. The front of the canoe swayed back and forth in the heavy current, making it difficult for the two of them to steady the boat. "It's going to float downstream without a captain. Al, can you climb in while we steady this thing?"

John said, "Here's the paddle. You take off and we'll catch up."

Al hauled himself over his canoe gear and crawled into the rear seat of the one-man canoe. He grabbed the paddle and the other two let go. Tom grabbed the nose of the next canoe and hefted it on top of the log.

When it was halfway through the opening, Paul climbed over the gear and into the front seat. John jumped in the back, with paddle in hand, as the back end cleared the tangle. Tom and Bob repeated the effort with the last canoe: Bob in front and Tom in back.

Paddling alone, out in front of the group, Al was a little concerned about their progress. They had been on the water for a little more than an hour and only covered about two miles. If the pace of obstacles and capsizes continued, they wouldn't reach their planned campsite before dark.

During the Saturday planning day, they spent an incredible amount of time laying out the trip's daily plans. They chose campsites and surveyed stop points for bathroom breaks and lunch. The stops determined the distance they needed to cover each day. The day-one strategy was to drop in just below the dam on Cotton Lake and pull out above the dam on Minong Lake. Via road, the distance was eighteen miles. On the twisting and turning Totagatic River, it was more like twenty-nine miles. A leisurely three miles per hour pace could cover the distance in just over nine hours. The pace on a river was always faster than that, and all five of them canoed faster than three miles per hour on lakes. He believed the distance was reasonable for a short day, especially if they paddled hard across Minong Lake.

After they cleared the downed trees, the pace picked up. They paddled continuously for the next two hours, not just to make up ground, but to keep from sweeping against the outer riverbank and capsizing in more debris. There were several other downed trees, but none that entirely blocked the river. Avoiding them took a lot of effort, and the continuous hard paddling made their arms and shoulders ache. The day was heating up and sweat rolled off their bodies, soaking shirts that weren't already wet from the river. They were deep in a heavily wooded area with fast water rushing over the river's banks. All five guys were in good shape, but if they stopped paddling, it would mean disaster. They needed a water break.

"Hey guys. Do you hear that?" Al called. The other two canoes were a short twenty yards behind him.

"Are those cars?" Paul yelled back.

Rounding another bend, they understood why the auto noise broke the north woods silence. In front of them was the US Highway 53 bridge. The highway was a major thoroughfare through rural central Wisconsin. It connected the cities of Duluth-Superior to the large town of Wausau in the middle of the state. Because it was a major US highway, the Army Corp of Engineers built up the road bed to cross the marshy areas of northwest Wisconsin. That didn't comfort Al as he neared the bridge. He called back to the rest of the group. "There's a good rest area on the right side just past the bridge, but we have a couple problems. Look at the clearance."

The four guys stretched out their necks to get a better view of what lay ahead. The river spread out for fifty yards on each side of the bridge structure. The opening acted as a funnel with a four-foot clearance from the water to the concrete beams.

"Can we get under that?" Bob yelled.

"Yes, but we can't paddle while we are under the bridge," Al replied. "The landing is tucked around the far side of the bridge, and we need to pull out of the current as soon as we clear the other side. If we don't, the current will sweep us past the stop. I need a break!"

John came up with an idea. "Hug the right side and use the last concrete beam to turn the canoe sideways when you clear the bridge. That will set you up to paddle out of the current."

The canoes formed a line, each ready to pass under the right side of the bridge. Al leaned back and lay on the stern's deck plate. He grabbed the first concrete beam and guided the boat straight under the bridge. He straightened the canoe each time he moved to the next beam, setting himself up for the opening on the other side. He heard the next canoe bang against the concrete pillar when he was halfway through. The two-man boats would find this easier than he did. No one was guiding the front of his canoe.

He had three beams left to go when a semi roared over the bridge. It shook dirt from the road deck and dropped it into Al's face.

"Ahhh! I can't see!" he cried. Panic set in for a second before his wrestling training kicked in and he thought, *When something goes wrong, think.* That's what his coach always told him. The unexpected always happened on the wrestling mat. When it did, they were trained to think about where they were and what they needed to do to get out of the situation.

He needed a little time for his eyes to clear the dirt, all while guiding the boat out from under the bridge. Wiping his eyes with one arm and feeling for the next beam with the other, he kept the canoe pointing downriver. He needed to sit up to clear the dirt but couldn't yet. He shook his head and wiped again, trying hard not to hit himself with the paddle. His hand hit the last beam. His fingers clawed at the concrete and he flexed his arm. The front of the canoe swung right and he let go of the bridge. When the sunlight streamed onto his closed eyelids, he sat up. He could just see the riverbank as he cracked one eye open and blinked. The front of the canoe was just out of the current and the river was sweeping the back end downstream. He dug in his paddle and with three strong strokes he was out of the main channel.

Leaning over the water, Al wet his face. The cool water washed both the dirt and the sweat from his eyes. A minute later he could see clearly again and he beached the canoe on the sloped roadway bank. Grabbing his water bottle and climbing onto the shore, he saw Paul and John clear the bridge. They used the same maneuver flawlessly. With Paul's power paddling in front, they were on the shore a minute later.

"Wow! What a workout," Paul said to Al.

"Yah, you should try it alone. My arms are like rubber. John, how deep is the water? I might take a dip before we move on." John dipped his paddle into the water at the back tip of the canoe. It struck bottom with about twelve inches of the paddle left out in the air.

"Not a bad idea, Al," John said as he stowed the paddle and crawled out of the canoe. "As long as we stay near the road and out of the current, we should be fine. Let's get Bob and Tom on shore and take a dip. I'm ready to get my butt out of this seat and stretch my arms."

After Bob and Tom were beached, all five drank their fill of water. The midafternoon sun had brought the temperature into the low eighties. All five of them pulled their shirts off and draped them across the canoes. Sweat covered their bodies and soaked each shirt from top to bottom. They needed a little salt to replace the electrolytes lost over the last couple hours, so Al uncovered the food pack and pulled out a five-pound pack of beef jerky.

Unrolling the white butcher's paper, Al said, "Here guys. Let's lighten the food pack a bit."

"Oh boy! Is that from Brine's Meat Market?" Tom asked.

"You bet. It's their secret recipe and it's salty enough to make you drink water all afternoon," Al replied.

All five reached for a few pieces, and Paul asked as he took his turn, "How far along are we? The last couple hours were intense and I don't know if I can keep it up for another three or four hours."

Al replied, "If I remember right, Highway Fifty-Three is more than halfway to our first campsite. Let me dig out my phone and check the map." He crawled into his original canoe and pulled out his dry bag. He wiped off the excess water, opened it, pulled out the GoPro, and tossed it to John. Digging deeper into the pack, a look of panic came over his face. "My phone! It's not here."

"Remember when Paul was collecting phones?" John asked. "I asked you and Bob if you were keeping yours. You threw your hand over your pocket faster than if someone was kicking you in the crotch."

Al kneeled up in the canoe to check his pocket and almost dumped into the river. "It's not here! What am I going to do?"

With all the sarcasm he could throw, Tom said, "Pull out the waterproof maps." John, Paul, and Bob choked on a laugh. They knew Al's mind was whirling. Tom jeeringly shook his head and said, "All of those apps just lying on the river bottom."

Bob pulled his phone out of his shirt pocket, captured the look on Al's face, and said, "I think I'll put this in my dry bag until we reach camp."

"No worries about saving this moment for history." John stopped the GoPro and tossed it back to Al. "Sorry man, the phone's gone. Nothing we can do."

Al's eyes formed that thousand-mile stare as he slowly reached into the dry bag for the old-fashioned maps. The guys gathered as he laid them across the gear. After a long sigh, he pointed to the map. "Here's where we started, and here's where we are now. We've already covered two-thirds of the first day's distance in a very short amount of time. I was really surprised to see Highway Fifty-Three."

"So help me gauge this. I can't see the map," Paul asked. "Do we have about another four hours until camp?"

"It might take us three hours, but the river is a lot less intense. After this bridge, the river twists and turns for a little while. Then it widens and slows as we near Minong Lake. Our campsite is here." Al pointed to a spot on the far end of the lake. "We will spend half of our time slow-paddling across this lake."

"That's fine with me," Paul said. "I could use an easy paddle."

"We should reach camp about seven," Al continued. "I see only one more obstacle before we camp, and that's right here." He pointed to a spot a few miles downstream where another roadway crossed the river. "This is a township road and it's tiny compared to this highway. I think we might need to portage around the township bridge if the clearance is low."

"Let's see how it looks when we get there," John said. "I know unpacking all of the gear will give us a chance to dump the water out of the canoes, but it will take us thirty minutes to portage around the bridge. The delay might force us to find our campsite in the dark. I don't like the thought of that."

Tom looked up from the map and said, "Let's not waste any more time." He stood up, grabbed his water bottle, and headed for the canoe. "Come on Bob. Let's go."

"I want to jump in the water and cool off first," Bob said. "I have this big knot in my shoulder from paddling. Maybe a dip in the water will help."

"I wouldn't do that if I were you," Paul yelled, but Bob was already in the water.

Bob had cooled down a little, and the water temperature was in the mid-sixties. It wasn't quite an ice bath, but the cool water had its effect. He was in for less than a minute when the other four heard, "Ow! Ow! Cramp!"

The other four were laughing as Bob stumbled out of the water. Pulling his left arm across his body with his right, he tried stretching his shoulder muscle. Next he tried bending over and touching the ground. None of this seemed to work.

"I don't know if I can paddle this way," Bob groaned in agony.

"Serves you right," Paul jeered back. "You know what happens when you throw a hot rock into cold water. It contracts really quickly and sometimes breaks in half. You're lucky that didn't happen to you."

"You're a funny guy," Bob said back. "What am I going to do?"

"Come-mere, I'll fix it," Tom said. The group always had knots and kinks in their backs when they went through tough wrestling practices. They often popped their own backs or had one of their teammates perform a version of gorilla chiropractic care to release stress points. Bob called this "chiro-magic" and never took part in the team's home cures.

"No way! You're not touching me," Bob said as he backed away from Tom.

"Come on, Bob. We don't have time for you to work out the kinks," Tom replied as he stepped toward Bob, intending to help him with his shoulder. Bob took another step back and put up his hand. Al had been watching this scene develop from behind Bob and quietly stood up. Tom saw Al smile and wink. He knew exactly what he was thinking. He continued stepping toward Bob.

"Come on, you wuss! A quick back adjustment and your shoulder will be great," he said as he smiled and took another step. Bob backed up again. On his tip-toes, Al grabbed him from behind. He wrapped his arms around his upper torso, capturing Bob's arms. Locking his hands across Bob's chest, he lifted him off the ground and squeezed.

POP-POP-POP.

"Ow! Ow!" Bob yelled as Al dropped him on the ground. Bob sat on the ground for a few seconds, wondering if his back was broken. He lifted his arm, twisted it around, and smiled. "Hey! That feels pretty good. This chiro-magic stuff really does work."

John pressed the button on the GoPro, ending the video. "That was great. We've worked for years to end your fears, Bob. Now we have a recording of a miracle cure. This should make a great media post when we get home."

The other four decided not to swim after Bob's cramping experience, so they crawled back into their seats and pushed off shore. They reentered the river's fast current. Twenty minutes later, Bob and Tom rounded a bend and saw the township bridge. From a distance, the bridge's shadow on the water made the clearance appear like twelve inches. There was no way they could travel under with so little room. Closing the distance, the shadows lightened and Tom could see that there might be a chance to sneak under the bridge.

"I think we can slide under the bridge," Tom called back to the other three. "We'll have to lie flat on top of the canoe and use the bridge deck to guide us again." Bob pulled gear from behind him and stowed it at his feet. He hoped to give himself more room to lie flat. They slowed the canoe, and Bob grabbed the bridge deck while leaning back. Bob just slid beneath the underside of the beams while lying flat on the gunwales. Tom saw this and knew he was in trouble. He was lying on the back deck, which was about three inches higher than the gunwales. His chest was also a few inches thicker than Bob's chest. He wasn't going to clear the bridge beams.

Tom grabbed the first beam with both arms and held the canoe in place while he thought about options. He couldn't pull the canoe back and start over because the current was too strong. He didn't think he should roll out of the canoe because that would leave Bob without a steersman when they cleared the bridge. Time was ticking and he knew he couldn't hold himself forever, so he pushed against the underside of the beam and continued under the bridge. His stomach and chest scraped the beam bottom as he benchpressed the canoe rear end down into the water. The freshly grown hair tugged and pulled away from his abdomen. The steel drug his nipples toward his chin as he pressed upward against the bridge. Each beam hurt more than the last as his arms started to tire. When Tom emerged from under the bridge and sat up, he looked down at the damage. Some of the freshly grown hair was torn away, and the high spots on his stomach and chest were red. Thankfully there were only a couple scrapes and no broken skin. John, Paul, and Al saw what happened to Tom and they had to come up with a different plan.

"That looked like it hurt," John said to Paul.

"What are we going to do? We have too much gear in our canoe to move things around, and you have no options in the back," Paul answered back.

"We have two choices. We portage or we jump into the water."

"I wanted to swim back at the first bridge and didn't, plus I'm really sweating again. Let's get in."

Paul and John slid into the water on opposite sides of the canoe and hung onto the gunwale. They occasionally felt the bottom and used it to guide the boat through the opening under the bridge. Al followed their example and slid off the canoe's back deck. He hung onto the back, acting like a rudder for the canoe, and steered it under the bridge.

Glancing back, Tom saw Paul and John near the river bank climbing back into their canoe. Al's arms and head were just coming out from under the bridge as the empty canoe glided toward the bank. "I wish we would have done that," Tom remarked.

Bob turned his head and caught the action happening upstream. Then he saw Tom's chest.

"Wow! You look like a red-striped zebra."

"Yah." Between paddles, Tom looked down at the four vertical red marks down the front of his body. "When I moved from one beam to the next, I couldn't push the canoe far enough into the water. My stomach and chest took the brunt of the pressure. The steel acted like an ice scrapper."

"It doesn't look like it broke the skin."

"No, but it looks and feels just like the hair removal I had done for the bodybuilding competition." Bob chuckled and paddled again as they rounded another bend.

An hour later, the water slowed and the canoes no longer moved in and out of shade as they rounded bend after bend. Instead of water flowing over a sunken bank, the water began to spread out and the trees dropped back away from the channel. All five guys relaxed and slowed their strokes, welcoming the break in effort. Rather than strung out in a narrow channel, the three canoes used the widening river and closed the distance between them. Al used the middle of the channel with John and Paul just next to him. Tom and Bob paddled a good thirty yards left, trying to shorten the distance between what were now long sweeping bends in the river. Suddenly, their canoe bumped something under the water and deflected the canoe bow.

"What was that?" Tom asked.

Bob pulled his oar up, laid it across in front of him, and leaned on it to look over the edge. "I don't see anything. No, wait." They bumped another object. "There are dead trees cut off just below the surface."

"We must be coming into Minong Lake. Those trees probably grew on the riverbank, and when the dam filled the lake, their trunks submerged. I'm betting the locals cut off the dead trees during the winter and used them for firewood."

Bob gave Tom a puzzled look. "How did they cut them off underwater?"

"These stumps probably stuck out of the water at least two feet when the water was at a normal level. The tree tops naturally dried in the sun and made great firewood. The locals probably drove four-wheelers out here in January, cut off the trees, and hauled them out in a trailer."

"Hey Al! How long will we canoe on the lake?" Bob asked.

"The river opens up into a small bay where we turn west. We make our way through some wide channels between a couple more bays before turning south on the main lake. It's about four or five miles to our campsite. We should be there in a couple of hours."

9

The Wendigo

The paddle across Minong Lake was a welcome change from the day's relentless survival effort. The remnants of their exertion showed on the cotton shirts Al and Bob wore. The fronts were soaked from their shoulders to their belt line, and the water mark on their backs formed a 'V,' stopping where the loose-fitting shirts left their backs. When they moved out into the main part of the lake, both of them pulled off their shirts and rinsed them in the water. Rather than putting on a cold, wet shirt, they laid them across the canoe in front of them. The light south breeze and the warm afternoon sun would dry them before they reached camp. Even though the others' performance shirts dried quickly while they wore them, each of them rinsed their shirts to get rid of lingering body odor transmitted to the fabric. Al pulled out the GoPro and captured four shirtless young men lake canoeing on a perfect early summer day. Future viewers would have no clue of the nightmare they went through.

Their first campsite was located at the end of the lake, just above a small dam. All five were exhausted from the day's efforts, and they were looking forward to getting off the water, setting up camp, and relaxing. They knew they were close to day's end because the map showed how the lake narrowed before it reached the dam. The shore on each side was now less than twenty yards from their canoes.

As the group rounded a point, they saw the bright orange buoys marking the danger area above the dam's spillway. A fisherman stood next to the landing, casting a line and bobber out next to the nearest buoy. The man seemed unmoved by the three approaching canoes. He brushed the gray and black hair away from his eyes and continued to focus on his bobber. His arms were tan, with wrinkled skin hanging loosely over muscle deteriorated by age. His face was broad, with wear lines etched into his forehead and cheeks from days in the sun. His demeanor seemed calm and patient. Perfect fisherman's traits.

The young men approached the landing slowly because they knew any change in natural conditions could change the fisherman's luck. Fishermen were usually suspicious and sometimes grouchy when fish stopped biting. They beached their canoes just upstream of where the man was casting, taking care not to drift into his line. After the canoes were secured, John and Al walked over, smiled, and greeted him.

"Hey," John said. "Any luck?"

"The warm weather has slowed the fishing," the man replied. "This evening I've only caught six small trout."

"That's actually a good evening's catch in my book," Al said. "Sorry about landing so close to your fishing spot, but there's not a lot of room. We are looking for a campsite. Our map tells us that it's somewhere near this landing."

"Yes," the man answered, pointing behind himself. "It is just up that trail. I often cook fish there before walking home, if no one is using the site. There is a fire grate and plenty of dead wood."

"Thanks," Al said. "Is there more than one site? We don't want to set up camp if you're already using it."

"No," the man replied. "There is only one site. Since you are camping, I will go home and cook up the fish."

"Well, we plan to cook supper after we set up camp. Why don't you join us," John said. "My name is John and this is Al."

"Ben Fischbach," the man said. "I would like that. You have enough to share with a stranger?"

"We do, and if you're willing to share some trout, we have cooking gear to share as well," Al said. "Come join us when you're ready."

"I'll fish a while longer while you set up camp," Ben replied. "Hopefully I'll catch enough for all."

It took less than an hour for the five to set up camp. Tom, Paul, and Bob set up the three tents and stowed the gear while John collected wood and started a fire. Al unpacked the food and readied the cooking gear for supper. He was just about to pull out a dry food pack when he saw Ben standing at the edge of camp. No one heard him come up the trail.

"Hey Ben," Al greeted as he watched Ben hobble over and set the bucket by the fire. "Fischbach is a German name?" He continued in a doubtful tone. "Are you German?"

"No, I am Ojibwe," Ben replied. "My name is actually Giigoonyike. It means *He Fishes*. The best translation I could find was Fischbach, which is easier for others to spell and pronounce. It means *he lives by a stream*."

"That explains a lot," Al said as he glanced in the bucket.

"I now have twelve trout. I filleted them by the river to feed the eagles and keep the bears away from the campsite. It should be a good meal," Ben said as he set the bucket down next to Al.

"Wow! They really started biting after we left," Al said. "How did you do this? It's only been an hour since we walked up the trail and here's a bucket of fresh cleaned fish."

Ben replied, "My grandfather would say that the forest provides when travelers are welcome. Your invitation to me was a good sign."

Al grabbed the fish, began breading them with crushed crackers and laying them in the freshly heated oil. John walked over with an armful of wood and asked, "Do you live around here, Ben?"

"I live a short walk from the landing, not far from the edge of the swamp. I was born here before this dam was built and the river altered." Ben sat on a log and began staring into the fire. "Are you leaving the river tomorrow morning?" Ben asked.

"No," Al replied. "We're canoeing all the way to St. Croix Falls."

"You should not travel through the Dismal Swamp," cautioned Ben. "Many bad things have happened to those who go into the area."

"Bad things; like what?" John asked. "If you mean getting lost and starving for a few days, I think we will be okay."

"No," Ben said. "I have seen strange things and heard dark stories about the swamp. Travelers should not venture there."

John's eyes went wide and he jokingly said, "That sounds spooky. What kind of things are you taking about? Bears? Quicksand? Bigfoot?"

Ben looked up from the fire and narrowed his dark eyes as he said to John in a low voice, "You should not joke about what you do not know. Let us eat first, then I will tell you a story about the Dismal Swamp."

The smell of wood smoke and freshly cooked fish filled the campsite. Side dishes of trail mix and apples were set out. Al scooped fish onto the camp kit plates, and the group made idle chat about the day's events while they ate. They were all eager to hear Ben's story.

When they finished eating and cleaning up the gear, John stoked the fire. The sun was setting, and the spring's coolness, still lingering in the woods, crept into their campsite and pushed the early season mosquitos toward the warmer rocky shore. All six sat on makeshift log benches, close enough to the fire to feel its heat. Ben grabbed a short stick and began drawing a wavy pattern in the dirt. Then he started the story:

There is a legend about a forest spirit my people tell. It is from a time when the fur traders first came to this area. Back then, the swamp was much larger, wild and untouched. The forest was old growth, with many animals, and the water flowed unbound. My people rarely entered the swamp. They only visited it to harvest rice and to retrieve game wounded outside the swamp. My ancestors respected the spirit and left tribute anytime they visited its home. In return, the spirit would allow them to enter and leave without incident. The legend describes the spirit as a shadow, never seen and only occasionally heard. My ancestors named the spirit Wendigo.

When the fur traders came, they found many animals in the swamp. They would trap beaver, mink, and muskrat along its edge. They would bring back full packs of pelts when they first trapped the area. That is, until they troubled the Wendigo.

Returning from weeks on a trap line, some men would talk of trails through the tall grass and cat tails. These trails showed strange prints in the mud. The prints were large with pads and claws like a bear, but long like human feet. The trappers talked of the animal at times walking on four legs and sometimes on two legs. They would see shadows in the woods and hear unfamiliar sounds breaking deep silence. They would sense something following them. When they turned to see the shadow or find what made the sound, there was nothing.

Later, the trappers found only the animals' feet in their traps. They returned with fewer pelts even though they traveled further into the swamp. Some men feared the Wendigo. Others wanted to find the spirit and kill it for taking their pelts.

My people knew that the spirit emptied traps to collect its tribute, but the trappers only saw this as stealing. My ancestors warned trappers not to anger the Wendigo, for it would protect the swamp and the animals in it. Some men ignored the warnings and continued trapping. Soon their traps disappeared and they returned with nothing.

One trapper claimed a visit by the Wendigo while he slept. The story told says he entered the swamp with food, a musket, and his traps. He placed traps for a full day and camped for the night. When he woke in the morning, all of his supplies and equipment were gone. The strange tracks were all around his camp, but he heard nothing during *the night. Following his trail back out of the swamp, he could not find the traps placed the day before. He told the others at the trading post of his encounter and left this area in fear.*

Two men who heard the frightened man's story vowed to find the Wendigo and kill it. They left the trading post the next morning and entered the swamp. They were never heard from again. Their empty packs were found floating downstream. Many claim this was the Wendigo's message to all who would enter its lair.

Many years passed and the swamp was left alone. Then the loggers came. They cut the trees and pushed the forest deeper into the bogs. The loggers would find damaged equipment, and men would disappear, but this would not stop the loggers. The crews would glimpse the spirit's shadow prowling nearby but would not leave their equipment to search. Eventually they could log no further, for the water stopped their machines. This left the remaining swampy forest that begins just below this dam and ends just upstream from the Namekagon River. This is the area you will canoe tomorrow.

The Wendigo is still angry because man destroyed its home. It still protects the untouched area today. The Dismal Swamp is named for the grave things that happened to the people who entered it. Few have entered the swamp since the loggers left, but all have told stories about the same shadows and how strange events happen while they are there. When you leave camp tomorrow, remember that the swamp belongs to the Wendigo.

Ben went silent and just stared into the fire. He let the story sink into the five young men's minds before he stood and said, "It is late and I do not like walking on the trails to my home after dark. Sleep well tonight. You must be alert tomorrow."

"Good night," the group said as Ben left the camp.

All five guys just sat and stared into the fire. They were tired, so it was hard processing what they had just heard. The Midwest was full of legends and stories. Most of them were from the big logging era when

Paul Bunyan and Babe the Blue Ox walked the landscape. They were stories of heroics, battles, and fantastic feats. This was something entirely different. None of them had much experience with Native American lore, so they tried to explain away the uncomfortable feelings Ben had left in the camp.

Bob stood and stretched his arms into the air as he headed for his tent. "I think the trappers and loggers bumped against local natives that didn't want them ravaging their home. The Wendigo was just a tool the Ojibwe used to drive fear into the intruders."

Since Paul was tenting with Bob, he stood as well. "That could be, but then how do you explain the strange tracks Ben described? What did he say they looked like, human-bear feet? Where's the latrine? I need to use it before hitting the sack."

Tom pointed to the edge of the campsite. "It's just up that trail, far enough away that we won't smell it. Let us know if you see any of those tracks." Paul didn't say a word as he grabbed a headlamp and walked to the trail. He paused where the trail entered the woods. He shined the headlamp into the darkness, then looked back at the group. Tom ribbed him further because he knew Paul's imagination was running wild. "Go for it Paul. Nobody is going to hold your hand."

As Paul made his way up the trail, he felt irritated at Tom's poking fun of his fear. It was typical good-natured ribbing, but the timing was bad. Everyone was tired and grouchy. A small stick snapped under his foot, and that gave him an idea. He picked up a couple branches from the edge of the trail and continued on. He found the latrine about twenty yards from the campsite. It was the typical formed plastic tube with the toilet seat cover. It sat on an open platform over a shallow hole. He set the sticks down behind him, did his business, then he carried out his revenge.

Back at the campsite Tom, Al, and John were stowing gear for the night. Tom was picking up the area. John and Al found a large tree just out of camp and tossed a rope over a branch to hang the food pack. They were in the middle of the hoist when the loud cracking of branches came from the latrine trail. Then a blood-curdling scream came from Paul. The food pack hit the ground and all three guys ran up the trail. Bob zipped his way out of the tent and followed close behind. The first three reached the latrine and stopped where the trail opened up to the latrine area. They spotted Paul's headlamp lying on the platform, shining on the plastic tube. Green leaves were scattered across and left of the platform.

"Are those drag marks across the leaves?" Al asked.

Bob stumbled up in bare feet and his underwear. "Where's Paul?"

"No idea." John stepped up onto the platform, reached down, and picked up the lamp. He shined it briefly into the open latrine. "Well, he's not in there." Nobody laughed. He walked over to the drag marks leading off from the platform and followed them toward the wall of brush at the woods edge. The others were on his heels. A twig snapped and they all froze.

"*Arrrrr!!*" Paul jumped out of the woods behind the group while swinging two branches against the brush around him. All four guys scattered and dove into the woods. Paul jumped onto the platform, raised the branches into the air, and let out the most sinister laugh he could muster. When John shined the headlamp on him, Paul brought the branches down and formed a body-builder's double bicep pose. He arched his back, bore his teeth, and gave his best Wendigo growl. Then he stood up straight, dropped the branches, and let out a joyous *'Got you'* laugh.

"Not funny!" Bob yelled as he returned to the latrine platform. His fists were clenched at his side and his jaw locked closed, pursing his lips. Paul could tell he was mad because he turned and stomped back down the trail toward camp.

"I'm sorry!" he called after him. "I was just trying to have some fun with Ben's story."

Tom, John, and Al stared at Paul in silence for a few seconds before Tom said, "You're lucky we don't tie you to a tree for the night and let the mosquitos drain you dry."

"Come on, guys. This was no worse than what Al and John did to Tom with the Mountain Dew this morning."

Al glared at Paul. "Shut up, Paul. I already paid for that when Tom tossed me around back by the truck."

Paul was trying to shift the focus away from him and onto someone else. "Yah, but what about John? He was in on it too."

"I just got a bruised ego and a full bladder from that," Tom replied. "If I'm up all night because I think every little sound is the Wendigo, you're going to pay." Then he turned and walked down the trail.

Paul just smiled at Al and John. He felt guilty about trying to shift blame for his practical joke. He just wanted to diffuse the intense scrutiny of the moment. Just like the others, Paul had been the brunt of past jokes. He saw a great opportunity and took it. He just didn't think his friends would take the joke so seriously.

Al just shook his head in disbelief. "You got us, Paul. Good one."

By the time the last three reached the campsite, Tom was zipping his tent fly shut. Bob was already in the tent he and Paul were sharing. When Paul gingerly unzipped his tent, he expected some kind of revenge from Bob. He peered in when the flap fell open, then crawled inside for the night. Al and John picked up the last pieces of gear and stowed them. John grabbed a bucket of water, doused the fire, and they both turned in.

♦ ♦ ♦

Even though the group was exhausted from the first day's efforts, all five had trouble falling asleep because Ben's story weighed on their minds. The sound of water pouring over the dam was soothing, but it was also a constant reminder of the next day's trip through the swamp.

When sleep came, sounds in the night would wake them. Eerie wolf cries in the night. A splash in the river that could have been a fish collecting a mayfly—or was it something thrown into the water? A snapped twig that could have been an animal moving in the woods—or was it the Wendigo scrutinizing visitors at the edge of its lair?

John awoke shortly after the five thirty sunrise created a glow on the tent's skin. He'd slept horribly. Rolling away from the brightening tent wall, he hoped to drift off again. Then Anne crept into his mind. *Wow, I'm really glad Anne came back Sunday. She really looked great in the hiking boots, cargo shorts, and t-shirt. Very sexy and outdoorsy.*

Even though she's a year younger than me, she seems smart and really mature. Anne already has a college career plan, and she's working on admission before the start of senior year. She thinks ahead.

We really don't know each other very well. How can I get to know her better? We said 'hi' passing in the school hallways, and sometimes we talked after wrestling matches. I didn't know what to talk about, so I asked her about the school newspaper and her expensive camera. She seemed happy to talk about them even though she knew I didn't have a clue.

We didn't have any classes together, and we only had a few common friends—my friends, I think. Even though we don't know each other well, I still feel comfortable around her. We seem to click each time we talk.

John rolled onto his back, and his thoughts about Anne continued. *How should I act and talk around Anne? Should I joke like I do with the guys? Should I act tough because I'm a wrestler? I know; I should be serious because she thinks about the future.*

None of the approaches seemed right. John knew that a false façade took a lot of effort and that cracks always developed. He'd seen a couple classmates start a band and claim they were musicians. Their terrible music and stuttering rhythm told everyone they weren't. He remembered others who talked about all the countries they've visited just so friends thought they were big world travelers. Turns out they never left airports in countries where they had connecting flights. When these myth builders were pushed on their stories, they couldn't back up their claims. John knew that a hollow character tarnished friendships and that Anne would eventually see through a false image. Finally he decided that being himself was best.

John also wanted to stay true to his close friends. Dating was a new thing to him, but he saw some relationships in school that he didn't want to mimic. It was like a dating game where one week a new couple formed and a month later the pair split. Two months later, the two were dating someone else. When the couples were together, they were so absorbed with each other that they rarely talked with their friends. Why couldn't couples just mix with each other's friends? Getting to know someone includes finding out who they hang out with. If the relationship works out, the couple would have a larger circle of friends. Anne already knew the guys because her school newspaper job followed the team. She seemed okay with them so far. The unfortunate thing was he didn't know any of Anne's friends. That was something to work on.

John was wide awake by the time he settled this in his mind. He finally unzipped his bag, put on his shoes, and pulled a flannel shirt out of his pack. He crawled out of the tent and began puttering around the campsite. Five minutes later, Al unzipped his tent flap, squinted up at John, and crawled out into the morning air.

"Sleep well?" John asked.

"Nope. Especially after you started tossing and turning. I could hear your sleeping bag sliding against the nylon tent." Al zipped the tent shut and headed for the latrine trail.

After Al returned, he and John undertook small tasks to begin the day. The northern forest was awake and they wordlessly listened to the conversations coming from the woods around them. Cardinal and chickadee calls defined territories and signaled for mates. Red squirrel chatter broke in occasionally as the furry little rodents scurried to find food on the forest floor. Trout chased mayflies at the water surface, sounding frequent splashes in the river. The low roar of water flowing over the dam filled the silence in between. Listening to the forest told them much about their day. Quiet mornings often meant a storm was coming soon. A brisk morning wind in the trees meant a shift in weather patterns. Screaming blue jays meant something was crossing the bird's territory. This morning the forest felt confined. Even though the morning noises were there, they sounded muffled in the campsite. It was almost like there was an invisible blanket over them. A very light southwest breeze carried in a sickly smell of rotting plants. It was an odor usually trapped in the reeds of large low-lying areas. It was puzzling why the smell migrated into their camp.

When the sun came over the treetops, Al was looking at the maps near the small campfire he built. John had pulled out breakfast for the group. They heard the other guys stir as the sun poured into their east-facing campsite. The tents began absorbing the morning sun, quickly raising the inside temperature. The sounds of sleeping bag zippers came first and then the soft fluff of bags thrown back. Soon there were sounds of bodies tossing and turning, craving sleep but losing the battle with the rising temperature. Within twenty minutes, the last three unzipped their tent flaps and crawled out into the cooler morning air.

The group was silent for the first few minutes, and each went about the task of waking up their bodies. Tom was bending his arms back against a tree, stretching them in preparation for the day's paddling. Paul was standing by the fire pit poking at the embers with a long stick. John occasionally glanced at him, wondering if Paul was going to stoke the fire before breakfast.

John broke the silence with, "Oh no!"

The other three heads snapped around and saw John pointing at Paul. Paul's face was contorted and turning red. He was leaning over slightly with his left leg up on a tip-toe. He strained for almost ten seconds before he let out an ominous early morning sound.

"Pffffffffftttt!" Looking relieved, Paul followed the fart with a long "Ahhhh."

John was the first to comment, "You're lucky your butt was facing away from the fire pit. If that gas reached any of the embers, the explosion might have killed us all."

Paul had a big smile on his face, like he'd just accomplished something epic.

"I'm just trying to clear the mosquitos out of camp," Paul commented.

Tom, who was down wind of Paul, said, "Oooo-wee! I can see the mosquitos dropping out of the air."

"I'm just glad you didn't do that in the tent," said Bob. "With that much hot air, our tent would have lifted off the ground."

Al chimed in and said, "I call the single canoe today. I don't want to be around Paul when the Wendigo smells him polluting the swamp air."

"I don't believe in old legends, but I sure had a hard time sleeping last night." John was heating water on the camp stove to pour into the cups filled with instant oatmeal. "How could something like the Wendigo exist when people are everywhere? Somebody would have seen it and taken a picture."

Al brought a topographic map over to John and said, "Look at this area. We're at this dam and here's where the Totagatic dumps into the Namekagon River. The river twists and turns through the swamp, there are no roads and no campsites. This stretch of river covers fifteen miles of remote and rugged swamp before we'll see any hills or elevation change. I don't believe in that stuff either, but if the Wendigo could live anywhere unseen, it would be here."

Paul walked over and sat down next to Al and John. "Remember what Ben said. The Wendigo is a spirit. I was taught that spirits can appear and disappear at will. You can't see the Wendigo unless it allows you."

Tom walked over and grabbed a cup of hot oatmeal and said, "Come on, you guys. Don't let your imaginations run away on you. Besides, where else can we go?"

Tom's comment drove home the point. They were stuck. The truck was eighteen miles upriver and there was a good chance the area held no cell towers. That meant they couldn't call for someone to pull them out.

"Good point, Tom," John said finally. "Besides, you wanted to canoe somewhere new and Bob wanted adventure. All of this high water and the Wendigo chasing us through the swamp should make it an exciting ride."

The group generally agreed. Why would they pull out? Ben's story added unknown excitement to paddling through a swamp. Even if there was a kernel of truth to the legend, whatever roots created the forest spirit so many years ago were long dead. Their intuition told them that they could handle whatever the river could throw at them.

They finished breakfast and packed the gear. It was about fifty yards around the dam to the landing below, and it took only an hour to pack and portage. Since sunrise was before six, they were getting an early start on another day of sharp river bends and fast water. By eight, Al was first to push off. Bob and Paul followed right after him. John and Tom checked the riverbank to make sure nothing was left behind and then pushed off. John glanced back toward the dam from his front seat as they moved away from the landing. On the shore next to the dam stood Ben, both hands wrapped around his fishing pole, holding it like a walking stick. His face was somber and his dark eyes watched the group round the first bend. As John lost sight of him, a quick gust of wind blew through the pines. He could have sworn it whispered 'BEWARE.'

10

Day 2 – The Dismal Swamp

Soon after the sound of the dam disappeared, the river banks flattened and more reeds lined the edges of the Totagatic. The twists and bends became sharper, and water occasionally flowed over the center bank. Even though the water was still high, navigating the bends was less of an issue than the day before because the swamp was a flood plain and the water slowed as it spread out across the shallower expanse. It was a welcome change from the previous day because their muscles were sore and the day was already heating up.

Paddling out front, Al occasionally lost sight of the other two canoes when he rounded meandering bends. He could tell they were not far behind because he could hear the sporadic paddle banging on a canoe or the voices of brief conversation. On one occasion, he saw Bob and Paul through the reeds across a bank where the water had cut a shallow path between the two channels. This gave Al an idea.

Looking at the map that morning, Al dreaded the boredom on this leg of the trip. The Totagatic River visibly snaked across the page, with few straight lengths where they could make good progress. Maps rarely contained detail that truly existed in real life. Here was another case. They had easily paddled over a mile, but as the crow flies they had covered less than half the distance. If he was right, they could speed their progress by taking shortcuts. In front of him he spotted another path where the water flowed over the low bank. It was an opportunity to skip the next bend. He slowed his canoe, waiting for Bob and Paul to come into view.

"Hey! Shortcut," Al called out as he used his paddle to rudder the canoe sideways in the current. Then paddling hard, the canoe cut into the reed opening along the bank. After a couple of hard strokes, the canoe easily navigated the ten-yard shortcut and popped out into the main channel. "Follow me guys. I must have cut off a hundred yards."

Bob and Paul missed the opening and had to round the bend. John and Tom came around the last bend just as Al disappeared in the opening and they caught on to the idea. Tom turned their boat sideways in the current and the two paddled into the reeds. After popping back into the main channel, they saw their friends coming around the bend behind them.

"Come on guys. Keep up," Tom called back to the last canoe. He chuckled and heckled his friends. His competitive nature had just turned this into a race, at least in his own mind. Tom's joy was short-lived though. No sooner had he straightened their canoe when Paul dug his paddle into the water and turned sideways in the channel. There was another shortcut behind the first two canoes. When he and John rounded the bend, Paul and Bob had slipped between them and Al.

"Wow, this is great," Paul called to Al as he and Bob cleared the reeds. "If this keeps up, we'll be out of this swamp by noon."

Tom and Paul spent the next half hour steering their canoes in a game of leap frog. When the distance between bends was long, both boats could make the next shortcut. When it was short, one of them would sometimes miss the opportunity because the current carried them too far from an opening. It was a game. How many shortcuts could they find and who would pop out in front of whom.

Al heard the bantering behind him and caught on quickly. His canoe was lighter and more maneuverable than the two-man canoes. He managed to stay in front of the others, hitting a half dozen shortcuts in a row. He needed them to offset the faster two-person canoes. Between shortcuts, his four friends would close the distance between their boats. Hitting every shortcut allowed him to stay in front.

John and Tom were now in second, gaining on the one-man canoe. Desperate to stay in front, Al looked for another opening. He saw nothing in the stretch of tall brown grass in front of him. As he approached, the high water seemed to push back the grass and present a clear opening. Glancing back, he saw a canoe's nose just coming around the bend behind him. He took a sharp left and disappeared into a six-foot-high corridor of last year's wild rice.

Tom spotted the back of the canoe just as it disappeared. "There goes Al. Paddle harder, John! We need to move through the opening before Bob and Paul round the corner." Thirty seconds later they were into the grass.

This shortcut was definitely different. The opening was very clear, but rather than dumping immediately into the next channel, the path continued into an expanse of wild rice. It narrowed and grew taller until last year's rice heads were above the canoers' heads. It was difficult paddling through the dense grass. Any effort to turn around forced the canoes against the wall of stalks and their paddles had trouble breaking through the dense root system. They could only manage long, slow turns.

Tom occasionally saw Al in front of them. He seemed headed for a line of trees that could be the river channel. When he and John first entered the grass, Tom recognized that something was different about the shortcut. He considered backing out of the rice field. The strange part was that the path seemed to close in behind them and disappear. He also knew that Al was in the same position they were and they couldn't leave him to tackle a wild rice paddy alone.

When they reached the line of trees, the river channel was nowhere in sight. Al stopped paddling and was looking left and right, trying to get his bearings. Tom and John slowed to a crawl in shallow water next to him. They were at the edge of a tall forest understory filled with old swamp oak trees. The tree trunks were more than two feet in diameter and the canopy was more than thirty feet above the water. The group could perhaps see thirty yards into the old-growth forest before the background turned into a dark vertical wall of wood.

John grabbed the gunwale of Al's canoe and commented, "This ain't no shortcut."

"Got that right," Tom added. "We've definitely left the main channel." Tom stuck his paddle straight into the water. "Look. The water doesn't even come up to the handle. I wonder if Bob and Paul followed us into the grass."

"They hadn't come around the bend by the time we left the channel. They may not have seen us leave the river," John said.

Al let out a piercing whistle and yelled, "Hey!" His call echoed in the understory.

"Yo," came back after a couple seconds. The other canoe was already some distance away.

"That definitely sounded like they were downstream. They didn't follow us into the grass." Al continued, "What do we do now? We could try paddling against the flow and back to the main channel." All three glanced back at the grass line. There was no trace of where they had been.

John swatted the back of his neck and replied, "I don't think that's a good idea. We could get lost in that grass. We can see fairly well through the woods. The water is still flowing well and it's just over a foot deep. We can canoe the shallow backwater, and I'm betting it eventually dumps back into the main channel. Anyone have their DEET handy?"

Both Tom and Al were waving their arms and swatting mosquitos. Nobody had put on bug dope that morning, thinking the mosquitos wouldn't bother them if they kept moving on the fast water. Now they were in the quiet shallows and at the mercy of the season's first mosquito hatching.

"Mine is packed away," Al said as he waved his hat through midair. "These bugs are the size of crows. They'll suck us dry and leave our bodies floating in the river if we don't keep moving." Tom dug out his bug dope, squeezed a puddle into his hand, then tossed the bottle to Al.

John pursed his lips, furled his eyebrows in worry, and began thinking to himself, *Oh great. We're lost. I'm not too worried about finding the main channel again, but if it takes a lot of extra time we might miss Anne and her friend at Nevers Dam. We made up time the first day after overcoming early obstacles. This is a little different. We could spend a half day or more trying to find our way back to the main channel. We've got to figure this out.*

John pulled out his compass and took a reading. The water was still moving southwest in the general direction where the Totogatic flowed into the Namekagon River. He was about to encourage Tom and Al to move into the woods, then he hesitated. The flowing water made no sound as it moved into and around the trees. John heightened his senses and the hair on the back of his neck stood up. There was no sound at all coming from the woods: no bird sounds, no animal noises, no wind. It seemed that every noise they made was sucked into the oaks and swallowed by the dark wall of wood. The swamp just moved from dismal to haunted.

John's mind began to spiral as he thought, *Maybe there is something to the stories about the Wendigo.* Then he shook his head and let his body shudder off the growing fear. *This is the kind of thing that scared off the trappers and formed the legends told by people like Ben. The woods are always quieter than the prairies because the trees act like a sound buffer. We're just sitting on the noisier side of the boundary.* Al and Tom were still pondering their choice when John made up his mind. He pointed his paddle toward the oaks and forcefully said, "Downstream!"

They finished rubbing DEET on their bodies and paddled into the woods.

♦ ♦ ♦

Paul and Bob rounded the bend, hoping to catch a glimpse of the other three guys. The river straightened for fifty yards in front of them before meandering around a gentle corner. Short scrub brush grew on the corner's inside bank, hiding the continuing channel. An unbroken wall of grass grew on the outside bank. As they navigated the meandering corner, they found an empty channel flowing toward the next bend.

Bob cupped his ear and listened for a banging paddle or conversation. "We need to pick up the pace. Both boats are already around the next bend."

"I'm not too worried, Bob. They can only go downstream. Let's just keep our eyes open for shortcuts. I know we missed a few, but we'll catch up if we hit a few in a row."

They searched for the telltale reeds that grew on the river's long point bars. Spotting them ahead of time gave them the chance to position the canoe for a shortcut. Two more bends went by before Bob expressed his worry again.

"The riverbanks seem a little higher again. The channel is narrowing and I only see scrub brush on each side. The strange thing is we haven't heard any noise in front of us." Bob swatted his arm and waved his hat across his back.

An echoing whistle broke the silence and then, "Hey!"

Bob spun his head around and looked at Paul. "They're behind us. How is that possible?" Bob cupped his hands and faced backward. "Yo!"

Paul continued steering, but the expression on his face had changed. Rather than his usual calm and relaxed expression, his lips were pursed and his eyebrows furrowed, creating two crevasses above his nose. Bob had seen this look on Paul during the wrestling season. Every man on the team accepted the fact that individual matches were a one-on-one contest with the whole gymnasium focused on the mat. Part of their training was dealing with the individual competition. Each team member also struggled with an imaginary foe that hung in the back of their minds. For some it was prematch nervousness, and for others it was lack of experience. Paul's imaginary foe was a fear of tall, lanky opponents. They worried Paul endlessly because his five-foot six-inch frame struggled with competitors over six feet. He developed a worried tell that surfaced every time he met a tall opponent. Paul wore that same genuine look of concern.

"I don't understand either," Paul replied. "They were in front of us twenty minutes ago. I didn't see any back channels leading off from the main water."

"Maybe they're playing a practical joke and are right behind us?"

"I don't think so. They sounded a long way off and they wouldn't have called out if they were joking."

"Should we stop and wait? It shouldn't take them long to catch up."

"That's not a bad idea and I need a bathroom break. I'll pull out of the current on the back side of a point. Find us something to tie off the canoe."

Paul hugged the inside bank of a sharp point and pivoted the canoe when the river bent around the corner. Normally they would find a sandbar at the end of the point, but the high water left them with a knee-deep shallow area. They both stepped out into the shallow water and Bob tied off the canoe on a scrub brush branch, letting the canoe sweep against the shore downstream of the point.

"This is a great opportunity to relieve some bladder pressure." Paul stepped into the scrub on solid ground to do his business. Bob grabbed a snack from his bag and walked across the narrow point to watch for their friends. Less than a minute went by before Bob heard Paul crashing out of the brush.

"Ow! These mosquitos are thick. Where's the DEET?" Paul was rubbing his arms and reaching back to scratch his shoulder through his thin Garth Brooks t-shirt.

"It's in the front of my bag. I'll grab it."

As Bob started back across the point, he heard a branch snap. Both he and Paul watched in horror as the canoe rope and a piece of scrub brush dropped into the water. Both of them sprinted across the point toward the drifting canoe. They closed the distance quickly, but the current was just strong enough to pull the canoe away from shore before either of them could reach it. Paul waded into the deeper water following it and feeling the sandy bottom as he went. He stretched his arm out hoping to catch hold of the rope floating behind the moving canoe. He was inches away when the river bottom dropped out from under him and he submerged.

"Paul!" Bob stepped further off from the point but hesitated. He didn't want to step off the edge as well.

Within a few seconds, Paul's head popped up at midstream. He broke into a freestyle crawl and captured the floating rope. Pulling hard, he reeled in the canoe and grabbed both sides of the front deck. Planting his feet, Paul tried to stop the downstream progress. Unfortunately it was a losing battle. The water was neck deep and pushing both him and the canoe toward the opposite riverbank.

Taking another step, Bob asked, "Are you okay? Do you want some help?"

"I'm all right. Stay where you are. I'll try to jump into the canoe and paddle back to get you."

Paul lifted his feet and let the canoe sweep sideways. He worked his way along the upstream gunwale, kicking his legs as he moved. When the back end hit the far bank, Paul was next to the rear seat. As the water pushed against the side and pivoted the canoe, he quickly boosted himself halfway over the side. The canoe rocked in the water but stopped before capsizing. The water pushing against the side gave Paul enough time to shimmy further into the boat, effectively balancing it before taking on water. He swung his feet onto the floor and grabbed the paddle.

Looking back at his partner, he saw Bob pacing across the point trying to stay ahead of a mosquito cloud. He was only twenty yards downstream from where the canoe was tied off, but it would take a few minutes to paddle upriver. Bob was swatting mosquitos with both hands. He slapped his cheek and then the back of his neck. His right hand rubbed the length of his left arm and he splashed across the shallows in an effort to dislodge mosquitos from his legs.

Paul quickened his strokes. His friend was being eaten alive and he needed to reach him before he panicked. By the time he was halfway back upstream, Bob was swinging his arms wildly, swatting his neck, shoulders, and arms. Bob was running back and forth across the point, experiencing mosquito overload.

"Bob! Look at me! Look at me! I'll be there in a minute. When I hit the point, crawl in the canoe and put on your hoodie."

Paul had seen overload before. The perception that mosquitos inflict immediate irreversible damage was a trick the mind plays on wilderness newcomers. While a lot of bites can give you a serious rash, it's a lot less painful than running uncontrollably through the woods or plunging into unsafe water just to get away.

Bob snapped out of the panic state when Paul yelled but was still swinging his arms wildly. He tried to time Paul's arrival with his movements across the point. *Focus,* he told himself. *Hoodie. I need the hoodie.*

When Paul reached the point, Bob brought up his left foot to step into the canoe. He caught it on the gunwale and stumbled face-first onto the gear behind his seat. "Go!" he yelled.

Paul backpaddled and swung the canoe into the current. Bob slid into his seat and reached inside his pack for a hoodie.

"You okay, Bob?"

Leaving the hood over his head, Bob pulled his hands out of the sleeves. He was breathing fast and hard from the panicked adrenaline surge. "Yah, I just need a minute to settle." He reached down and rubbed the shin he banged on the canoe edge. "I thought they were going to carry me away."

"That was a classic woodsman panic attack. I've heard stories of people running off cliffs just trying to get away from mosquitos. Next time, if there is one, pause and think like coach taught us."

"Now I understand why you call me the new guy. There are still a few things I haven't experienced. I was ready to dive into the water just to get away from the swarm of mosquitos."

"No worries. We all go through it. At least you haven't gotten lost."

"Speaking of lost, how could our three veteran campers disappear on a river. It's a one way trip and we stopped long enough for them to catch us."

"I don't know. Let's take our time paddling, look for signs, and listen for clues. If they don't show up on this river, we know they are moving downstream. They'll show up on Namekagon River."

♦ ♦ ♦

Both canoes left the open sky and entered the woods. The bright midmorning turned darker with every stroke. Even though the trees hadn't fully leafed out yet, the sun eventually disappeared, leaving them in what seemed to be twilight. The small breeze they felt in the rice field had disappeared. Tom glanced back after five minutes and could see the forest closing in behind them. It was musty and warm, with that sickly smell of rotting plants they'd experienced earlier that morning. The mosquito buzz reminded him of the boiler's hum in the mechanical room next to his workout space. The sound was a constant high-pitched whine that seemed to have no source, but it filled the air.

"Any guesses on how far before we reach the main channel again?" Tom asked John.

"Hard to tell. This looks like a good size mud flat. The trees are huge, which means logging equipment couldn't get into this area to cut."

"I hear you. Every time I push my paddle against the bottom, it sinks into the mud."

"As long as the water keeps flowing we should come right out into the main channel again. Maybe this is actually a long-shortcut."

"I'll believe it's a shortcut when Bob and Paul pull into the next campsite after us."

Progress was slow because long canoes weren't meant to navigate a labyrinth of oaks. Al led the group, zig-zagging his canoe through the trees and occasionally glancing back to see how his friends were doing. He was a little worried because the water seemed shallower than when they entered the woods. "Hey, you guys doing okay?" he called back to them. "I'm almost dragging bottom."

"We're scraping once in a while," Tom replied. "We're a little heavier than you are. I hope we don't have to get out and pull our canoes in this mud."

"I hear-ya," Al said. "I don't think there are leeches in the river, but I don't want to find out. Are we heading in the right direction? I'm a little disoriented because we've made so many turns."

John pulled out his compass again and tried to get a reading. "We were heading southwest when we entered the woods, but it's acting weird right now. With these high trees, I can't see the sun to get a bearing. Just keep following the water. It has to flow back into the channel sometime."

"Okay. I hope you're right. It just seems like the water is leading us somewhere other than the main channel."

Another ten minutes of zig-zagging went by before Al noticed a thinning in the treetops. "Hey guys. Do you see the opening ahead? I think we are coming to the main channel. The water is flowing straight toward it."

Both canoes picked up the pace. They wanted to get out of the woods and away from the mosquito swarms. The DEET was doing its job keeping the bugs off their bodies, but their breath and body heat signature drew swarms close to the canoes. The high-pitched whine was constant.

The view at ground level began opening in front of Al. John and Tom could see him strain to see the channel ahead. They were hoping for good news when they saw him pause midstroke. Al rose slightly off his seat, then plopped down in what seemed to be frustration.

"What's up?" John called to him.

"I think we are in trouble. That opening is not the main channel, it's a deadfall."

Both canoes moved closer to the opening, and as the vertical wall of wood thinned, they could see dozens of trees lying across the forest floor. Some past thunderstorm had blown through the swath of woods and created a monstrous tangle of downed wood. Large trunks lay in the water with bulky branches draped across them. They looked like arms hanging in midair with clawed ends ready to drop onto anything that ventured by.

Tom navigated next to Al and grabbed the side of his canoe. "Not a big deal. We'll just go around it."

"I don't think it will be that easy," Al replied. "The main flow, what little there is of it, goes right through the deadfall. It's obvious that we can't go through this, and I'm sure we'll run out of water as soon as we try to go around."

John was surveying the area and jumped into the conversation. "I see what you mean. The only option is to circle around the opening. Let's hope there's still water for the boats."

Tom shook his head in frustration. "This isn't what I had in mind when we left this morning. I was hoping to find a way to get back at Paul today. After his stunt last night, I didn't sleep well. Paul and Bob will be way out in front of us by the time we get out of these woods. Today is a lost opportunity."

"There's plenty of trip time left, Tom," John replied. "We'll get the chance before we leave the river. Besides, the funniest payback is spontaneous." In the back of his mind, he was thinking about the Mountain Dew challenge in the truck and wondering what Tom was scheming to even the score with him.

The silence persisted as the three took in the impassable deadfall. Large trunks lay half-submerged, supported by large branches snapped from what was the forest canopy. To the left were several fallen treetops, their branches hanging like a comb just above the water. To the right, the deadfall perimeter circled away toward what seemed to be downstream.

Al recognized the better option and dug in his paddle, turning the canoe right. "This way. The deadfall is about a hundred yards wide and we are right of the halfway point. This way is shorter and easier." His two friends turned their boat and fell in behind him.

Moving around the deadfall was no simple task. When they turned right, the cross current began pushing against their canoes, forcing them toward the opening. They had to work to keep the boats straight and to keep them from bumping against trees. By the time they again turned with the current, the water did just what John predicted. The twelve inches of water had decreased to eight inches, and the heavier canoe was scraping bottom. With each stroke, Tom and John pushed their paddles against the mud bottom just to keep them moving forward.

Al noticed the water depth change as well. The farther they moved from the deadfall's center, the shallower the water became. He tried moving closer to the opening as they circled, keeping a watch on what lay ahead. Large branches had fallen from trees at the deadfall's boundary. They made it impossible to edge closer to the deeper water. The further from the opening, the shallower the water became. It seemed like the deadfall and the shallows were funneling them to a specific location.

When they were halfway around the opening, Al scraped bottom and could no longer paddle forward. He glanced back and saw that John and Tom were already out of their canoe, pulling it. Their steps were labored, high-stepping each leg just to pull their feet out of the mud. Occasionally their feet would break the water line. He assumed they were wearing shoes, but he could not tell because black muck clung to everything below their ankles. Before he stepped out of his canoe, he grabbed his water bottle and took a long pull. Even though they were not working as hard as yesterday, it was warm and humid in the woods, and he was sweating. When he tilted his head back, he could see a swarm of mosquitos just above his head. A few would occasionally dip toward him, tempting to cross the DEET boundary lifting off his skin.

"It should get easier after this," Al called back to his friends. "We are halfway around the deadfall." Before Tom or John could respond, there was a deep crack of breaking wood followed by a massive splash of water. All three gawked at the site in front of them. Twenty yards away, a dead branch broke off from an old oak and crashed across their path. It was a major limb, breaking at the crotch. Its smaller upper branches flew everywhere and created a staccato of echoing splashes when they hit the water. When the sound of falling branches settled, they heard the most unimaginably eerie sound: the rhythmic sound of running in water.

Al crouched and pointed beyond the fallen limb. "There! I see something but it's too far away to tell what it is." John and Tom quickly waded up next to Al, where they all stood silently for a minute, looking and listening. The muffled silence had returned.

John raised his arm and pointed to an area near where the limb landed. "There seems to be a small knoll of ground over there. I'm betting there was an old swamp buck bedded down and the falling tree spooked him. Could you tell if it was a deer?"

"No clue. All I could see was a shape moving away from us in the woods."

"The falling branch might have spooked a bedded animal, but…" Tom's pause left a thought hanging in each of their minds. They stared at each other, eyes wide and jaws dropped. The rice paddy seemed to lead them to the woods, then the deadfall had forced them to leave the deeper flowing water. Then a huge branch dropped right across their path. Now they heard footsteps splashing in the water.

Al sneered at Tom. "Stop it! Last night you harassed Paul about his imagination. Sounds like you're as paranoid as he is. Do you really think the Wendigo is doing this?"

Tom didn't say anything. He just looked toward the knoll, back to Al, then scanned the woods.

John grabbed the front of their canoe and said, "It was either the Wendigo or gravity and a deer. Regardless, we're not leaving these woods unless we keep moving. We have some heavy lifting ahead. I don't think we want to drag the canoes over the knoll, and the deadfall has a lot of debris. We need to pull our boats over that limb."

The three mucked their way to the downed limb and chose a spot midway between its dead canopy branches and the debris at the deadfall's edge. Tom and Al grabbed the front seat of the first canoe, lifted the point onto the log, and all three pushed the boat forward. The aluminum sounded off, popping and crinkling as it scraped across the bark. When it neared the balance point, Al hopped over the limb and pulled the front deck. In less than two minutes the back end splashed back into the shallow, flowing water. After the second canoe cleared the limb, they took a water break. Tom leaned over, placed his hand on the limb, and looked down its length. "I can't believe how close to us this fell."

"Coincidence. Just coincidence," John answered.

The group pulled their canoes back to the deeper flow on the far side of the deadfall. They climbed into their seats, still hoping the flow would soon take them back to the main channel.

♦ ♦ ♦

Paul and Bob continued downriver at a much slower pace. They paddled only when they needed to navigate sharp bends or to avoid objects. Slowing the pace allowed them to watch and listen to the surroundings in hopes of picking up some sign of the others' whereabouts. After almost losing their canoe, the river had taken an extended northerly bend. This wasn't odd for a smaller river, but it worried Paul and Bob. There had been no sign of their friends for over an hour and they felt their northward heading was taking them further away from the others.

"You would think we would have heard some sound that would tell us which direction they went," Bob said after a long stretch of silence.

"I wondered about that too," replied Paul. "We haven't heard a civilized sound for an hour. Did you notice that there are no automobile sounds in the distance? I don't think we've even seen an airplane. It's kind of peaceful and eerie at the same time."

"This river is like a sound booth. The scrub brush muffles outside noises, and the humming mosquitos drown out any other sounds. The only thing we hear is the water under our canoe."

"We did hear that tree fall a little while ago, but even that was muffled and a long way off. I was glad when the river turned south again. That headed us back toward the Namekagon flowage. After we get there, we turn west before it flows into the St. Croix."

"Is the Namekagon River like this one?" Bob wondered aloud.

"Way up river, but not near its end where we will meet it. I'm looking forward to seeing the small rapids near the end of the Namekagon. It's wide and fairly straight. It will be a nice change from this twisting river."

The two went quiet again, carefully listening for human sounds that might be muffled by the sound booth they were in. After a short while, Paul broke the silence. "By the way, Bob, I never thanked you for pulling me out of the river yesterday. With the fast water, the adrenaline, and the exhaustion, we all kind of blew through the day only thinking about how to reach our campsite. I can always buy a new pair of glasses, but if I got seriously hurt we'd be in trouble."

"That's what friends are for, Paul. They are there when you need them."

"No really." Paul's voice quivered slightly. "I think you saved my life. Thanks."

Bob turned his head and briefly looked at Paul with a smile. He was a little embarrassed because he wasn't used to receiving personal recognition for something of this magnitude. He'd just acted when there was a crisis, and it never occurred to him that things could have turned out differently. He didn't want to show his embarrassment, so he paddled a few strokes and changed the subject.

"I can see why this place was called the Dismal Swamp. It's all scrub brush, swamp grass, and rice paddies. There are no roads and the place stinks."

"Don't forget about the mosquitos. Look at the swarms in front and behind us."

Bob continued, "I can see why Native Americans believed the Wendigo lived here and why the pioneers believed it was true. The Wendigo took our friends. The Wendigo broke the branch holding our canoe. The Wendigo grows mosquitos to torment travelers. If one bad thing happens, you deal with it. If two things happen, it's coincidence. If three or four occur, it's a wilderness vigilante."

"I know what you mean. And, when someone comes back from the swamp and nothing happened to them, everyone wants to know what they did differently. Then their fearful story about abandoning food or game grows into a legend about leaving offerings to appease the spirit."

Bob stopped paddling for a moment, then turned his head toward Paul. His face lit up with an idea and he shouted at Paul, "That's it!" Bob turned and unzipped his pack. After a few seconds, he pulled out the rolled up package of white butcher's paper.

Paul couldn't believe what he was seeing. "Is that the beef jerky?"

"Yes, I grabbed it from the food pack before we left this morning. I planned to pull it out when we took a break. We never gave a Wendigo offering when we left this morning."

"Come on Bob. You can't be serious."

"It can't hurt. Let's see if the Wendigo has a taste for Brine's secret recipe."

Bob unwrapped the package and laid the paper and beef in the water beside him. The paper raft floated past Paul, and the two watched it sweep against the outer bank. It floated a few more feet before getting caught in a tangle of branches that hung into the river. The branches bounced and swayed as the current swirled around them. The paper boat spun in the water and was swept under a bush covering the bank's edge. The bush and brown water seemed to absorb the white paper. One second it was there, the next it was gone.

"Did you see how the swamp swallowed up the beef?" asked Bob. "It was like the Wendigo reached down into the water and grabbed the jerky. I'm betting that it's been a while since someone offered such a tasty offering."

"I'm not holding my breath that any of this will end quickly."

The two young men continued canoeing in silence, again hoping to hear their friends. They rounded another bend and noticed the scrub brush was ending on one side of the river. A little distance in front of them, the brush changed over to tall hardwoods. The channel in front of them also looked strange. Between the two banks, the air seemed to have a fluid motion. It was like seeing a water mirage over a desert highway or a black-and-white film on a grainy old television set. The image was there, but you couldn't entirely tell what it was. As they approached the area, the fuzziness changed to dots darting back and forth. Bob and Paul began hearing a low buzzing sound.

"What is that?" Paul asked.

Bob laid his paddle across the canoe and listened. "I don't know. The mosquitos up river made a much higher-pitched sound. When I lived down south, I heard swarms of locust, but this isn't anything like that."

"Look what just landed on the end of your paddle. It's a dragonfly."

Bob looked down and smiled. There on the end of his paddle was a turquoise, blue, and black dragonfly. Its wingspan was almost three inches across. Between its front legs was a large mosquito. The dragonfly was lifting the bug to its mouth, crushing the pest between its jowls and tearing off lunch. When it was finished, it took flight to look for another meal. When Bob looked up, the rest of the dragonfly swarm moved across their canoe, punching holes in the cloud of mosquitos following them.

Paul laughed and said, "This is incredible. Look at the dragonfly colors. Some are red and black, some are green, and more are like the blue one that landed on your paddle."

Bob joined the laughter as they watched the swarm move around them. They were like little X-Wing fighters moving with incredible speed and precision. Some cruised the top of the river, angling upward to skim the gear in the canoe, then diving back to the water surface. Others blew by at high speed, punching a hole in the mosquito cloud. Most of the dragonflies flew well above their heads, circling and diving to capture bugs.

"This is great!" Bob exclaimed. "Where were these dragonflies when I suffered my mosquito overload? They could have feasted on the swarm that attacked me."

"Wow! Look at that." Paul pointed his paddle downstream.

Bob's jaw dropped when he looked up and saw a canoe. It was some distance out, poking its empty front seat out of the wooded riverbank. Soon the back end appeared with Al paddling hard to point the boat downstream. Bob cupped his hands and let out, "Hey!" He waved his paddle over his head as Al turned to look upstream. As Bob brought his paddle down, John and Tom appeared at the woods edge. Bob turned to Paul and saw a look of complete relief wash over his face.

"That explains a lot," Paul commented with a broad smile. "They probably took a shortcut that really wasn't a shortcut. This is a swamp after all, and high water tends to flood into surrounding areas. I have to give them credit though. They're still in front of us," Paul finished with a chuckle.

Bob and Paul paddled hard while their friends navigated at a leisurely pace. The gap between them closed, and soon they were paddling downstream together.

"Look at these dragonflies," Al exclaimed. He too watched the air acrobatics overhead and the precision flying around his canoe. "There are at least three different species sitting on my gear." He pulled out the GoPro, snapped a few close up pictures, then switched to video mode.

"They showed up about fifteen minutes ago when we rounded the last bend and came up on these tall oaks," Bob said.

Paul cut in and corrected him. "You mean they showed up right after we gave an offering to the Wendigo."

John looked puzzled and a little tired from the morning's efforts. "Offering?"

"Yah," Paul continued. "Bob sacrificed the rest of our beef jerky. He floated the package next to the canoe. After a couple minutes, it swept against the riverbank and the brush seemed to swallow it up. Really mystic."

"Coincidentally, we spotted the edge of the woods about fifteen minutes ago," John replied.

Tom added, "We were moving in twelve inches of water for quite a while. We didn't know how long we would have to paddle in those woods. All I can say is thank goodness for bug dope."

"Maybe there is a kernel of reality to Ben's story about the swamp," Al said. "We had three or four strange things happen to us that just seemed too convenient to occur randomly." He swung the camera around to pick up the other two canoes and then ended the video.

Then John said without thinking, "Maybe Anne can write about them." His mind panicked for a moment and he stopped before saying more. Unfortunately, it was too late. All four guys turned to look at him.

"Anne?" Tom asked. "I'd forgotten that we have two ladies joining us on the last day."

Al jumped in with a couple more jabs. "Now I understand why you didn't sleep well last night. It wasn't the Wendigo keeping you awake, it was your girlfriend. I'm betting you were thinking about her rather than canoeing and that's why we got lost."

"Wait a minute," John complained. "You're the navigator reading the maps and you led us into the rice field. Besides, I'm not steering this boat. Tom is."

"He has some good points, Al," Bob said. He knew that their lost adventure didn't show up on planning maps, so he continued with a little sarcastic humor in his voice. "All I can say is that you're lucky the maps showed you the way through the woods. You'd still be lost if you didn't have them. By the way, John, how will Anne know when to meet us? I bet there's no signal out here."

John reached for his dry bag. One bar is all he needed for signal.

When Paul saw John pull out his phone, he threw his arms into the air. "What is this world coming to? I think the last fortress of rugged sanctuary has been breached. Technology has broken into our camping trips. Al is playing with a GoPro and John needs to call his Honey. Is there nothing sacred left?"

"Come on, guys," John said. "I'm not planning to use the phone for anything other than the call to Anne. Besides, we've all learned that backup plans are a good thing. A cell phone is the perfect tool to help us out of a serious jam. If someone gets hurt, help can find us a lot faster than if we didn't have it." He pursed his lips when he looked at his screen: no signal.

As the four of them jabbed at John, they seemed to forget about river hazards until they rounded a corner and discovered another downed tree against the far bank. That seemed to end the conversation about the mobile phone, Anne, and the swamp. Al stowed the GoPro, and the group focused on navigating the meandering river again.

The scrub brush and grass gave way to taller trees, and the riverbanks seemed to confine the flooding water. That meant that they were close to where the Totagatic River joined the larger Namekagon River. The day so far hadn't been perfect, but they had made it through the Dismal Swamp. Now the group could focus on reaching their next campsite.

11

Confluences

Even though the conversation about Anne was dropped, John continued to think about her. He wanted the rendezvous to go according to plan. She and a friend were supposed to meet them Thursday at Nevers Dam, and he needed to call her about their possible arrival time. John looked at his watch. It was a little before noon on Tuesday and the group didn't seem to be off track. Day one was a little long, but then again they spent a lot of time overcoming obstacles. If things had slowed down significantly, they would have camped further upstream. Today the group was separated, and three of them spent a lot of time dragging canoes through shallow wooded floodplain. He needed to know how fast they were moving, so he asked the navigator.

"Hey Al, can you dig out the maps and tell me where we are?"

Al reached into his day pack, pulled out the maps, and laid them across the gear in front of him. The river's twists and turns still demanded his attention, but it was nothing like the first day. The turns were gentler, and fewer obstacles hung into the water. The fewer hazards allowed him to glance at the maps and narrow down their location.

"The Namekagon River is about sixteen miles from our first campsite. The Totagatic River flows southwest from the dam for about half that distance, then turns northwest until it reaches the Namekagon. We've traveled northwest for at least ninety minutes."

John did some quick math in his head. "That means we should reach the Namekagon River any minute, right?"

Al thought about it for a minute, then said, "That should be right. Where the rivers merge, that should give us an exact location and tell us how fast we've moved. There's a campground and picnic area less than a mile after the confluence. The landing is on the far riverbank, just after a county road that crosses the river. We can stop for lunch and pick a campsite for tonight."

"Sounds like a good plan."

Everyone was surprised when the Namekagon River appeared in less than ten minutes. All three boats hit the cross current when the rivers merged, and they pointed their bows downstream. Bob spotted the bridge first and pointed it out to his steersman, Paul. All three canoes moved to the far bank and prepared for a landing.

Tom pulled the food pack out of Al's canoe and dug into it. He tossed around snack bars, beef sticks, and trail mix before opening a bar for himself. With his mouth half full, he said to Paul and Bob, "We could have been lost in those woods for days. You guys would have had to live off tree bark and frogs after you sacrificed that beef jerky. You would have starved."

Al was looking at the maps and chimed in. "No way! The map shows the river flows south and then takes a sharp turn west. We went into the grass just before the bend. The high water just took a shortcut and took us with it."

John was less concerned about where they were and more about where they were going. The phone call was on his mind, so he asked, "How fast are we traveling?"

Al did a couple thumbnail measurements on the map and then looked at his watch. "The best I can estimate, we averaged somewhere between four and five miles per hour this morning. Because of the twisting river and the obstacles we encountered, I'd actually guess over five."

"How far is it to Nevers Dam?" John continued.

Al flipped over one of the maps. Since the upper St. Croix River was a canoeist haven, the DNR expanded map information to include distance charts. These charts helped people easily plan day trips and weeklong excursions on the waterway. Al ran his fingers down the distance chart and matched up Nevers Dam to the Namekagon confluence.

"It says that we are about seventy-five miles from Nevers Dam." Al sat and thought for a few seconds, then pulled out a pen. He scribbled a few numbers on the map and then thought a little more while chewing on the end of the pen. He wrote down a few more numbers, drew a line and totaled the list. He tapped the map with the pen tip, looked up at the group and said, "We are moving faster than our original plan. According to this, we will reach Nevers Dam late Wednesday and not on Thursday."

"What!" the group said in astonishment.

"Yah, that's right," Al continued. "It's Tuesday today. We based our plan on a typical speed between three and four miles per hour. We navigated the Totagatic River moving over five miles per hour on average, even with all of our problems. I'm betting our progress will only pick up when we canoe the St. Croix. It's relatively straight and probably moving faster in the high water. We will knock off almost a full day and end the trip in St. Croix Falls on Thursday."

John panicked and walked back to his canoe. "I need to make a phone call. If we are a day ahead of schedule, our guests need to know."

"Your new girlfriend will be a little irritated if we've come and gone by the time she arrives," Paul jeered.

"She's not a girlfriend, but I have to admit that she has good qualifications," John replied. "I'm just trying to be courteous. They are expecting us to camp and then paddle with them the next day. It wouldn't be right for us to leave and not tell them." In reality, John wanted to give Anne every opportunity to meet them. "Hopefully they can shift their schedule, but if they can't they can make other plans."

John dug his phone out of his pack and turned it on. The system came up after a minute, and an antenna with a little bar through it appeared in the upper right corner. His face grew that same worried look he had when they were lost. He turned off the phone.

Paul watched John trying to make the call. As John walked back to the group, Paul commented, "I've seen that worried look before, John. What's up?"

"No signal out here."

"You really want this meet to happen. I haven't seen you this concerned since the sectional wrestling meet last season. I'm sure we'll cross an area where there's enough signal for a call. Al, how long does John have to wait?"

"It's strange that we don't have signal. We are only about eight miles away from Danbury. There is a casino in town so I'm sure there is good signal there. Out here the mobile phone companies direct their antennas toward towns and highway traffic. We'll cross under two major highways in the next couple hours. That should solve your problem, John. There's always good signal along highways."

"Sounds good. I'll try again when we come to a bridge. Let's figure out where the next camp is and get back on the water."

With lunch and water bottles in hand, they crowded around the map and watched Al trace his fingers along their route. "We're here, just after the Totagatic confluence. We'll cross over the shallow rapids at the bottom of the Namekagon just before dumping into the St. Croix River. It's shortly after one o'clock, and we should pass Danbury, going under the Minnesota/Wisconsin bridge around four." He flipped over the map and continued tracing the route on the back side. "We have a choice to make for this next stretch of river." He pointed to the bottom corner of the back side. "There are some major rapids along this five-mile stretch. We could pull off from the river around six and tackle the rough water first thing tomorrow morning. That places camp around twenty miles south of Danbury. Or, we could push through the rapids today and get off the water around seven. That will leave thirty-five miles to Never's Dam instead of forty miles tomorrow."

Tom raised his hand and said, "I vote for rapids tomorrow. Rough water means wet gear, and if we leave the river around seven, we will sleep in wet tents tonight."

Bob stood up and leaned over the maps for a closer look. "How serious are these rapids? Are we talking splashing water that gets things a little wet or are we talking possible capsize?"

Tom just smiled and looked at Bob. "These rapids are rated level two. There are some huge boulders we typically avoid and some troughs where the water moves pretty fast between large underwater rocks. That means there is a chance of capsizing for inexperienced canoers under normal conditions. We usually make it through these rapids with some water in the bottom of the canoe. With this high water, there's no telling what we'll find. I don't think any of us have canoed this stretch of river under these conditions."

John, Paul, and Al nodded their heads and reinforced Tom's thoughts.

Bob looked a little worried over the uncertainty involved with tackling uncharted whitewater. His friends didn't look overly concerned, but then again they had run the St. Croix River a few times. "What do level-one and level-two rapids look like? I'd sure like to know what I'm getting into."

Al paged through the maps on his lap, folded over one of the sheets, and handed it to Bob. "Here are the official descriptions provided by the DNR." Bob grabbed the map and read.

Class One: Easy - Fast moving water with riffles and small waves. Few obstructions, all obvious and easily missed with little training. Risk to swimmers is slight; self-rescue is easy.

Class Two: Novice - Straightforward rapids with wide, clear channels which are evident without scouting. Occasional maneuvering may be required, but rocks and medium-sized waves are easily avoided by trained paddlers. Swimmers are seldom injured and group assistance, while helpful, is seldom needed.

Class Three: Intermediate - Rapids with moderate, irregular waves which may be difficult to avoid and which can swamp an open canoe. Complex maneuvers in fast current and good boat control in tight passages or around ledges are often required; large waves or strainers may be present but are easily avoided. Strong eddies and powerful current effects can be found, particularly on large-volume rivers. Scouting is advisable for inexperienced parties. Injuries while swimming are rare; self-rescue is usually easy but group assistance may be required to avoid long swims.

Class Four: Advanced - Intense, powerful but predictable rapids requiring precise boat handling in turbulent water. Depending on the character of the river, it may feature large, unavoidable waves and holes or constricted passages demanding fast maneuvers under pressure. A fast, reliable eddy turn may be needed to initiate maneuvers, scout rapids, or rest. Rapids may require "must make" moves above dangerous hazards. Scouting may be necessary the first time down. Risk of injury to swimmers is moderate to high, and water conditions may make self-rescue difficult. Group assistance for rescue is often essential but requires practiced skills. For kayakers, a strong roll is highly recommended.

When Bob finished reading, he looked at the group. "Based on what we found yesterday and today, I'm thinking these rapids are more difficult in high water. Al and Tom tipped over in the first hundred yards yesterday and we nearly lost Paul when he was swept under our canoe. Today you three were lost in the woods for more than an hour. Paul and I nearly lost our canoe. I'm with Tom. It would be nice to have fresh arms and a clear head when we tackle the white water."

"Also, the forty miles to reach Nevers Dam leaves us a quiet and easy day of paddling after the rapids," John added to the vote. "I think we should camp north of the rapids."

Al took one last look at the maps. "It's settled then. There are state parks on both sides of the river south of Danbury. There are plenty of sites to choose from. Let's pull into one of the sites sometime between five and six."

Al folded up the maps and got up. The others got up, stashed their snacks, and headed for their canoes. John shoved his phone in his back pocket, thinking he would periodically check for a good signal. They were only five miles from the St. Croix River, and all of them were looking forward to moving from the twisting and turning on the Totagatic River to the open water and rapids on the Namekagon and St. Croix Rivers. They pushed off all three boats to finish the day.

12

Early Camp

Soon after the lunch stop, the Namekagon River presented a long open stretch of water. This last stretch widened before the St. Croix confluence, and in a typical early season, the group would have experienced class one rapids. Not that day. The river was a rough, rippled surface, with not a stone in sight.

"This is incredible!" Paul yelled to the group. "I've canoed through here several times in the early season. Usually you can look down and see fist-sized stones on the bottom and a few larger rocks sticking out of the water. I've never seen the river so flat and deep."

Bob commented back to Paul. "Is this where I would have used the old tennis shoes you told me to bring?"

"It sure is. Walking barefoot over the rocky bottom is really tough on your feet. One time I did it in the late season when we had to drag our canoe through a field of slimy wet stones. It took us an hour to cross the rapids because our canoe was loaded down. I didn't have shoes, and we were too stubborn to portage. I ended up with cuts on the bottom of my feet."

"I'm not disappointed that we can stay in our canoes, but I hope the downstream rapids aren't submerged. That would make tomorrow kind of a boring day."

Paul just chuckled and used his most haunting voice to say, "Wait until you see the boulder field on the last set of rapids tomorrow."

The submerged rapids gave the group a chance to take in the scenery. Normally, the shallow whitewater demanded their attention, but now each of them noticed that the Namekagon River actually had a several islands and submerged sandbars near its end. Most of these created back channels with slower water that formed a delta with submerged islands. Seeing the back channel detours, Tom couldn't resist poking fun. "Wanna try one of those shortcuts, Al?"

"You're a funny guy, Tom," Al said with a large dose of sarcasm in his voice.

"Have you guys noticed how fast we are moving?" Tom asked. "Usually someone on shore could keep up with us at a fast walking pace. Today they'd need to run."

Al just smiled, knowing his number-crunching was right. "You can see why we will trim a day off from our trip. The river is moving us twice as fast as normal."

John occasionally pulled out his mobile phone to check for signal. He knew there was a cell tower in Danbury, and the Namekagon River was located just northeast of town. Unfortunately, there was a sharp signal drop-off northeast of the tower. The mobile phone companies probably didn't see the urgency in covering the wilderness area they were canoeing. On other trips, he had seen his phone display no bars at one location and then full strength within a few hundred yards. He knew it had something to do with the antenna array but didn't know the technology behind it. He wanted to call Anne as soon as possible and let her know they would arrive a day early at Nevers Dam.

The fast rippling water over the submerged rapids moved the three canoes into the St. Croix River cross current within ten minutes. After the Namekagon River ended, it was five miles to Riverside Landing and the Wisconsin Highway 35 bridge. After John and Tom pointed their canoe downstream, John didn't waste any time checking his phone again. Seeing the three bars in the display's upper right corner he thought, *Great! About time.* He accessed Anne's contact information and tapped the send button.

After five rings, John heard, "Hello this is Anne. If it's early morning, I'm probably still sleeping and my phone is off. If it's evening, I'm delivering pizzas and can't talk while I'm driving. Otherwise I'm out taking incredibly scenic photos. Leave me a message and I'll call you back."

"Hey Anne, this is John. It's about two thirty on Tuesday. The trip has been exciting so far. I'm looking forward to sharing the stories with you at Nevers Dam. The problem is, we will reach the campsite a day early. The rivers are flowing fast and hard, moving us much faster than we planned. We should reach the campsite by early evening tomorrow. Call me when you get this message." John ended the call and stuffed the phone in his back pocket. He was a little worried that Anne might not listen to the message until tomorrow, but it was only midafternoon. If she didn't call him back by the time they set up camp, he would call her again.

This far from its headwaters, the St. Croix River was completely different than the Totagatic River. Its width easily spanned fifty yards between the east and west banks. While the channel still occasionally curved enough to hide the downstream views, it was nothing like the serpentine Totagatic channel. The gentler turns provided easy navigation for the group. If he chose to, the steersman only needed to rudder and allow the river to do the work. The energy level of five wrestlers and their drive to reach camp at day's end compelled them to continue paddling, although at a much lighter pace than earlier that day.

"Hey Al," Bob called out. "What's between here and our campsite? Is it just four hours of open river?"

"We go under three bridges here at Danbury. One is Highway Seventy-Seven that crosses into Minnesota. There's an old railroad bridge converted to a bike trail crossing, and shortly we will see

Highway Thirty-Five that runs north to Superior, Wisconsin, and Duluth, Minnesota. We might have to flatten ourselves to go under the bridges, but there should be plenty of room to maneuver."

"The river looks different out in front of us. What is that?"

"That is the first set of two rapids we'll cross on the St. Croix today. The first is a long class one, and the second is called the State Line Rapids." Out in front of the canoes, the water surface looked slightly broken and bumpy. Six-inch ripples formed on the right side of the channel near a big island with campsites. "We should just breeze over this first rapids in the high water. The right side has a rocky sandbar we would totally avoid under normal conditions. It might be fun for you to veer that way and see if you can spot any rocks just under the surface." Al was only kidding about veering right, but Paul started the canoe toward the island.

"Hey Paul!" Bob yelled from the front of the canoe. "What are you doing? You're not thinking about shooting the rapids without your glasses?"

"You sound worried, Bob. Don't you trust my driving? Al's right. This might add a little excitement to our last couple of hours today. Besides, you can practice these little speed bumps before tomorrow's heavier class two rapids."

"Okay, okay, what do I do?"

"First, you need to relax. There's nothing dangerous about this little bit of whitewater. I'll give you a couple tips, and then we can practice as we head through. Number one, unless I tell you otherwise, you need to keep paddling while we navigate the rapids. The power you apply up front helps me steer through narrow openings between rocks. If you stop paddling, the current can carry the canoe right into a rock."

"Got it, keep paddling."

"Number two, you are fourteen feet in front of me and can see sneaky underwater rocks I might miss. Let me know what you see."

"Got it. What happens if we hit a rock?"

"Probably not much in this little rapids, but that's number three. Don't panic. Just steady the canoe by leaning into the rock to keep the canoe balanced. Depending on how we hit a rock governs what we do. We might just scrape over it or we might power around it."

"That's it? Sounds pretty simple."

"It is. I might even do this with my eyes closed." Bob turned and glared, but Paul just showed him a bright smile. Then Paul said, "Pay attention. Here we go."

The six-inch ripples started slapping the canoe's bow, and they picked up speed as Paul steered them down the side of the island. Paul saw Bob sit up straight and hyper-focus on the water's surface. He was showing his rookie experience by holding his paddle across his chest as he watched for rocks in the water ahead.

"Keep paddling!" Paul wasn't worried about navigating the harmless stretch of river. The water was deep enough that they were gliding over everything. The water passing over the rocky bar created a churning surface that looked challenging to the inexperienced eye, but the canoe was clearing the largest rocks by six to twelve inches. It was a good lesson for Bob about how people focus on danger they think lies in front of them.

"Oops. Sorry about that." Bob dug in his paddle and relaxed a little. "There's a big one." Bob briefly pointed his paddle off to the left and then dug in again. Paul made a slight adjustment and they continued on. Within two minutes they passed through the churning water and joined the other two canoes.

"Whoop! Whoop!" Tom yelled out, half poking fun and half in congratulations. "Bob survived his first whitewater challenge." The other three cheered, and Bob pumped his paddle over his head in mock celebration. He quickly realized that the rapids were no big deal, but the adrenaline surge beforehand and his friends recognizing the experience afterward made it worthwhile.

Bob turned and smiled at Paul. "Thanks Paul. That was a first-rate whitewater baptism. I'm ready for the second rapids. How far is it?"

"I think it's just after the first bridge."

Within fifteen minutes, the group rounded a bend and saw Riverside Landing and the Highway 35 bridge. The high water presented a thirty-six-inch clearance under the concrete beams. All five guys lay back on their gear and easily drifted under the two-lane highway. Within a couple minutes, they picked up the dull roar of the State Line Rapids. The short class two rapids were named for its location right on the Minnesota and Wisconsin border. After the rapids, the St. Croix River became the dividing line between the two states.

"That sounds like our next challenge," Tom called out as he stretched his neck to see the river ahead. "I'm seeing a little more whitewater." The rapids were indeed short. The group was a quarter mile away, and at that distance, they couldn't see the bottom of the rapids. The river beyond appeared flat and smooth, but the water pouring over the rapids created a fat white line across the river. There was no transition between the rapids and the river beyond. The site made all five canoeists sit up and pay attention because it meant that the river dropped a couple feet in the short distance and the riverbed held larger rocks or boulders. They had to choose a route and set their course before heading into the rapids. "Al, what does the map recommend?"

Al quickly pulled the map out of his pack and found the detailed description. "There's an island on the left side of the channel with shallows at the tip. Stay far right just until the island's point and then work back across the channel. The river bends left and there's another rocky bar on the Minnesota side where the channel turns east. The rapids are only about fifty yards long."

There was whitewater higher than the canoes' sides as Paul and Bob headed into the fast-moving straight. Al was in the single-person canoe ten yards to their left. John and Tom followed directly behind them. Paul called out to Bob, "What's the first rule for running rapids?"

"Keep paddling!"

"Right. We don't want to hang up on a rock with Tom and John right behind us. They can't stop."

Paul and Bob crossed the threshold from flat water into the churning ripples of the early rapids. Paul recognized patches of deceiving smooth black water in front of them as small boulders just below the surface. He steered the canoe left and right of large rocks toward churning white waves just either side of the hidden stones. Water slapped the canoe's bow and threw droplets into Bob's lap. The path through the right side of the rapids was fairly straight, but the current bent toward the left as the river made its way around the island. Paul fought the river, trying to point the canoe downstream until it was time to cut across the river and avoid the lower rocky bar on the Minnesota side. Each time they passed over a small ledge or avoided a rock, the river would try to sweep the canoe sideways. Bob used his adrenaline surge to paddle hard rather than freeze up. With the power in front, Paul was free to rudder and pivot the canoe in a moment's notice. Bob glanced at the large submerged rocks as they passed by the rapids midpoint. He saw silver streaks left by some past canoer whose bottom scraped over the stone. Tom and John were three canoe lengths back, following as if they were cutting a narrow trail through a jungle. The distance closed when Paul pivoted the canoe left to cross the channel and avoid the rock bar on the Minnesota side of the river. Paul dug in his paddle to avoid a collision and their canoe shot through the last line of whitewater.

Al's path took him through a more difficult part of the rapids. The boulders were larger and closer together, so he was zig-zagging to thread through narrow troughs. The canoe's bow met tall white-tipped waves every time it passed a boulder. This rolled water over the canoe's edge and threw spray across the entire boat. Thankfully, the gear in front of Al's canoe was covered with a tarp that saved the tents from taking the brunt of the incoming water. No one wanted to sleep in a wet tent.

The more intense flow between the larger rocks also threatened to sweep Al's boat sideways, but the lighter bow allowed him to quickly pivot his canoe between zig and zag. Occasionally he would bounce against the side of a boulder, using it to straighten out when shooting down a churning trough. His path set him up for a straight run through the lower half of the rapids. He didn't need to pivot mid-channel as his friends did, and his shorter route popped him out of the rapids ahead of them. He pulled out the GoPro and turned to watch as the two canoes navigated the last of the rocks. Boulders and side currents jerked Paul and Bob right and left. They shot through troughs, digging their paddles into the waves to keep their bow pointed downstream. The canoe behind them was so close that it appeared as if a rope was tied between them. The second boat's motion and the paddling effort appeared like a time delay of Paul and Bob.

When the two canoes cleared the rapids, Al yelled to Bob and Paul. "Way to blaze a trail for John and Tom. I got it on video. They didn't even need to think about their course."

Paul glanced back to John and Tom and said, "I should guide and get paid for this."

"We're just lucky you didn't hit a boulder," John replied. "It would have slowed you enough that we might have rammed you."

They navigated the State Line Rapids in less than three minutes, coming out the bottom end with only a few wet spots on the front passengers' shirts. They all looked back with smiles on their faces as their adrenaline subsided. John continued his thoughts. "I've never run those rapids at this water level. The rocks were less of a challenge, but the wave action was incredible. We finished a little wetter than normal."

"Those were true class two rapids," Al added. "They were not as bad as I thought they would be."

"That was great!" Bob yelled. "I was a little worried when we came up to them, but my partner flew through them like he was using The Force. They don't look so tough now."

Tom looked back upstream, then turned to Bob. "Yah, rapids always look easier after you've run them. Wait until tomorrow's rapids. They are longer and the boulders are bigger. I can't wait to see your face when you first see them."

Thinking about planning a route through the rapids, Al jumped back into the conversation. "We can pull out the maps this evening in camp and plan how we should run tomorrow's whitewater. We should start looking for campsites in a couple of hours when the river reaches the north end of St. Croix State Park."

The group rounded a bend in the river, and the second of the three bridges came into view. The old railroad bridge was part of the Gandy Dancer trail that ran between St. Croix Falls and Superior, Wisconsin. The trail crossed the river right on the edge of town and was often used to bike, walk, or four-wheel across the river. The group could see three boys fishing from the bridge. Their poles hung off the upstream side, and the strong current pulled their lines beneath the bridge where they were hoping to catch sturgeon that sometimes lurked under the trestle.

The three canoes spread apart and approached the Wisconsin side of the bridge. The three young boys watched them approach from the west half, curious how the five young men would navigate under the trestle. Like the other bridges on the trip, the high water crept close to the underside, making it impossible to sit upright while passing underneath. Al lined up his canoe, expertly lay back on the rear deck, and disappeared under the bridge. Tom and John slid in behind him.

"Cool trick!" one of the boys called from above. Two of the boys pulled their lines out of the water and ran across the trail to watch the canoes pop out the other side.

Bob called out to the third boy, "It's easy. This is our fourth bridge. Caught any fish?"

"Nothing. The current's too strong."

Bob thought about the delicious fresh fish they ate the previous evening. As Paul lined up their canoe, he commented back, "You know the old Ojibwe named Ben? He lives near the Minong Lake dam. He never goes hungry."

The boy responded as Paul and Bob passed under the bridge. "Yah. He's a legend around here, but only the old-timers have met him."

"Good luck fishing," Bob called back as they paddled away from the bridge. The boys waved and went back to their poles.

The group crossed under the third bridge using the same technique as before and cleared the two-lane Highway 77 without incident. The water still moved fast, but the need for heavy navigation dwindled to almost nothing. They had time to take in the wooded shoreline and enjoy the wild and scenic riverway. They began picking up blue jay and raven screeching over the sound of running water. Those species were the forest alarm system that warned about predators high on the food chain. A lot of times it was man wandering clueless into the bird's territory, but today the calls warned of something else. Some distance ahead of them they could see blue and black birds flitting between treetops. As the canoes closed the distance, the five guys soon saw the reason for the noise. A pair of bald eagles sat camouflaged just inside the treetop canopy, watching the water surface for their next meal. The smaller birds made sure every animal knew their location by moving in measured circles around the majestic hunters. The eagles ignored the ravens and blue jays as they watched the three canoes pass by.

The trip shifted to a more serene quiet, broken only by occasional idle chat. Bob began to sigh in the front seat of the canoe as they entered the second hour of leisurely paddling. They had reached St. Croix State Park with its deep woods and abundant wildlife, but Bob saw little excitement in the passing forest shoreline. His eyes pictured only trees, trees, and more trees. It reminded him of old movies where you could tell Hollywood had a tight budget and car scenes were shot on a movie set. After short intervals, the same scene passed by the car window again and again. After the fourth sigh, Paul decided to pester him.

"Are you bored, Bob?"

"Just a little. We haven't experienced this much continuous downtime anywhere on this trip. We paddled nonstop just to keep from capsizing both yesterday and today. When things slowed down yesterday on that long lake before we camped above the dam, I was too tired to notice. Today there was the Dismal Swamp, the Namekagon River, the bridges near Danbury, and the State Line Rapids. Now we are just paddling down river."

"I'm glad to hear the trip hasn't disappointed you so far."

"It's been great! I'm glad you came up with the idea. Maybe the last day and a half conditioned me to expect something exciting around every river bend."

Paul chuckled a little and thought about how different this trip was. "Yah, this trip has been a little more exciting than the other times we've canoed this stretch of river. The high water really adds a different dimension. Most people take this trip to relax and get away from urban hustle. This part of the river is what they savor most."

"Maybe you're right. I should enjoy the scenery and quiet time a little more. Do you think I'll beg for downtime like this when I'm at the Air Force Academy?"

"I have no doubt in my mind. You will be sleeping with at least twenty other guys in the dorms, and upper classmen will kick your butt all day long. The only downtime you'll have is when you're asleep. The upside is that boot camp is only eight weeks long. I just don't know if that's long enough to turn you into a real man."

Bob swung his head around and sneered at Paul. "Hey! If you don't think it's that tough, why don't you sign up and join me? If the academy really changes a person, they might even have a way to make you taller."

"If I did that who would plan your welcome home party? No thanks. All I know is that it will be different not hanging out with you this summer."

Paul's last sentence drove the point home about life changing. *I'm going to miss you too, Paul,* he thought. *I have a feeling that I'm going to miss a lot of things.*

Bob and Paul fell behind the other two canoes during their conversation. There were a few small islands that offered an occasional back channel to explore if they wanted, but they decided to catch up to the others. Their stomachs were growling. When they found a campsite, they could grab a quick snack while the group set up camp.

Al had dug out the maps again, surveying the possibilities and sharing them with Tom and John. "It's almost four thirty. I see four campsites on the Minnesota side and two on the Wisconsin side. The four are in St. Croix State Park with access to fresh drinking water. They also require fees for camping. Any thoughts?"

"We still have plenty of water," Tom replied. "I vote for the free camping. Which one has the best accommodations?"

"That would be Norway Point Landing. It has a toilet and picnic area, but it's still an hour away."

John glanced at his phone to check the signal strength. He was worried that he hadn't heard from Anne yet. "I'm good with another hour of paddling if it means a decent place to set up cooking gear for supper. Let's land at Norway Point." He stuffed his phone into his day bag, wondering if she got his message. By the time they reached camp, it would be almost five thirty and Anne would be at work. With so many forms of communication, some people just ignored voicemail if they didn't recognize the number or if a call wasn't expected. Maybe Anne was one of those people. He pulled his phone out again to text her, just to see if she received his voice message. There was a good chance she would miss them at Nevers Dam if she didn't check her phone.

13

Norway Point Landing

Norway Point Landing sat next to a bend in the river that created a sand bar just downstream of the river access. It was a small semi-modern campsite with a narrow paved boat launch accessing the river. The group beached their boats just upstream from the pavement to avoid scraping the canoes on the hard surface. There was thirty yards of roughly mowed grass between the river and the camp area. A single picnic table sat next to a fire pit, where a rusty hinged grate sat waiting for the next pot of camp coffee. The area was flat, clean, and perfect for their tents. While the site had no electricity or running water, the Wisconsin DNR had recently built a permanent outhouse. Busier sites with both camping and a boat launch took a toll on Mother Nature. The DNR wanted people to use the permanent structure rather than the woods.

As the group stepped from their canoes, they couldn't tell if the effort was entirely successful. There were small openings in the wooded perimeter with worn trails ending several yards off from the grassy campsite. John wrinkled his nose at the thought of how many people it took to wear in trails like they were seeing. "Watch your step if you're looking for firewood down one of those trails. It looks like that new outhouse is badly needed here." He knew that Mother Nature would swallow up the human impact in time, but she wasn't there yet. One misstep and somebody might discover an aging wilderness commode.

The five guys moved back and forth between the canoes and picnic area, quickly emptying the boats. Each bag was simply tossed in the area near the fire ring for sorting and unpacking. Al and John made the last trip to the river and pulled the canoes onto the grass near the wooded boundary. They flipped the canoes to empty what little water lay in the bottom and tucked the paddles up underneath. Even though they were confident that the river wouldn't rise high enough to float their boats during the night, they tied them to brush with small ropes. The river had ways of surprising people and they didn't want to swim for their canoes the next morning.

Bob grabbed the food pack and heaved it onto the picnic table. He carried the cooking gear over between the fire pit and the table, where he pulled out the camp stove and set it on the end of the picnic bench. No one yet complained about hunger, but Bob heard more than one stomach grumble during the procession emptying the canoes. If he timed it right, supper would be almost ready by the time the rest of camp was set up.

Tom and Paul began setting up tents a reasonable distance from the fire pit and picnic table. Floating embers sometimes drifted a short distance from the pit. While all of their tents were fireproof, no one wanted a small annoying drip hole melted through their tent fly. Food scraps were another concern. Local vermin always visited picnic areas and focused their attention around the food source. Pitching tents a little distance from where they ate decreased the chance that something might wake them in the middle of the night.

John and Al returned from the river's edge and grabbed the last tent bag. Tom looked over at them when he heard them zip open the nylon bag and dump the fiberglass poles on the ground. He got off his knees, leaving the last few stakes for Paul to pound into the ground. He picked up a small blue tarp and walked it over to John and Al.

"Here, use this on the ground first. It will help with the morning dew around the tent edge." Handing off the tarp, Tom felt he was out of earshot from Paul. With his back to Paul, he whispered to Al and John, "We need to find a way to get back at Paul for the latrine scare he gave us last night." Both of them looked up from where they were unrolling the tent, then quickly went back to their task, hoping Paul didn't notice their change in focus. A moment later, John glanced over at Paul and saw he was busy hammering in stakes. He handed Tom the tent fly and winked at him before going back to what he was doing. Tom smiled and unfolded the fly. John had something in mind and he just needed to wait.

When Paul finished with the tent stakes, he stood up and looked at the three working on the tent and then at Bob fixing supper. "Looks like you guys can take care of the tent. Want me to help Bob?"

John looked over toward Bob and the fire pit. "All of the firewood is gone. Do you think there is any dead wood anywhere close by?"

Bob replied, "We could use a couple arms full for the evening."

"I'll wander into the woods and see what's available." Paul turned, grabbed the saw from the gear pack, and walked toward the wooded perimeter.

"That should keep him busy for a while," Tom said as he watched Paul disappear into the woods. "This place is picked clean near the campsite. He'll have to walk a ways to find dry wood. Any payback ideas?"

Al paused from slipping a fiberglass pole through the tent sleeve. "I saw a great one on an episode of M*A*S*H*. Hawkeye and BJ Honeycut carried Frank Burns out of their tent while he was asleep and set him down in the middle of a field. When he woke, the camp was nowhere in sight."

"That would be great except they had an army cot to move Frank," Tom replied. "Paul would wake up when we pulled him out of the tent. Besides, I think they slipped something in Frank's coffee so he wouldn't wake up."

Another idea sparked in John's mind when he glanced over at Bob's efforts with supper. "We could stuff a peanut butter sandwich in the bottom of Paul's sleeping bag. The raccoons will pick up the scent and pester him all night."

"That would be really funny," Tom replied again. "Two problems with that joke. Bob wouldn't go for it since he is tenting with Paul and the peanut butter might attract bears rather than raccoons. I want to scare Paul, not kill him. Although, that gives me an idea."

Tom outlined his idea for Al and John while they finished raising the tent. They talked more while driving in stakes. The three of them began to chuckle as they attached the tent fly and shared ideas to improve the essence of the payback. The last thing they needed to do was bring Bob into the plan. Paul had just finished dropping an armful of wood near the fire ring and started for the woods a second time. As he walked away, the three of them stood and walked over to Bob.

Bob had just sampled the Noodle Helper that was bubbling in the cook pot. When he turned to see John, Tom, and Al, they were walking toward him and glancing at Paul walking back into the woods. Bob looked at Paul, then looked back to his three friends.

"What?" was all Bob said when his three friends sat down at the table and broke into devious smiles.

Tom checked the woods for Paul one last time and then said, "We have something planned for Paul and we need your help. Here's the plan…"

It was sunset before the five guys were ready to sit down around the fire ring. The high-carb supper of bacon bits and Cheese Noodle Helper went down well. Bob mixed a triple batch with a whole box of macaroni noodles. The result was a half pot of sticky, starchy, and fragrant camp food the five of them couldn't quite finish. It was sitting in their stomachs like a ball of soft dough that would eventually woo them to sleep after they sat down. Since Bob made supper, he was excused from clean-up duty. He sat on one of the logs that surrounded the fire ring and poked at the burning embers. John and Tom rinsed everything with a little river water, then heated some fresh water from their reserve to wash the dishes.

John pulled dish after dish from the pot full of soapy water and dipped them in the rinse bucket. Tom stood off from the end of the picnic table wiping the dishes after John handed them to him. He kidded John while he finished the last couple plates. "Anne is really going to like those nice soft dishpan hands."

John was getting tired and grumbled at Tom's one-liner. He ignored the comment and said, "I just wish she would call or text me back. There, I'm done. Can you handle storing everything while I take care of the food pack and cooking gear?"

"Yes, I've got it." Tom recognized that the lack of response from Anne was really bugging John. He decided to drop it, knowing that they had no control over when or if she would reply.

Tom finished putting away the plates and flatware, emptied the wash water into the woods, and then set the large pot on the picnic table to dry. Al dug out the map that detailed the rapids they were going to tackle the next morning. When John sat down, returning from hanging the food pack and cooking gear, Al began outlining the next day's rapids run.

"About three miles downstream there is a four-mile section of faster water sprinkled with six to eight sets of rapids. The channel splits just past the first set at a place called Head of the Rapids Island. That's where we have a choice to run the western set of rapids where the Kettle River flows into the St. Croix or run the eastern rapids in the wider channel."

"What's the difference?" Paul asked.

"The west is shallower with shorter and narrower rapids that step down toward the Kettle. That's why it's called the Kettle River Slough. In low water we would have to get out and walk canoes through the rocky steps. With the high water we stay in our canoes, but we bang against boulders just below the surface. The east channel has longer stretches of whitewater with a wider area to navigate the hard parts. The water is probably moving faster in the main channel than it is in the western back channel, so more class two wave action."

"Both are a challenge, but I like to avoid banging on rocks," Paul said. "We might as well pick the one with faster water that doesn't damage the boats."

John jumped in. "Since we have three canoes, we should choose the wider channel. That will help us avoid ramming each other if the water pushes us close together."

"I like the idea of more wave action," Tom said. "It will challenge us to maneuver the canoes. Wave action tends to push you around, and it's tough to control a long boat. If you're trying to line up for a run between a pair of rocks, you really need to work hard to push through the river current."

Al chimed in and looked over at Bob. "I agree. We haven't heard from you, Bob. Any thoughts?"

Bob was just recovering from an arm stretch and a long yawn. "Remember, I haven't canoed rapids before. I'm just along for the ride and I don't plan to steer tomorrow. The east channel sounds fine."

"Okay then," Al continued as he folded the maps. "East channel. Remember to bag everything when we pack up tomorrow and tie everything down in the canoes."

They stoked the fire and gathered around the ring to stare into flames. The orange glow of dusk was gone and the nighttime forest voices filled the spaces between the crackle of burning wood. Not many words were shared as they listened to the high notes produced by the crickets and frogs and the background bass of the river droning on behind them. Paul would occasionally break their trance when he poked at the fire with the long stick, tipping over a small log or flipping another into the flame from the edge. The motion would send off a small shower of sparks and expose the orange underbelly of embers. Yawns were the first signs of slumber creeping into camp. Soon the hypnotizing effects of the fire closed Al's eyes and his chin dropped to his chest. He looked somewhat comfortable and warm sitting on the ground with his back against one of the log benches. After a minute, he snorted and eyes snapped open. Embarrassed, he got up, stretched, and headed for his tent.

"I'm turning in. I can't keep my eyes open."

Bob followed a few minutes later, leaving the last three to enjoy nature's quiet time as long as their tired bodies would allow.

Paul picked up his stick again and twirled it in his fingers. That prompted Tom to get up from the picnic table, stretch, and yawn. John watched him as he walked past Paul at the fire ring. On his way to his tent, Tom looked back at John. They smiled at each other and then looked at Paul poking his stick into the fire. It was almost payback time.

After another minute, John stood up. "Paul, can you douse the fire before turning in?"

"Sure. I won't be up much longer. I just need to let Bob's gourmet supper settle a little more before I turn in."

John climbed into the tent he shared with Al and left Paul to his quiet time.

♦ ♦ ♦

Paul's eyes snapped open. He was alert and focused. He knew he was staring up at the tent ceiling but there was no distinguishable form or color beyond the blackness that filled the air. He wasn't quite sure if his half-conscious mind heard something or if it was part of the dream he could no longer remember. He pulled his arms out of his sleeping bag and fumbled for his glasses but then remembered he had lost them over a day ago. Touching the backlight button on his watch, he moved his wrist closer and further away from his face, trying to form the numbers. It was 3:39 a.m. He slid his arms back into his bag and listened to the night. His bladder was talking to him a little and he contemplated getting up to visit the toilet, but he was warm and comfortable, so he decided to stay in his bag. It was pitch black outside with the new moon and it would start getting light in about an hour. He could wait that long. He closed his eyes, laid his head back on the camping pillow, and let his mind drift back toward sleep.

Just as Paul slipped back into a dream, he heard the cooking pot tip over and roll off from the picnic table. Before turning in, he had used it to gather river water to douse the fire and then he had set it on the table. Paul got up on his elbows, poked his tent mate Bob and whispered to him.

"Hey, did you hear that?"

Bob rolled over and gave him a groggy response. "Hear what?"

"Something just tipped over the cook pot and rolled it onto the ground."

Bob lifted his head, listened for a few seconds, and said, "You're dreaming. Go back to sleep." As he lay back down, there was a quiet scraping of metal against dirt. Now Bob was up on his elbows as well.

The two of them were in the tent closest to the fire pit and picnic table. While the other three guys may have heard the pot fall, they probably didn't hear it dragging on the ground. Whatever had their pot would soon drag it across the grass and into the woods.

"I didn't pack away the cook pot because John already hung the cooking gear in a tree. I need to shoo away whatever is dragging it into the woods." Paul was already out of his sleeping bag and slipping on his shoes. "Where is the flashlight?"

"Here it is." Bob handed the light to Paul and began unzipping his bag. "Wait until you are outside to turn on the light. You will get a better look at whatever it is if your eyes are still used to the dark after you get out of the tent."

Paul quietly unzipped the door while Bob hunted for his shoes. He slipped his head through a small opening and strained to see any shapes in the darkness. Nothing seemed to move, and he could barely see the horizontal lines of the picnic table just beyond the fire pit.

Another quiet scrape prompted Paul to zip the door wider and step out of the tent. He tip-toed a half dozen steps toward the table and brought up the flashlight. As he touched the button on the end of the light, he pictured seeing eyes reflecting back from under the table and raccoons scampering away from their campsite. When he pushed the button, nothing happened.

Paul looked down at the light, shook it, and pushed the button twice more. When the button released the second time, the pot clanked against the metal table leg. Paul raised his head and saw a figure slowly rising from behind the table. Time seemed to slow as the figure rose. At first he thought it was a bear as he saw its back arch. Then the figure continued extending upward. Paul took a couple steps backward as the hooded figure reached its full height. There were no details in the outline against the wooded background, but he could tell this thing was over six feet tall, stretching half a body length over the top of the picnic table. He was about twenty-five feet from where they ate last evening and wondered what the thing would do next. There was a sliver of comfort knowing the table stood between him and the figure, that is until it turned and stepped toward the fire ring. Panic set in as the figure raised its cloaked arms and rounded the end of the table. Paul let out a high-pitched scream, turned, and ran.

"Run!" Paul sprinted past his tent where Bob was just climbing out of the door. He weaved between the other two tents, trying to use them as camouflage in his retreat. In another dozen adrenaline-laced steps, Paul slammed his shin into a canoe and sprawled face first into the wet dewy grass. He scrambled back to his feet and leapt over the riverbank into knee-deep water. When he turned and looked back to camp, he saw flashlights weaving patterns on the grass and making their way around the tents. Instead of panicked yelling, he heard laughing and howling.

Paul's four friends were out of their tents, following his wet footprints toward the river.

"Hey Paul! You can come out now." It was Tom taunting Paul's quick exit from the campsite. He was mockingly waving his sleeping bag–cloaked arms over his head and leading the other three guys around the canoes.

A flashlight caught Paul's eyes looking back through the grassy riverbank as he made his way out of the water. "Very funny, Tom. I can't believe you were able to pull this off without the other guys interfering."

"This was pretty easy to do once everyone knew their role."

"You mean all of you were in on this?"

Al reached out his hand and helped Paul up the small bank. "It was Tom's idea, but we all built on the concept. John hung the food and gear without stowing the pot, knowing we wanted to use it to wake you up."

"Let me guess," Paul said. "When the pot tipped over, you weren't really sleeping. You were lying in your sleeping bags enjoying the beginning of the show."

"Pretty much," John said. "Tom told us that he usually visits the bathroom every night between three and four. Since his tent was behind ours, we heard him get up and quietly unzip his tent. We just needed to wait until he woke you up."

Bob jumped in to outline his part. "It didn't matter if I heard Tom or not. We knew you would wake me whether I was asleep or just pretending. It was my job to disable your flashlight and suggest that you not use it until you left the tent. All I needed to do was twist the end halfway off."

Paul complimented his friends. "Very ingenious. Even Mother Nature cooperated. It was so dark out here that I couldn't tell what was standing behind the picnic table. Ben's story about the Wendigo and the Dismal Swamp raced through my mind when Tom stood up. When he came around the table, my half-asleep brain screamed one thing; RUN!"

"We had to do something after your stunt last night," Tom said. "Scaring the hell out of us meant we all needed payback."

Bob added, "You're lucky we decided to gang up on you. Otherwise, you'd have to look over your shoulder the rest of the trip."

The four schemers shared high-fives as they walked back to their tents. Paul grabbed a towel from his day bag to dry off as the mood settled down. It was still pitch black around the camp, and two of the guys yawned. That prompted Al to ask Paul, "Do you think you can fall asleep again? It's over an hour until sunrise and we have a busy day on the river."

Paul could feel his heart still pounding in his chest, but the initial adrenaline surge was wearing off. "I don't know, but it's cold out here." He turned and walked toward his tent. "I'd rather crawl back in a warm sleeping bag than start a fire. Maybe a little more sleep will help me dream of a way to return the favor for getting me up so early."

They all laughed and crawled back into their tents.

14

A Change in Plans

Anne saw mist rising from the river where the water impacted the rocks at the bottom of the dam. It created a perfect shot. The eastern sun shed a warm orange glow across the massive concrete structure. Below the dam, water flowed through a blue trap rock gorge that created fast running narrows where kayakers honed their swift water skills. This photo she took of the St. Croix Falls dam would make a perfect cover picture for her college entrance portfolio. Anne was certain it would seal a "Yes" at any college she applied to. Now she needed to get off the ledge where she photographed the dam. She thought the rope was right behind her, but now there was nothing but a flowering vine snaking its way up the vertical blue cliff. She couldn't recall how she reached the small ledge, but she knew climbing up the smooth rock face was impossible without a rope. Maybe she could use the vine. It looked strong enough, but could she trust it to hold her weight if she used it to climb up the cliff?

The faint rhythmic sound of a car horn echoed in the gorge, and Anne wondered if whoever was parked above had a rope in their trunk. They could toss it down to her and pull her up. She tried calling out, but her voice was muted. Frustration crept into her mind as the horn grew in intensity and became more annoying. Suddenly the trap rock cliffs disappeared without warning. Anne's eyes snapped open and she realized the car horn was her phone alarm. It was five thirty a.m. and her dad would soon leave for work. She kicked back the blankets and slid her legs over the bedside where her slippers waited. Reaching for her phone to silence the alarm, she recalled the previous evening's frustrating situation. In the rush to leave for work, she ran out of her house with less than 10 percent battery and left her charger cord in her bedroom. Her phone died while she listened to music on the way to work.

Lifting the phone off the nightstand, she unplugged the cord. As she swiped her finger across the screen, she saw the text message from John asking about whether she heard his voicemail. It took her less than five seconds to access voice messaging and begin the playback. Panic set in when John's voice described how the rivers' high water sped up their schedule by one day. They would reach the meeting point this evening.

The schedule change created huge problems. She was slated to work tonight, and swapping schedules with someone seemed impossible. What was Sandy's schedule, and could she still make the trip? They were all packed to leave, but they still had no river transportation. She had to catch her dad at breakfast and ask about using the prized wooden canoe. If he said no, where would she find a canoe?

She looked at John's contact name on her phone and anger surged in her mind. How could he do this to her? Moving the schedule up by a day on such short notice was rude. She thought about calling off the trip, but then some other thoughts occurred to her. It had rained for three weeks and the water was very high. John said that they never canoed the Totagatic River and didn't know what to expect. He called her and left a message early yesterday afternoon. Then he sent a text asking if she got the message.

Anne's anger subsided when she realized that John probably called her as soon as he realized that Mother Nature had affected their plan.

Then he followed up when he didn't hear from her. John was doing everything he could to make sure she could meet them.

Anne replied to John's text as she slid out of bed. *Sorry. My phone died. Got your message. Will get back to you.*

When she opened her bedroom door, Anne heard three beeps from downstairs in the kitchen. Dad was still making microwave oatmeal or reheating his coffee. She had a minute or two, so she swung into the bathroom to relieve the pressure nagging her midsection. The extra time gave her a chance to rehearse what she wanted to say. The canoe was beautiful, but it hung in the garage more than it touched water. Both she and her dad were busy with their individual schedules and rarely had time to spend a half day or more canoeing. What sense did it make to have something made for the water and have it hang in a dusty garage forever? She would promise to be careful with the canoe and not land it on a rocky shore. She could also throw in how she was saving money for college and shouldn't rent a canoe when the family had one.

As she walked downstairs, the sound of a sliding chair came from the kitchen and a spoon clanked on a bowl. Anne rounded the corner and saw her dad sitting at the table, first spoonful of oatmeal entering his mouth. "Morning, Dad."

His eyes lifted from the bowl in amazement, and he set down his spoon. "This is a surprise! I remember hearing you come in after ten thirty. Don't you usually stay up a couple hours after you're done with work and sleep in until midmorning? I'll start a second pot of coffee before I leave. You're going to need it today."

Anne smiled at the bad dad humor and sat down at the table. He knew that she didn't drink coffee but knew she understood the value of caffeine. "I'll probably go back to bed after you leave. I wanted to catch you and ask a favor."

"Does this have something do to with the overnight canoe trip?"

"I guess Mom told you about what is going on?"

"You know that Mom and I share everything involving you. What do you need?"

"Well, I've searched and searched for a canoe to borrow and all of my friends' canoes are still in storage. I really don't want to spend the money to rent a canoe because I'm supposed to save for college. I'm kind of stuck." Anne let her statements hang for a few seconds before asking the question. "So, I'm wondering if I can use the wood canoe for the trip?"

Dad took another spoon full of oatmeal and acted like he was really savoring the bland morning meal. Then he laid his spoon in the bowl and picked up his cup of coffee. This was all part of the game Anne had gotten used to over the years. Anytime she asked a favor, she and her dad would play this waiting game. He wanted to see how badly she needed the favor and teased her into begging for what she wanted. When she was younger, she would ramble on and share all her reasoning, saving nothing for debate. Now the older and wiser Anne just waited for his next move.

He took a small sip of coffee, then blew across the cup to cool the hot liquid. "That's a big ask. You know that you and I spent a lot of time building that canoe, and so far the two of us are the only people who have used it."

"Yes, I know. Think about though, that canoe sees water so little, and it's a shame to let it hang in the garage unused."

"I don't know if you should use it." He stalled a few more seconds. "I was planning to dust it off and sell it to the Minneapolis Museum of Art or have the whole canoe bronzed as a memento of the time we spent building it."

Anne smiled. Dad was shifting into humor mode. That meant he had no intention of arguing about the subject of the favor. All she had to do was finish playing the game with him. "Would it make sense to have weeds stuck to the canoe when it's bronzed? That would give it a more realistic look. I could take the canoe through some boggy backwater before bringing it home."

Her dad smiled, knowing she'd already read his mind. "Now that would give it some character. Seriously though, that wooden canoe has gathered way too much dust lately. Take it out and use it but PLEASE remember the care it needs to stay beautiful. You and I spent a lot of time gluing and sanding when we built it."

"Great Dad, thanks." Anne slid back her chair and began to get up from the table.

"Two more things, Anne." She stopped halfway to a standing position, then plopped her butt back into the chair. "Mom tells me there are five guys on this trip. We realize that you spend every day with guys at school and work, but social boundaries tend to change in small groups isolated from everyday life. Because this is reality, can you promise me some things?"

"Sure Dad, what?"

"Keep Sandy and your phone with you at all times. They can help you deal with any awkward situation you might not want to be in. Second, if you decide you like this guy, I want to meet him sooner rather than later. I'm betting we can share some great canoeing and camping stories."

"I can do that. Thanks for the advice." Anne stood, walked around the table, hugged her dad, then headed back upstairs. "Have a good day at work. I'm going back to bed."

◆ ◆ ◆

Anne woke about nine thirty. It was later than she'd hoped to get up, but the extra sleep felt great, and it didn't affect her day. The tasks needed to change her departure from Thursday to Wednesday really couldn't begin until later in the morning. She ticked them off in her head as she trudged down the steps to find some breakfast. There were three things that could cancel the trip entirely, and she needed to jump on them as soon as she finished eating.

The first was work. The pizza shop opened at eleven, and the owner arrived an hour earlier to start preparations for lunch deliveries. The work schedule hung on the back room wall, and Anne couldn't recall who worked Wednesday afternoon and evening. The owner usually had one full-time person working daytime and a team of three part-time people rotating work shifts in the evenings. Anne needed the schedule to find out who was working Thursday evening to ask if they would switch and take her Wednesday evening instead.

Sandy's company on the trip really helped convince Mom that Anne could do the overnight camping. Anne knew Sandy didn't start work until next week, but she had no idea whether Sandy had anything planned for Wednesday evening. Anne pictured her irritation when she broke the news and hoped her schedule was flexible enough to change dates on a moment's notice. Sandy had no idea the date change was coming, and she was probably just getting up, so Anne could give her a call after checking the work schedule. If she could still go, then they could load up everything that afternoon.

Anne's mom was still hesitant about the trip, and the change in schedule would give her another reason to question whether she should let her go. It wasn't hard to convince Mom to drive her and Sandy Thursday morning, but Wednesday afternoon was a different story. Wednesdays, her mom volunteered at their church, reading stories to the children at the daycare. It was only an hour in the early afternoon, but she usually followed that with an afternoon workout and grocery shopping. Upsetting Wednesday routine was taboo. Anne had tried it before and rarely won over her mom.

Anne pulled the milk out of the refrigerator, grabbed the new box of Captain Crunch, and stuffed it under her arm. With her free hand, she grabbed a bowl and spoon, then headed for the back porch for breakfast. The weather was perfect for camping. The skies were clear, and there was just enough breeze to keep the bugs at bay. The guys were probably on the river, already heading for Nevers Dam.

Anne was crunching away on breakfast and mulling over everything that needed to fall into place when her mom stomped onto the porch. With a huff, her mom sat in the chair next to her and crossed her arms. *Not a good sign,* Anne thought. She took another spoonful of cereal and silently debated whether this was a good time to bring up the subject of camping. Poking a bear was never a good idea.

Her mom grumbled under her breath, then voiced her irritation. "Why do people always change plans at the last second? It's so inconsiderate."

"I'm sorry, Mom." Anne panicked, set down her cereal, and stared at her mom. How could she have found out about the overnight schedule change? John's voice message and text were the only clues. "I didn't know it was going to happen either," Anne continued.

"It's not your fault, honey. My yoga instructor is just a poor planner. She knew her sister was planning a long family weekend event over a month ago. The thoughtless part is that yesterday she decided to leave town early to help with setup."

Anne half smiled, then flattened her expression, trying not to give anything away. "That means she canceled this afternoon's class and dropped that bomb on all of her clients?"

"Yes, she sent us all an email last night and I saw it first thing this morning. I hope she has a customer service plan to pacify her angry class."

"You could ask for a couple free passes to soothe your anger. You said some friends wanted to share the yoga experience. Get a couple passes and take them to class with you."

"That's a great idea, Anne! I'll corner the instructor next week and tell her what a good idea a couple passes could be for business, especially when she cancels class at the last second."

With the change in her mom's mood, Anne decided to take a chance and bring up the other schedule change. "Well, your Wednesday afternoon isn't totally wasted. You still read for the preschoolers and there's still grocery shopping. Have you figured out what to do with the extra time?"

"No, not yet. I actually dread visiting the grocery store before the long Memorial Day weekend. The aisles are packed, and it takes forever to check out."

Anne put on her sweetest begging smile and asked, "Can I make a suggestion? John texted me and said that they are ahead of schedule and will arrive at Nevers Dam this evening rather than tomorrow afternoon."

"What! How could that be?" Anne's mom was visibly frustrated.

"Hold on, Mom. Please hear me out." Anne reached out, hoping her mom would take her hand. "John said the recent rain really sped up the rivers, and it naturally shortened their schedule. We can blame Mother Nature." Hearing that it was really no one's fault, Anne's mom calmed down a little and took her hand. Anne continued, "Since it's only an hour drive to Nevers Dam, we don't need to leave until sometime after you're finished reading at the preschool. We were planning to leave tomorrow morning. Why don't you grocery shop then, rather than this afternoon? Mornings are less crowded anyway."

Much as Anne's mom hated changing routines, her face softened. There was really no reason why the new plan wouldn't work for her. "I see your point, but what about your schedule? Don't you have to work tonight? Also, have you checked with Sandy?"

"Great minds think alike, Mom. Since I just heard about the change this morning, I'm still working on those two things. You were just lucky to be first on the list. Does the plan work for you?"

"I suppose so. I'm not happy about it, but life never stops throwing us changes, does it? Let me know if things fall into place with Sandy and work. I'll let your father know. After I drop you off, maybe he and I will have dinner downtown and do some people-watching."

Anne's mom got up and went back into the house. Anne finished her cereal and then went to her bedroom to change. The pizza shop would be open soon, and the work schedule change would probably take some time. She needed to be there right when the owner arrived.

While Anne pulled on her clothes, she touched the phone app on her mobile's screen and called Sandy's number. It rang four times before a gravelly voice answered. "Hello?"

"Sandy, this is Anne. There's a change in our little camping trip."

Anne made sure Sandy was awake and paying attention before she went into the details of the change. She told her about the high water speeding up the guys' trip and their new arrival time that evening. She also shared a short version of the conversation she and her mom just finished and told Sandy about her work schedule logistics. Anne was happy to hear that Sandy really had no plans since the week was a mini vacation before starting her summer job. The two talked about loading the car and pulling down the canoe after Anne, hopefully, rearranged her work schedule.

"What time should I come to your house?" Sandy asked.

"If all goes well, we can start loading gear by two thirty. My mom should be home from the preschool by then." Anne was heading down the stairs to her car. "I'll text you if changing work schedules become a problem."

"Sounds good. See you at two thirty, I hope."

Anne pulled into the short alleyway behind the pizza shop. The back door stood open, allowing the fresh spring air into the building. As she stepped through the door, she could see the papers pinned to the bulletin board flapping in the breezy hallway. Reaching up, she flattened down the work schedule and ran her finger down the days. She was scheduled on Wednesday, Friday, and Sunday evenings. All three of the part-timers were scheduled to work twice on the long weekend, with two of them on every evening just to keep up with the orders. A guy named Troy had Thursday, Saturday, and Monday evenings. The boss's son was working opposite Anne as the second driver on Friday and Sunday evenings.

Anne walked to the kitchen area and found the owner at the mixer tending to a batch of fresh dough made for the shop's popular garlic crust. She smiled and greeted him. "Hey boss. What's DOUGHing on?"

He just chuckled and shook his head. "Morning Anne. What brings you in so early?"

"I'm wondering if it's okay to switch my schedule. A friend invited me to take some photos on the river and we are planning to drive up north tonight and camp before canoeing tomorrow."

"It's kind of a late change. What happened to camping tomorrow night?"

"They're already into their third day on the river and the fast water shaved a day off from their trip. I'm meeting them for the last day of canoeing."

"You could take a day trip on any of your off days this summer. Why is this day so important?"

Anne hesitated a few seconds and blushed a little. Then she said, "Well… There's this guy."

The owner laughed out loud, then said, "As long as the customers receive their pizzas on time, I'm happy. If you can arrange a switch with someone, I'm good with it."

"Thanks, Boss." Anne smiled, turned, and walked back to the bulletin board to grab the phone numbers for Jack and Troy, the other drivers. She knew these calls would involve some begging and thought about calling Troy first. He worked Wednesday, and it made the most sense to ask him to swap for Thursday. The problem was, Troy was kind of a jerk. He would probably want something else in return for the "BIG FAVOR" he was doing for her.

Anne pulled both drivers' phone numbers from the hallway bulletin board and called Jack, the owner's son. She reached his voicemail and her heart sank as she listened to the message.

"This is Jack. I will be at scout camp the whole week before Memorial Day weekend. I'm coming back Friday afternoon. Don't bother calling me because I won't have my phone. I'm working on survival merit badges. Please leave a message and I will call you back. – BEEP."

This left her with no choice. She ended the first call without a message and dialed Troy.

He answered on the second ring. "Hello?"

"Hey Troy, this is Anne from work. Got a minute?"

"Sure, what's up?"

"Well…" Anne asked Troy to switch Thursday for Wednesday and received exactly what she expected. Troy was hard-nosed about trading nights and used her request to gain something he really wanted: the weekend off.

"There's no way I'm working both Saturday and Monday evenings for you. That means I'd work every evening from Thursday through the end of the holiday weekend. Besides, if you don't work, how are you going to earn any spending cash for the summer? Some of the biggest tips come on holiday weekends."

"Good points, Anne, but I really need to have the weekend off so I can visit my friends over in Green Bay. I'll make you a deal. I'll take Wednesday and Thursday. You take Friday through Monday."

Anne thought about it for a few seconds. She felt like she was getting the short end of things but graciously said, "Thanks, Troy. I really appreciate it. I'll tell the boss and make the change on the schedule." She hung up and thought in the back of her mind, *Wow, is he a schemer.*

On her way back to her car, Anne smiled as her thumbs flew across the phone's qwerty keyboard. *John – Just finished rearranging everything. Will see you later today.* ☺

15

Day 3 - Angry Water

Paul spent fifteen to twenty minutes calming down after he crawled back into his sleeping bag, but when the adrenaline left his bloodstream, he fell into a deep and uninterrupted sleep. When he opened his eyes again, he could tell the sun was well over the horizon by the amount of light in the tent. The noise outside told him he was the last to rise, and his watch definitely confirmed it. The time was 8:10. When he unzipped the tent flap, the smell of cooking summer sausage hit his nostrils. John was tending the fry pan, flipping over the two-inch medallions carved from a Brine's smoke cured sausage they bought for the trip. It was a simple recipe that fried them over an open flame in a pool of margarine squeezed from a bottle. Paul's mouth began to water when John plucked one of the medallions out of the pan, smiled, and stared at the meat as the margarine dripped off the bottom. He lightly blew on the meat and popped it into his mouth. John closed his eyes and slowly chewed the camping delicacy.

Steam rose from the percolating coffee pot that sat on the camp stove. Sliding his shoes on, Paul walked over and poured a cup. He savored his morning coffee and loved the way the metal camp cup warmed his hands on cool mornings.

Tom and Al had already flipped the canoes upright and pulled them to the water's edge at the boat launch. They were busy rolling up sleeping bags, sweeping out tents, and storing gear in bags for the day's trip through the rapids. Bob pulled tent stakes and removed the tent flies so the morning breeze would dry the dew more quickly. Half of the work to break camp was already done.

"I should sleep in more often," Paul remarked as he sat down at the picnic table and sipped at his coffee. "I missed most of the morning chores."

John flipped a couple of sausage patties onto a plate and handed it to Paul. "We all thought you would be in a better mood if we let you sleep in. Last night really scared you."

"You're right about both items. I was terrified when Tom stood up behind the picnic table, and now I feel great. Nothing like an extra few hours of sleep to help start a day." Paul took another sip of coffee, then continued, "You must have slept well. You seem extra cheerful."

"It's a beautiful morning." John took the pan off the fire and set it on the table. "Come and get it guys!" Reaching into the gear bag, he pulled out another four plates and scattered them around the trail mix, cheese curds, and protein bars already sitting on the table. The others instantly dropped what they were doing and came over to satisfy their hunger pangs.

As Bob slid his legs under the table, Paul nudged him in the ribs and whispered, "What's with John? He's extra cheery this morning."

"Remember yesterday when John was so worried that Anne blew him off? He heard from Anne this morning. Her phone died yesterday afternoon. She must not have gotten his messages until this morning."

"She still coming on the trip?" Paul whispered back.

"She didn't say, but John's just grateful to hear from her."

"Mmm-mmm, I love these little sausages." Tom needed fuel for the day and didn't hesitate when meat protein was involved. He grabbed four of the medallions, then reached over for a handful of cheese curds. The others dug in as well, nearly emptying the pan on the first round.

Al moved a few bags around the table, looking for something particular. "Didn't we buy cashews for the trip?" Not finding any on the table, he stretched his neck out and glanced at the food bag. "By the way, who is riding with who today?"

John picked up on the hint and reached into the bag for the nuts. Then he jumped on Al's question. "I paddled solo just a little on day one. I'd love to try the rapids alone."

"I have no problem with that," Tom said with one cheek full of cheese. "After running the State Line Rapids alone yesterday, I have to say it's a little scary controlling these long canoes alone in tough water. It'll challenge you, John, but I think you will have some fun."

Paul smiled at Tom and then asked him, "Do you want to ride with me today? After you scared the life out of me last night, I have no fears about you steering us through a couple class two rapids."

"You mean I would have a blind lifeless zombie paddling up front?" Paul hunched over, dropped his left shoulder, crooked his jaw, and moaned. A couple pieces of food dropped out of his mouth as he gave the guys his best zombie performance.

Al laughed and then took a sip from his water bottle. "That leaves me and the new guy. Do you want to steer today, Bob?" Bob's fork stopped halfway to his mouth. Al saw the hesitation and twinge of fear, then he reinforced his question. "You know how to steer a canoe. Navigating rapids are just another version of moving along a channel. You just have to know what to look for and what to avoid."

"That's the problem. I don't know how to read a rapids."

"Tell you what, I'll coach you from the front and we'll select the easiest side of the rapids to navigate. All you need to do is line up the canoe and rudder left or right when I point out rocks."

"It sounds easy enough, but why do I have the feeling that it's not that simple."

"Think about it this way," Al continued. "We rehearsed wrestling moves over and over during practice. When we wrestled an opponent, the same moves applied. The difference was that we didn't know which moves were needed at which time. That meant your brain needed to react to a situation, decide what to do, and then do it. The concept is the same here. You know how to steer a canoe and have done it for years. You have run a couple sets of rapids and seen how we navigate them. Now it's time to just do it."

"I suppose I can't sit on the sidelines forever, and this is the last opportunity to steer through rapids on this trip. I'll take the helm."

It took the group another hour to finish breakfast, clean up the gear, and finish packing up camp. When they pushed off from the boat launch, the sun had already warmed the air enough that no one needed a sweatshirt. The morning breeze had changed to a steady wind that now created ripples across the widest part of the channel. When the group paddled away from shore, those ripples slapped the bows, creating that lulling telltale sound of a steady headwind.

Even though it was a beautiful spring day, Bob really didn't notice the scenery. His mind was on what lay downstream. "How long before the first set of rapids?"

Al smiled, knowing that Bob would be a little nervous. "We should reach Head of the Rapids Island in just a few minutes. It's just around the next bend." He paused for a moment, then tried to reassure Bob. "Relax, you got this. In fact, I'm so sure you'll survive that we're going to record it." Al released the clip on his waterproof day bag, unrolled the top, and pulled out the GoPro. He clicked the clamp mount accessory onto the bottom and slid the jaws over the canoe's center support rail. When he activated the camera, Bob's image appeared. Al adjusted the mount for the best viewing angle and then resealed his day bag.

Bob waved to the camera, but he was too nervous to smile. "I hope you're right, Al. If you're wrong, we both end up in the river."

A few minutes after the island came into view, the guys could see the change in water surface marking the first of the rapids. Instead of the windswept ripples, the water appeared more like rolling waves. The first rapids were class one, and it was just downriver of a campsite that offered people a great basecamp to spend a day enjoying the exciting stretch of river.

As they approached the top of the rapids, the front men in the canoes focused on finding the telltale signs of rocks at the surface. Neither Paul nor Al saw any frothy whitewater signaling obstacles. The canoes just moved over a narrow choppy channel.

Bob remained hyper alert but relaxed a little. "Where are the rapids?"

"They're here, but the high water submerged all of the rocks," Al responded.

The current picked up and moved the boats quickly past the Head of the Rapids Island. They steered left, sticking to their plan to take the wider east channel. The second set of rapids didn't take long to announce themselves. Instead of rolling waves, there were definite signs of difficulty ahead. They saw a gradual elevation change in the river where water passed over what appeared to be small boulders. The closer they came, the louder the rushing water grew. The two hundred yards of whitewater was moving fast. After they entered the rapids, there was little chance to change course, so the group lined up their canoes and chose their routes.

"Let's keep to the left, Bob. The channel bends to the right near the end of the run. There are more rocks and shallower water on that inside bank. We'll stay in the deeper part of the channel."

Bob veered left and moved away from the other two boats. He watched John drop back from Paul and Tom to create a buffer and then he returned his attention to what lay ahead. Al was right. He could see that the channel's right side contained more debris. There were white wings spreading out on each side of lone rocks and wavy backwash below large boulders where water dropped off from a smooth back edge. The channel in front of he and Al was littered with bucket-sized stones that initially looked like an impassible minefield of white waves. Moving closer, Bob began to see where the stones broke the surface and where deeper water simply created wave action. He ruddered left and right, zig-zagging through a path that was unseen until the last moment. Al paddled hard up front to allow Bob's steering to change course at a moment's notice.

"Rock to the right!" Al called out. A half second later, Bob saw it and ruddered hard on the left side. That swung the canoe left, and they glanced off from the hidden stone. Water splashed over the canoe's bow, wetting Al's right arm and chest.

"Thanks for the bath," Al chided from up front.

"Sorry about that." Bob made another course correction and their canoe reached a short break in the rapids. As the river bent, the outside part of the channel was deeper and the rocks were submerged. He and Al glanced at the other two boats in the center of the river. Paul and Tom were briefly hung up between a pair of submerged stones. They tried to thread the needle and run the chute of water flowing between the rocks. The depth wasn't as great as anticipated, and their canoe scrapped across the stones. John recognized the trouble and veered left as he approached. He cleared their boat by less than ten feet.

John heckled them as he passed by. "Did you guys throw out an anchor?"

Bob steered the canoe to the channel's center for the last twenty yards of rapids. His confidence had built up and he realized that class two rapids were more fun than dangerous. He weaved left and right again, avoiding smaller obstacles, then lined up the canoe to take a wide chute. Two large boulders stuck a few inches above the surface. They created a lip where water flowed between them like a pitcher spout. Below the rocks was a twelve-inch high white wave where the water curled back on itself. As the bow passed between the stones, it crashed into the wave and threw water as high as Al's head. A few gallons flowed over the canoe edge and into the floor.

"Yee-haw!" Bob called out as he passed between the boulders and out of the last of the rapids.

Al's shirt front and crotch were soaked. He hadn't expected Bob's enthusiasm for whitewater and paid the price for encouraging him to take the helm. "Nice job, Bob. We came through that pretty well unscathed."

"That was awesome! You were absolutely right about the just do it thing. After seeing rocks in front of us, I only had a few seconds to react and turn the canoe."

The other two boats pulled in closer and complemented Bob as well.

"You're a whitewater pro, Bob," John said. "There was more wave action than I expected, and you handled it really well."

"You picked a better chute to run than I did," Tom remarked. "I wish we could have followed you, but the current pulled us too far right. It would have been fun to soak Paul."

Al chimed in to encourage Tom. "You might get your chance. There are three more class one and one long class two rapids left."

"I think we are just starting one of them," said Bob. "Look at the waves."

The group was so caught up in commending their friend that they hardly noticed the surface change just in front of them. It seemed the high water had again submerged the class one rapids, leaving nothing but waves across the channel. They paddled through that set of rapids and the two following with little concern. That would not be the case for the last section of whitewater.

They could hear the rapids before they could see them. It started off as background noise blending in with the brisk wind. The farther downstream they traveled, the more pronounced the sound became.

When they finally saw the defining white line across the channel, the noise had turned to a dull roar.

"Hey Al, what's the best way to handle these rapids?" Bob asked.

"They break into two separate sets that stretch over almost a mile of river. The first set is fairly short and you can steer us right down the middle. The second set is a lot longer. Keep to the left at the beginning and then cut to the middle of the channel as the river bends to the right."

"Sounds simple, I'll see what I can do." Bob was confident that he could navigate the whitewater. The question was whether he could do it without slamming into rocks or losing control of the canoe.

As they entered the first set of rapids, the group could tell the class two rating was seriously shy of describing what was in front of them. The channel had a lot of wave action, with crests higher than the side of their canoes. That meant there were some large rocks completely submerged. The heavy current flowed over the boulder tops and created back current on the downstream side. Some of them were large enough to form mini waterfalls. If anyone went over the top of one, they would bury the canoe's nose in the river.

John led the way, taking his canoe down the middle and then breaking to the right. Paul and Tom followed close behind and then broke left. They threaded their way around the large rocks and tried not to take on too much water. Boulders created two-foot waves that slapped against their boats and threatened to turn them sideways in the channel. Tom and Paul had no problem pointing their canoe downstream, but each time a wave hit the front of the canoe, Paul took a dousing from water slapping the bow.

Without the power paddler in the front seat, John's canoe swung like a pendulum as he made his way through the maze of submerged rocks. He paddled frantically to correct his course and barely missed sweeping sideways over a mini waterfall. The river slapped the front of his canoe as well, throwing water onto the tarp-covered tents tied just behind the front seat.

Bob and Al followed John's route through the rapids. They could feel the canoe jerk every time a wave slapped the bow, and Al was getting wetter with every wave. Bob looked for another chute to run and saw an opportunity farther right. There appeared to be a pair of submerged boulders spaced ten feet apart, with a small wall of white water just downstream between them. As Bob lined up the canoe, he realized that he focused too much on the chute and misread the upstream water. There was another boulder just right of the chute's mouth that created a good-sized bow-slapping wave. The wave swung the canoe left and forced them to go directly over the boulder. As Al cleared the rock and went down the back side, the bow dug into the river. He was relieved when the bow didn't submerge, but a second later he took a quick breath, held it, and squeezed his eyes shut. The huge backwash downstream of the boulder slammed into Al's face and chest. Water washed over both sides of the canoe, half-filling their boat.

The upper rapids ended quickly, dumping into a brief passage of calm before the second longer set. To their right was a long island that separated the main channel from the Kettle River Slough. The DNR set up a campsite at the island's downstream endpoint, and the group could see tents pitched between the trees. The site was used primarily by kayakers who loved to run the rapids over and over. The island ended at the head of the lower class two rapids, and spectators could watch their friends navigate the half-mile stretch of whitewater.

"Looks like we will have an audience judging the rapids run," Tom said. "They're all sitting around the picnic table eating lunch. Somebody is bound to spot us as we move by their camp." He whistled at the campers and waved his paddle.

"I won't have any time for grandstanding," John replied. "I need to keep my canoe pointing downriver. Zig-zagging between the boulders didn't work very well for me. The river threw around the front of my boat and my arms are aching from the quick overexertion."

"We have about four inches of water in the bottom of our canoe," Al commented. "I'm hoping to stay a little drier this time." He turned and sneered at Bob. In return, Bob just smiled, then stuck his tongue out at Al. He liked running chutes and planned to find more if he could.

The roar of water picked up again and the group staggered their boats for the whitewater entry. John steered down the middle while the other two canoes broke left. The channel narrowed between the point of the island and the Wisconsin shore. Ahead of them, they could see the river drop several feet in the half-mile stretch of rapids. The combination of these two items sped up the water and created wave action that dwarfed the upper rapids. Near the campsite, there were several boulders sticking three to four feet out of the water. The river crashed against them, creating a boiling torrent not meant for their long sluggish canoes.

From the channel's middle to the Wisconsin side, the river was deeper, and the submerged boulders created three-foot-high wave action. It looked like Bob would get his wish. No one could navigate the rapids without running several chutes or rolling over boulder tops. Paul howled as they entered the rush because he knew he would get wet. Tom read the first two chutes well, moving from left to right after passing through the first. The third chute was too close for their canoe to abruptly turn, and they passed over a large boulder. Paul's thighs took the brunt of water washing over the sides. He yelped as the cold liquid ran up his legs and settled in his crotch.

By now the campers had left their lunch behind and were standing on the shoreline. When they ran the rapids, their small maneuverable kayaks easily moved through the whitewater. They could turn on a dime and take full advantage of thrills the river currents produced. More experienced kayakers could turn back upstream below a boulder, spin around, and surf the backwash. The canoes were more like semi-trucks pushing through a tight obstacle course. There was no way they could navigate the course without hitting a few orange cones. The campers wanted to see the canoeists clumsily move through their playground.

Bob read the river beautifully. He looked well ahead of their position and lined up their boat for chute after chute. Occasionally they would bump against a rock when they passed through a narrower opening. Halfway through the rapids, Al complemented him.

"Nice job Bob, but I just wish there was some way to keep from getting wet." Water washed over the bow at every chute. "Looks like I won't be that lucky because the rapids intensifies near the bottom."

John was taking a brute-force approach to the rapids. Instead of letting the river slap his front end around, he pointed his canoe directly over the submerged boulders. This allowed him to move straight down river using his paddle as a rudder rather than straining to paddle against side currents. The drawback was he was burying his bow in the backwash of just about every boulder. He hoped to stay afloat through the end of the rapids.

The island campers were entertained instantly. They enjoyed watching Tom and Al getting wet in front of their respective canoes. They clapped a few times as John drove his canoe over larger and larger boulders. Near the end of the rapids, the river was a minefield of bigger boulders and submerged rocks. The Minnesota side of the channel had a few car-sized rocks near the shore. The water rushing from the Kettle River Slough slammed against them, throwing mist into the air.

John was closest to the Minnesota shore and had two submerged monsters to cross over before exiting the rapids. When he passed over the first, the canoe front hung three feet off from the water before slamming down into the river. The canoe's rear followed and slammed the back side hard enough to force water over the canoe's edge. The river flowed over the second monster rather than dropping off like the first. The canoe's front hung out of the water briefly before diving down the rock's back side. The rolling water created a wavy backwash big enough for a surfboarder to ride. The bow hit the wave point first and buried the canoe's front end. John came down the rock's back side and followed his bow right through the wave. Cheers came from the shoreline when the kayakers saw the canoe's bow punch through the wave and come out the other side. They watched water slam into John's midsection and thought it would knock him out of the boat. Instead, John reached out with his paddle and dug into the wave before it hit him. This countered the water's force and left him sitting soaked in his seat.

Al and Bob were navigating what looked like a minefield of small pillars sticking out of the water. They no longer had the choice of running a chute or pouring over a rock. They had to maneuver between rocks like gates on a slalom ski hill. Their boat had taken on enough liquid that the top edge was inches from the waterline. This made the canoe hard to steer. Once again a close group of boulders pushed Al and Bob over the top of a submerged rock. Instead of clearing the rock, their front end hung up and the back end swung around into the chute. They leaned into the current and avoided capsizing, but the canoe was now backing down the river. They still had fifty yards of whitewater to navigate, and Bob was panicking. He couldn't steer because he was downstream of Al and facing upriver.

Al quickly gave Bob a crash course in mid-river canoe tactics. "Spin around and kneel on the canoe floor," Al ordered Bob. "I'll do the same and steer from back here." They could hear cheers and whistles from shore as they pulled off their spin move and navigated the last of the rapids.

Paul and Tom were the first out of the whitewater. They navigated the river almost flawlessly and continued floating downstream, watching their friends finish their work. Even with the expert run, they still had six inches of water in their boat. They guessed that the others were barely floating after seeing how little waterline their canoes showed.

"Great run guys!" Paul called out from downstream. "I have never seen that much action on this river. I'm betting that last set of rapids ranked a temporary class three."

"Talk about baptism under fire," Al added. "Bob did a great job handling something that was probably over his head!"

John pulled up alongside Bob and they bumped paddles in celebration. "Yah, nice job Bob. You even had an audience cheering you on." Then John glanced at their two canoes and continued, "Speaking of paddling over your head, neither of us have a waterline. The air in the gear and the foam in the ends of the boats are the only things keeping us afloat. We better beach these things and bail them out before we are literally over our heads."

Paul and Tom were far enough ahead that they could see a campsite on the Wisconsin shore. "Can you guys make it another hundred yards?" Paul called out. "There's a nice beach at a campsite just ahead. We can empty out and see if any gear is wet."

"Yah," they called back. "Lead on."

16

Nevers Dam

When they reached the campsite's landing, none of them could beach their canoe by merely paddling. When each bow hit bottom in the shallows, the water that filled their canoes became dead weight, stopping them while still in the current. When Al and Paul jumped from their front seats to pull the boats to shore, the fingertip grip the bows had on the river bottom released. They each grabbed their canoe and pulled. Their feet dug into the sandy bottom as they strained to reach dry land. With each foot of progress, more aluminum scraped sand, lifting the long troughs of water from the river. Eventually, Al and Paul abandoned their effort because the canoes became too heavy to drag.

John's bow was still clinging to the sandy shallows, but his back end had swung downstream. He was frantically paddling against the current to keep his canoe from sliding back into deep water. If it did, the river would sweep him away from his friends and his canoe would continue sinking. When Bob and Tom stepped from their seats into the shallow water, Al and Paul ran to John's rescue. They grabbed his bow and pulled the canoe until it was solidly stuck in the sand.

All five guys began emptying their canoes, tossing the gear up onto dry land. It was the only way they could lighten the canoes enough to tip the water out. The last items to hit the beach were the three tents.

Back at Norway Point, the tents were laid in the canoe bottom and bulky packs lashed in over the top to prevent them from dumping into the river. What a mistake. John had to crawl into the canoe and deadlift each tent to pull them off the bottom. As he lifted, he tilted each bag and let the water run out the end. The other four watched him with sour faces. They all had slept in wet tents, usually from days of rain during long camping trips. No one enjoyed it.

"We'll be sleeping on waterbeds tonight," John remarked as he tossed the last tent on the riverbank. A group groan followed John's effort at humor.

"What if we unpack the tents and stretch them out for a while?" Paul asked. "The afternoon sun and wind will dry them out in an hour or so."

John looked a little concerned over the suggestion of an hour delay. "I'm not so sure I like that idea. That will delay our arrival at Nevers Dam."

"What's the big hurry, John?" Paul challenged. "I'm betting we have plenty of daylight to travel whatever distance is left to tonight's campsite. Al, how far do we have?"

While Al walked over and pulled out the maps, Tom jumped into the discussion. "I think there's someone John wants to see at the campsite. By the way, have you heard from her about changing her schedule?"

"Come to think of it, no. She hadn't texted back before we left Norway Point and we've been busy dealing with whitewater since then." John pulled out his phone and saw Anne's text. *John – Just finished rearranging everything. Will see you later today.* ☺ A smile came across his face. "Looks like she rearranged her schedule and can make it tonight. I know you guys will give me a hard time, but I'd really like to reach Nevers Dam sooner rather than later. How far do we have to paddle Al?"

"It's about thirty-five miles to Nevers Dam and the fast river current should take us there in six hours, at most."

"That means we reach camp at around eight if we dry the tents for an hour." John continued, "By the time we let the tents dry, repack the gear, and get back on the river, two o'clock will have come and gone. That's getting a little late."

"I agree. Sunset is about eight forty-five," Bob said. "That's a little late to set up camp and cook supper. I have an idea to save time and dry the tents. What if we repack the canoes placing the duffle bags on the bottom and the tents on top? Instead of packing them back in the bags, we stretch them out over the gear and use the travel time to air dry the tents."

"That's a great idea, Bob." Paul was impressed with his suggestion. "It's a sunny afternoon and the south wind has picked up. If I remember right, there is nothing but open uneventful river in front of us. The tents will be totally dry by the time we land this evening."

"I'm starting to figure out this real camping thing," Bob continued. "This way we make sure lover boy sees his new girlfriend before dark. Let's empty this foot of water out of the canoes and repack." As Bob walked over to his gear, he started singing. "*The kid is hot tonight, whoa-whoa so hot tonight, but where will he be tomorrow?*"

"Where did that come from?" Tom said as he grabbed his first pack.

"It's a song chorus from another one of my dad's old vinyl albums. It's from the early eighties—a group called Lover Boy."

John sneered at them as they laughed and then took out his phone. He texted Anne, "*Will be @ Nevers Dam by 7.*"

♦ ♦ ♦

Anne's mom stopped the car where the road ended at the river. To the right was the Nevers Dam camp area. It was a typical DNR river-access campsite. There were two tent sites about fifty feet apart. Each had a picnic table and fire ring. Near the road sat one blue port-a-potty to serve both sites and the boat launch. The toilet sat southeast of the campsites and just far enough away that the sickly chemical fragrance wouldn't bother campers unless there was a rare southeast prevailing wind. In front of the car was a narrow gravel drive lane that dropped down to the river. The DNR built it to improve small boat access. It was tucked in just downstream from what was left of the old earthen dam.

The three women got out of the car and did a quick survey of the area. They could see the river moving past the boat launch in front of them but couldn't hear the water movement. The wind was swaying the tree tops, creating just enough background noise to drown out the trickling sound of the river.

"Look at that," Anne's mom said as she pointed toward the woods in front of them. Between the car and the boat launch, the woods were cut back and a trap rock boulder stuck three feet out of the ground. The top was flat and slightly angled toward the road. "Looks like a plaque of some kind, anchored to the top of that rock."

Sandy started toward the rock. "I'm betting it's a historic monument. We covered the local lumbering industry in history class this spring. Nevers Dam was mentioned as a busy place for moving logs from the northern forests to the sawmills in Stillwater and Marine on St. Croix."

"I want to take a picture of that," Anne said as she opened the rear hatch to find her camera.

All three walked over and were surprised at the size of the boulder. While it only stuck three feet out of the ground, it easily extended a few feet down into the soil. Like most blue trap rock, the fracturing nature of the material left the boulder flat on all sides. Trap rock was often used for landscape steps, hard seating in outdoor amphitheaters, and monuments like this. The three-foot-wide bronze plaque was indeed a historic summary of the Nevers Dam site. Anne snapped a few pictures, then the three stood and read the plaque.

Nevers Dam

This dam played an important role on the St. Croix River during Minnesota's and Wisconsin's late logging industry period. Low water levels and spectacular down river log jams often hindered the industry's ability to process the millions of logs floating from the northern forests to the downstream lumber mills. The St. Croix Dam and Boom Company built the dam for a cost of $200,000 in 1890 to control water flow and sluice logs at a manageable rate.

This structure was rumored to be the largest pile driven dam of the time. The original 624 foot long earthen dam had thirteen Tainter gaits, 16' high by 24' wide and one Lang gate, 12' high by 80' long. The dam held back 17 feet of head, releasing water through its gates to sluice over 4,000,000 feet of logs per hour. The last log sluiced through its gates in 1912 after an estimated total of over 40 billion lineal feet passed over the dam.

High water often threatened this dam, including the flood of 1924 which washed out two 24 foot gates on the Wisconsin side. Following that flood the entire dam was rebuilt and reinforced, replacing the two gates with an extended earthen dike. It remained in place until the unprecedented flood in May of 1954 which undermined the dam and finally washed it out. Northern States Power Company removed the dam in 1955, leaving the earthen dike on the Wisconsin side as a remnant, creating a popular fishing hole in the eddy current behind the dike.

Anne's mom was amazed at how much lumber would have come from the logging. "Can you imagine over forty billion, with a 'B,' lineal feet of logs going by this spot?"

"I can't even imagine what it looked like when they opened the gate and let the logs pass over the dam," Sandy wanted to draw a visual in her mind of what the scene may have looked like, so she turned and walked toward the river's edge.

Anne snapped a few more photos, then followed Sandy to the boat launch. "Hey, what does that sign in the water say?" she called out to Sandy. Just beyond where the gravel lane met the water, the DNR posted one of their brown informational signs. The water had risen to cover nearly all of the post, now placing the sign almost twenty yards offshore.

Sandy reached the water's edge and made an effort to read the sign. "I can see the word *CAUTION*, but the rest of the wording is too small to read at this distance."

"Hey Mom, can you grab the binoculars out of the car? They should help us with the sign."

Anne's mom walked back to the car, pulled the binoculars out of the back and closed the hatch. "I wish you wouldn't have left the car open." She called out to Anne as she walked to the river. "The back is full of bugs and I'm the one driving home with them." She walked to the water's edge and brought the 4X lenses up to her eyes. "It says *CAUTION, Strong undertow off from the dike's tip. No swimming allowed.*"

"I wonder what causes the undertow?" Sandy asked. "The river is fairly straight between here and the Minnesota shore."

Anne stepped off from the gravel and walked a short distance down the shoreline. "There's a trail on top of the dike. Let's walk to the end and see if we can get a better view of what's causing the undertow."

Anne's mom followed the trail with her eyes and then said, "It looks like the trailhead is somewhere near the two campsites. Since we need to walk past the car to reach the trail, how about if we grab an armful of gear and drop it in one of the sites. That will save us at least one trip back to the car."

The three women almost emptied the car, strapping on the backpacks and loading their arms with gear. The dike blocked the river view from both camping areas even though the nearest site sat thirty yards from the water. They stopped at the site closest to the river, carefully placing everything on the picnic table until they returned to set up camp. The path to the dike left their campsite on the western edge of the grass, and they jogged up the short hill to the dike's summit. When they reached the tip, they had a clear view of the river's expanse over to the Minnesota shore. More brown DNR signs were spaced along the opposite shore designating a Minnesota state park across the river. There was a large island south of the landing, and the river stretched for over a mile beyond before gently bending east and out of sight. North of the dike, the river bent sharply west and disappeared within a half mile. It was the perfect place to see the group of guys when they rounded the bend.

Sandy picked up a large stick and tossed it off the dike. The three women watched the stick float normally for about ten feet and then upend at what seemed to be a line in the water. Quarter-sized whirlpools formed where half of the stick extended vertically from the water surface. The swirls rotated the stick and created the illusion of some invisible force screwing it into the river. Within five seconds it had completely disappeared from view. "Wow! Did you see how the water just pulled the stick down?" Sandy remarked.

"I'm betting that's the undertow the sign warned about," Anne's mom said.

Anne was awe-struck by the underwater forces that submerged the stick. "That was really cool! I want to see that again." She turned and walked back to a small brush pile behind them and picked out a two-inch diameter branch. Hefting it off from the ground, she slowly spun the ten-foot piece of wood and walked back to the point. At first, it floated normally after she heaved it into the river. When it reached the line, Mother Nature repeated her show. The stick's front point disappeared and the last four feet rose out of the water until it was perpendicular to the surface. With small whirlpools on each side, the branch looked like Excalibur when the Lady of the Lake drew it down into the water. After the sharp tip submerged, the whirlpools combined and formed a small hole on the water surface. They stood captivated and watched the hole disappear as quickly as it had formed.

"Look how the water flows backward behind the dike." Sandy pointed at the shoreline downriver from their position and swept her arm up to the spot in front of them. "When it flows back to the main river channel, the two currents collide."

"It's like a big whirlpool," Anne's mom commented. "Look at the debris circling downriver and then flowing back along the dike." About thirty yards offshore, there were clumps of branches and a few plastic water bottles circling like a merry-go-round. The swift water rushing past the dike's point was pulling the dormant water on the back side of the dike and creating a gigantic eddy.

Anne's mom looked at the undertow line and her face tightened, showing the lines of concern every parent shows when their children near something dangerous. "Promise me you will stay out of the water." She turned and looked at Anne and Sandy.

"No worries about that, Mom. That undertow is serious stuff."

"Good." Anne's mom relaxed and she smiled before turning back on the trail. "Let's go set up camp. It's almost five and that will keep us busy while we wait for the guys. I still want to meet the whole group."

Within an hour, the tent was pitched, gear stowed, and a small fire started. Sandy had just plopped into a folding-style camp chair when Anne came back from the car with an empty water jug and an unopened package of tent cord. She grabbed another camp chair, walked by

Sandy, and said, "Why don't we go sit on the dike? We can watch for the guys."

"What's the cord and jug for?" Sandy asked.

"I'm planning to tie this fifty-foot cord to the jug's handle and toss it in the river. I'm betting the water can't suck down an empty jug, but if I add a little water before each throw it will eventually sink."

Anne's mom chuckled and grabbed a chair. "That's what I love about camping. It lets you come up with creative ways to kill time."

The three women headed up the dike trail to wait for the guys to arrive.

◆ ◆ ◆

Tom jumped into the solo canoe for the last thirty-five miles. Even though paddling wasn't exactly bodybuilding, he wanted to work his arms and shoulders. He figured the wind blowing up river created a great opportunity to increase his stamina. He tied a red handkerchief around his head and called to John, "Can you push me off shore?"

John shoved Tom's canoe backward and briefly watched him glide out into the current. He quickly sidestepped into his canoe and crawled over the front seat. They had spent too much time emptying the canoes and repacking the gear. He didn't want Anne to wait any longer than she had to. As he made his way toward the back seat, the nylon tent slid sideways when John's knee pivoted on top of the gear. His whole leg slid out from under him and the canoe rocked sideways as John lost his balance. His foot barely caught the edge of the canoe, preventing him from rolling into the knee-deep water.

"Whoa! That was close," Al said as he grabbed the front of the canoe to steady it. "Maybe the quick bath would have been good. You want to look your best for Anne when we land this evening."

John pushed himself off from his belly and ignored Al's comment. His face was beet red from frustration and embarrassment. The fun little jabs from his friends usually didn't bother him, but this thing with Anne was new and for some reason it affected him. *Strange*, he thought as he crawled into the rear seat. Then he said to Al, "Can you reach back and tuck in the tent again before you push us off? The wind will grab that loose corner and flop it into the river."

"Sure." Al tucked the tent between the gear and the canoe wall, then leaned into the canoe's front point. His feet dug into the sandy bottom as the front slid toward deep water. "I can tell that we'll need to rotate the tents at least once. Otherwise, the parts tucked between the gear and the canoe's side won't dry."

Paul was already sitting in the rear seat waiting for Bob to finish the last walk around the shore area. Even though they really didn't unpack anything, double-checking a site before leaving was a good habit. Too often a small piece of gear was left as a donation to the next campers.

"Are you okay steering without your glasses?" Bob asked as he bent down to push into the canoe's front point to launch.

"Yah, I'm good. The river is wide enough and there aren't any rapids between here and tonight's camp. Let's go." Bob slid the boat back. In one fluid motion, his back foot left the ground and his body rotated into the front seat. "That's pretty good, Bob." Paul was smiling at his friend with a little pride in his voice. "Two days ago you would have landed face-first in the river if you tried a pivot move like that."

"Thanks. I've developed a little muscle memory. I just hope that I don't forget from one year to the next."

"You mean that you want to do this again next year? This trip's been a little rough."

"Are you kidding? This is way better than a one-night going-away party. The rough parts are some of the best experiences."

"You'll have to let us know when the Air Force gives you leave. We'll plan another trip when you come back." Paul pivoted the canoe and pointed it downriver.

"That might be a long time from now," Bob replied. "I'll apply for pilot training during freshman year. If I'm selected, I'll start training after graduation and I become an officer. Then I'd belong to Uncle Sam for a decade. I'm not sure when I could come back."

"The upside is the Air Force pays for your college and they'll train you to fly." Paul was trying to add a positive side to the conversation. "You'll see some fantastic parts of the world I'll never see. Also, being an officer means you'll develop leadership experience you can use when you return to civilian life."

"That's all great stuff, but the long commitment means I lose touch with friends and I miss family events and holidays."

Paul added a little empathy into his voice and said, "Those sound like regrets and you haven't even left yet. Look at it this way, Bob. Change happens whether you want it to or not. You're just smart enough to choose what that change will be. Besides, the others around you will be in the same spot."

"That's true. The recruiter said that the others around me will be like new family because they're in the same situation I am. We'll celebrate holidays together, party after graduating pilot training, and experience deployment hardships. He said the bonds that develop can't be found anywhere else."

"Are you worried about where the Air Force will send you?" Paul asked. "There are some really troubled spots in the world."

Bob paused a moment before answering. "I suppose dying somewhere in a foreign country will always be in the back of my mind. I try not to think about it. The hard part for me is the long commitment and being away from stuff like this. If I stayed here and just went to a local college, I could come home anytime and I would be done in four years."

"Don't worry, Bob," Paul reassured him. "We won't forget you and we'll get together whenever you come back."

"Thanks Paul. I appreciate it." Bob stopped paddling for a moment, glanced at the riverbanks, and took a long deep breath. "We're moving really well, even with the headwind. How long before we reach the Highway Seventy bridge?"

Paul was a little surprised about the sudden change in subject, but then realized Bob had left the topic behind to enjoy the rest of the trip. He knew Bob was excited about attending the academy and going on to be an aviator. When he'd received the acceptance letter, he'd talked about it for weeks. Bob had already made his decision, thought through what it meant, and there was no backing out now. His friend had set a good future in motion. Paul let the topic go and responded, "At this rate, it should be less than an hour."

An unbroken line of hardwood trees lined both shorelines for miles. Fate had been kind to this part of the river. The land bordering the upper St. Croix had been purchased by the power company during the first half of the twentieth century, giving them exclusive property rights for hydropower. After hydropower's decline, the power company negotiated land sales and grants to the states of Minnesota and Wisconsin. The states dedicated the land to the park systems that continued to protect the shorelines from development. This allowed the forest to regrow unhindered for a century after logging ended. That unbroken tree line buffered the group from a headwind blowing out of the southwest. It reduced the wind enough to dry the tents without blowing them off from the canoes.

Tom hugged the west bank to completely avoid the headwind. He was paddling hard in the single canoe and starting to distance himself from the rest of the group. The workout was fantastic. He snaked his canoe in the backwaters amongst Seven Islands, a mile below the last rapids. Turtles slipped from bare logs lying in the water when he approached. Herons walked along the islands' shallower sandy points, looking for minnows. Tom admired it all as he paddled past.

The river opened up for a few miles after Seven Islands. There was an increased water flow feeding the St. Croix from the Snake River and another small creek. This pushed sediment down river to another chain of islands where fisherman loved hanging a line in the water as they drifted between sandbars. The paddle was relaxing and scenic.

The shoreline began showing sandstone ledges, so Al pulled out the maps to check their progress. "Hey John, we're coming up on Sandrock Cliffs. Have you ever visited the hiking trails there?"

"Isn't that just north of Highway Seventy near Grantsburg, Wisconsin? You know, I've crossed the St. Croix River dozens of times to go fishing east of Grantsburg but never stopped."

"You should ask Anne if she has ever taken photographs there. I bet she would love hiking that unique area. Over the eons, the river carved its way through the sandstone and left a lot of cliffs. Now it's a state park with hiking trails scattered along the river and wooded area above. It's kind of like the Boom Site near Stillwater, but without the town."

"That wouldn't be a bad second date, if there is one. I hope this camping and canoeing thing works out."

"I don't see why it wouldn't. We've all met and talked with Anne during the wrestling season. We'll have to socialize instead of saying a few words before and after a match. The drawback is we've spent two days on the river and we smell worse than after a match."

"That's what I'm afraid of. She's seeing our wilderness side right away. That's not something entirely appealing."

"Look at it this way, her impression of you can go nowhere but up."

"Come on Al, be serious. I kind of like her."

"Sorry about that. I know we are giving you a hard time about Anne, but you know it's all envy. From what you've told us and what we know about her, you've got it made. She's really smart and she loves the outdoors. I get why she might like you. You've got a sense of humor, and you're a great friend. That's why we like hanging out with you."

"Thanks, Al. None of us are good at the mushy stuff, but I hope you're right. If she sees through the rough surface, there are a few good things underneath."

Al turned and smiled at John, then sarcastically said, "That's another thing I like about you. You're modest."

The ledges grew into one-hundred-foot sandstone cliffs. Trees clung to the soft rock, sinking roots into cracks and crevasses like giant rock climber's fingers clinging to a wall. The guys wondered if the trees ever lost their grip.

When the cliffs abruptly ended, truck noise broke through the sound barrier created by the high rock walls. "Hey, there's the highway bridge," Al said. "Let's stop and flip around the tents." He let out a piercing whistle and signaled for Tom to pull out at the bridge. He was a good half mile in front of the other two canoes and still paddling ferociously. The river had opened up and the wind stiffened against their southward travel. Tom probably needed a short break.

After the three canoes beached at the highway bridge landing, Al tossed Tom a jug of Gatorade and a salty granola bar. Sweat covered his shirtless torso and his red headband was soaked.

"Thanks Al. That's a stiff headwind. If I stopped paddling to drink water, it would have blown me upstream."

Paul chuckled and commented, "I don't think you need to worry about taking a break. You're easily outpacing the two-man canoes."

"That's going to change," Al added. "The river widens below the bridge and flows straight south for about ten miles. It heads straight into the teeth of the wind. You want to trade spots, Tom? You've already had a morning workout."

"Nah, I got this. It's not like there are whitecaps on the river. I'll let you know if I get tired. Can I have another bar and can I keep this Gatorade?"

After exposing the wet tent corners and resecuring them, the group finished a late-morning snack and hopped back onto the river. They still had twenty-six miles to Nevers Dam and it would take them all afternoon.

17

Incident at the Dam

The wind had died down with the coming evening and the waves created by the headwinds were gone. Anne and Sandy took turns tossing the gallon jug into the river's undertow and reeling it back with the long tent cord. Between tosses, they heard the occasional slosh of fast current against the dike's point and the undertow's gurgle where the main channel's flow met the back current. At first the empty jug just bobbed in the water and slid back and forth across the undertow line. After they added a little water to the jug, it would bob a little deeper and pull harder against the line. It was a game to kill time. How much water would it take before the undertow could pull the jug underwater?

Anne was down at the river's edge adding a little water to the jug when Sandy called out, "Hey, a canoe just came around the river bend."

Anne stood and screwed the top back onto the jug. She stepped up the short steep bank, careful not to slip on the loose sediment edge. After gaining her footing on the dike, she turned and shaded her eyes with her hand. She could see gear heaped in the canoe between the two paddlers. After a minute, a second canoe appeared. This one had only one person paddling. "That has to be them. Not many people canoe alone in long canoes like that." She turned her head toward the campsite and cupped her hands. "Mom, they're almost here!"

Anne's mom was poking at the fire pit with a stick when she heard Anne's call. She rose from her fold-up camp chair and grabbed Anne's camera before following the path to the dike. By the time she arrived at the river, the first pair was one hundred yards from the old dam site. "Who is that in the first canoe?" she asked Anne as she handed off the camera.

"That's Bob in the front and Paul steering in the back. I don't think you've ever met them. Tom is in the second canoe by himself." Anne snapped a few photos of the lead pair.

Sandy waved her hand in the air and yelled out to her brother. "Hey Al, how come you're the slow poke?" He and John were a half block back and letting the current carry them downstream.

Al stopped paddling and squinted toward the shoreline. "Sandy? What are you doing here?"

"Anne invited me. Surprise!"

John chuckled and said to Al, "Now we know who she invited to join her."

Al turned and looked at John. "I can't wait to hear the story behind this one."

The three women watched Bob and Paul angle their way across the channel toward the Wisconsin shoreline with Tom a half dozen canoe lengths behind them. The boat landing was nestled around the back side of the dike, and the shortest path to it brought the canoes just in front of them. Anne continued to shoot pictures as the current quickly carried the guys to the dike's tip.

"Careful, there's an undertow right out in front of us," Sandy called as the first canoe swung in close to the dike. Bob and Paul momentarily stopped paddling and stretched their necks out, looking for any signs of rough water. With the evening's dying winds, the water was flat and quietly serene.

When Bob and Paul were straight out in front of the women, the canoe spun in the water. Neither of them expected the sudden jerk that quickly turned their boat toward the shore. As soon as they were perpendicular to the point, their starboard canoe edge was sucked down and water rolled up over the gunwale. Both guys leaned away from the action, but the strong back current pushed against the gear and flipped the canoe. They were caught in the water pushing upstream against the river flow.

Tom recognized what happened. He'd seen it many times in rapids when someone swept sideways in strong current. He dug in his paddle, trying to swing back into the main channel. He didn't want to ram the capsized canoe or hit his two friends, but hoped he could offer some help.

"Somebody help them!" Sandy brought her hands to her mouth as she watched the canoe's bow go under like a sinking steamship. Both guys went underwater when they flipped, but she could see Paul's arm clinging to the canoe as the stern rose out of the water. Bob was nowhere to be seen.

The canoe's gear had a lot of air pockets and they delayed the river's pulling the Alumicraft under. Anne was snapping photos when the canoe flipped. She couldn't believe what had just happened. She saw Paul clinging to the back seat with everything he had, just keeping his head above water. It wouldn't take long before the river won. She dropped the camera and jumped into action.

Anne picked up the water jug and yelled, "Paul! Grab onto this!" She wrapped the tent cord around her wrist, took two steps toward the river, and launched it. The half-full jug thunked against the canoe and skidded beyond with a short hop. "Paul! Grab ahold."

As Paul groped for the cord, Sandy and Anne's mom slid down the bank and grabbed the back of Anne's cargo shorts. Paul found the cord with his right hand and wrapped it around his forearm. In his panic, he forgot to release the canoe from his left hand and it dragged him under as it submerged. Anne slid to the ground and cried out when the cord tightened and strangled her wrist. Sandy and Anne's mom held tight to

Anne's pants and then reached for the cord with their free hands. If they let go of Anne, she would be pulled into the river.

After a few seconds, the cord loosened. All three women pulled hard and Paul's head popped to the surface. Paul exhaled and took a deep breath just before his head went under again. They began reeling cord hand over hand, hoping Paul had the strength to hang on while they pulled him in. Paul's right arm surfaced first. It was stretched out over his head, and each time the women pulled, they could hear Paul gasping for air when his head broke the surface. In just over a minute, they pulled Paul from the water.

"Are you okay, Paul?" Anne's mom asked.

Paul coughed a few times and said, "My arm is killing me. Where's Bob?" All four of them looked out from the shore, hoping to see some sign of Bob. Paul yelled again. "Bob! Where are you?" He scrambled up the dike to gain a better vantage point. "Come on! Help me look. If we spot him, the other guys can help him from the canoes."

The three women followed Paul up the dike, turned, and scanned the water. All four began calling out. "Bob! Bob!"

The other two canoes had circled around the undertow area and were floating a short way downstream. The back current was carrying them upstream toward the dike's point, and they were uncertain where the current would carry Bob. Tom, John, and Al scanned the water in all directions, hoping to catch a first glimpse of their friend. They repeatedly yelled his name, "Bob! Bob!"

On top of the dike, Anne felt helpless because time was ticking for Bob and they needed to find him. "Mom, Sandy and I are taking the canoe out to help look for Bob. Can you call 911 and sit with Paul?" She didn't wait for an answer. "Come on Sandy."

The two of them ran down the trail to the campsite. Within minutes, they pushed off from the boat launch. Paddling their way around the dike's curved shoreline, they spotted the other two canoes. The guys were floating about ten yards apart, scanning the water in all directions.

When Anne felt they were within earshot, she yelled, "Let's split up. We can cover more area and find Bob sooner. Tom, go cover the edge of the wooded area just below the dike. That's where the water comes out of the woods moving upstream." She turned toward the other two. "Al and John, can you cover the main channel? The two of you have a better chance of paddling upstream if you see something. Sandy and I will hang around the dike's tip."

The St. Croix Falls volunteer fire department was located about ten miles south of the old dam. Even though Nevers Dam was at a rural location down small country roads, Paul heard the faint sound of sirens in less than twenty minutes. He sprinted down the trail, past the campsite, and up the drive toward the township road. His lungs burned as he climbed the last one hundred yards up the hill. He leaned over and placed his hands on his knees when he reached the tar road, trying to catch his breath before the trucks arrived. When the EMT vehicle rounded the curve before the entrance road, Paul threw his hands into the air and waved his arms. The EMTs slowed but didn't stop to talk with Paul. They turned and headed straight toward the boat launch. Anne's mom had let them know that this was a water rescue, so Paul saw a team of four divers in the truck and a trailer with three inflatable rescue boats as they passed by.

Paul was just about to walk back to the boat launch when a firetruck rounded the curve. It's red and blue lights reflected off the deepening shadows in the trees. Because the siren was off, Paul could hear the increasing roar of the big diesel engine. Directly behind the firetruck was a red pickup, its lights also flashing. The firetruck turned and bypassed Paul as well. The pickup, however, pulled up a short distance from Paul and stopped. As Paul walked over, he read the emblem on the pickup's door. "*St. Croix Falls Fire Department, Fire Chief.*"

The chief rolled down the passenger window and said, "Get in, son. You can tell me what happened as we drive in."

The three guys, along with Anne and Sandy, had spent the twenty minutes paddling the area below the dam, hoping to find Bob swimming downstream. They had only found the capsized canoe by the time the firemen called them into shore. Anne's mom was standing next to Paul on the gravel access road, a few yards from the water's edge. She had her arm around him, holding the EMT's blanket in place. Paul's face was tight with worry and he still scanned the water as his friends came to shore.

The fire chief met each canoe as they landed at the river access. He helped them pull their canoes out of the way to allow the rescue crews to set up and launch their boats. None of them wanted to abandon their friend, but the fire chief insisted that they let the professionals do their work. Their motorized boats could more quickly cover the channel and area around the dike. They wanted to take advantage of what time was left before the sun set, and the EMT's didn't need the worry of extra people out in the river while they worked.

John and Al were the last to return, pulling the capsized canoe. "Where did you find the canoe?" the chief asked. "Its location may give us a clue how the river current moves past the dike."

"We found it in the middle of the channel, about fifty yards downriver," Al responded. "Do you think Bob is that far away already?"

"We'll send one boat downriver a few hundred yards and have it work back this way. The other two will start here and work south. Why don't all of you go set up camp and start a fire? We'll let you know our progress in a little while."

John and Al just stared at the ground, their paddles hanging loosely from their hands. Tom was leaning on his paddle, hands over the top to cushion where he rested his chin. He too was staring off into space. Paul and the three women stood in a group, not knowing whether they should insist on helping or walk back to the campsite. Shock had set in.

"Go on," the fire chief insisted. "If you hang around here, you'll just get in the way. Let the professionals do their job. I promise to tell you as soon we know something." He turned and walked toward the boats, barking commands as he went. "Let's get these things in the water and find their friend!"

18

Quiet Camp

The group quietly moved about camp, listening to the sound of outboard motors move up and down the river. Paul pulled out the cooking gear and food while Al, Tom, and John worked on setting up two of the tents. A soaking wet third tent lay on the edge of the campsite. John and Al found it earlier while they were searching for Bob. It was floating a short distance from where it was tied onto the half-submerged canoe. Sandy, Anne, and her mom collected wood and stoked the fire.

Few words were said. When they spoke, the words came in short bursts, asking about how to start the fire, what to eat for supper, or how to tie the best knot for the tarp. It wasn't conversation. The words were more like the sharp sound of a book hitting the floor of a quiet library. When someone spoke, everyone turned to look where the sound came from, wondering why the reverent silence was broken.

Finally, Tom couldn't take it anymore and cut into the campsite's heavy atmosphere. "Maybe Bob floated way downriver and made it to shore on the Minnesota side. Wild River State Park is over there, and it would take him a long time to find help."

John had camped at Wild River State Park and knew the place fairly well. "There are some really remote places in the park. Some of the shoreline is more than a mile from any road or campsite. If he floated past the park's boat launch and swam to shore, the current would have carried him more than a mile south of here."

"He's a really good swimmer," Al commented. "He told me how he used to swim in the ocean when he lived in San Diego. The riptide was nothing to mess with and he was caught by it a few times."

Anne jumped into the conversation, trying to add a little hope. "If he could handle the ocean's riptide, he can handle a river like this."

"He'll show up. I'm sure of it," Anne's mom said. "We should call his parents."

"And tell them what?" Al asked. "Bob's lost and EMS is looking for him? We don't even know if he's alive! If he survived the undertow, we should let the firemen find him before we make that call."

Paul slammed the camp plates on the picnic table, and everyone turned toward him when the crashing metal clatter broke into their conversation. Paul just sat down on the bench and rested his face in his hands. "Are you okay, Paul?" Anne asked.

"No, not really." He ran his hands up his face and back through his thick curly hair. "I was caught in that undertow when you were pulling me out of the water. If that paracord broke, it would have pulled me under too. There's no way Bob could fight that river. I'm just afraid he's not coming back."

The group went silent and stared at Paul. He was staring into the fire but not really seeing the flames. His teeth were clenched behind tightened lips, giving him taught cheeks that forced water to his eyes. Everyone had hope, but they all witnessed the river's force pulling the canoe under, and the women remembered how hard they pulled to save Paul. The silence was like a vacuum sucking a stark realization into camp. Bob wasn't alive and the fire crew would bring bad news sometime during the night. The pain of anticipation hit Paul hard.

A loud pop from the fire broke their trance, and everyone but Paul silently went back to what they were doing. He just sat staring into the fire, thinking. *I was inches away from death and I didn't even realize it.*

There was no way to get out of the undertow without help from shore. I wonder if Bob realized what was happening or if he knew and just let go? The river grabbed the canoe and flipped both of us into the water. That was the last time I saw him. I would have never come up if the canoe hadn't upended before it went under. Why am I so lucky and he wasn't?

Sandy glanced over at Paul sitting on the picnic table's bench. His hands were folded with his elbows resting on his knees. There were tears running down his cheeks. Paul sniffed and rubbed his nose. Sandy walked over, picked up a few napkins from the end of the table and then sat down next to Paul. She handed them to him and then put her arm around him.

"Thanks," Paul said, taking the napkins. "I'm sorry about this. You probably had some other vision of what tonight and tomorrow would be like."

"There's nothing to be sorry for, Paul. I'm just glad we're here to help."

"This is my fault. I lost my glasses when Bob saved my life two days ago. I insisted on taking the back seat and never should have. I steered the canoe right over the undertow that flipped us. Now we're all here and Bob is somewhere out there."

Sandy rubbed his back with one hand and reached over to Paul's clasped hands with the other. "There's no one to blame here, Paul. No one could see the undertow from the river. Even if you knew it was there, who would have thought it could flip a canoe?"

"I know you're right, but that doesn't help how I feel. Bob is my closest friend and now there is a huge hole right where he used to be." Paul pulled one hand away from Sandy's grip and tapped his fist against his heart. "That's a tough spot to fill."

When John finished attaching the fly to his tent, he noticed Sandy and Paul talking at the table. His eyes went from the pair at the table to Anne across the fire from them, sitting on a makeshift log bench. She had just brought the camera down from her eye, and he saw firelight reflect off from a tear on her cheek. He walked over and sat down next to her. "It's great to see Sandy sitting and talking with Paul. He needs something different than what his wrestling buddies can offer him right now. How long have you two been friends?"

Anne glanced at John and then over to the pair sitting at the table. "We really haven't done much together since middle school. I should have made more effort to hang out with her."

John smiled at Anne, then looked in the same direction. "Yah, Al talks about his little sister once in a while. Everything he says about her tells me that she really cares about people. She sounds like a good friend to have."

"I'm going to rekindle that old friendship this summer. Delivering pizza and taking photos definitely falls short of finding a good friend like her." John just nodded his head and put his arm around Anne's shoulders.

Tom and Al picked up where Paul had left preparation for supper. They could see how devastated he was by the capsize and knew that pitching in around camp just wasn't in him. They could also see that Sandy was doing a great job comforting Paul and didn't want to upset the good coming from their conversation.

Al set plates around the picnic table, and Tom dumped the macaroni and cheese noodles into the pot of boiling water Paul had set on the fire grate. When the noodles were soft enough, Tom added the cheese mix, bacon bits, and then squeezed a half bottle of margarine into the pot. While he stirred the mixture, Al set out dried fruit and poured lemonade into cups. Sandy and Anne's mom brought over their contribution. After they set two gallon baggies of fresh fruit on the table, Tom called out, "Let's eat!"

Somber silence hung over the meal with only the occasional requests to pass something breaking the silence. The group could hear sporadic radio chirps from the firetruck down near the boat launch.

Everyone strained to hear word about their friend, but the distance muffled the messages beyond recognition.

It was dark by the time they finished their meal and cleaned up. John and Tom grabbed their flashlights and spent the better part of an hour gathering firewood. The temperature was still in the midseventies, and they really didn't need the wood for warmth, but their efforts gave them something to do. Each time they returned with more fuel, Paul would lay a few more branches on the fire. When they finally stopped making trips into the woods, they had gathered enough logs to keep the fire burning well into the morning. Paul finally sat down when the flames reached over six feet high. He had built more of a bonfire than a campfire.

One by one, each of them pulled out their camp chair and chose a place around the fire. The heat kept them from crowding into a tight perimeter so that conversations never really began. They mostly stared at the fire and the glowing faces across from them.

Around eleven p.m., an ambulance and the county sheriff's car turned off from the main road, rolled past the campsite and down to the boat launch. All heads turned to watch their arrival. Paul, Tom, and Al stood and stepped out of the circle. They started toward the boat launch but stopped, facing away from the remaining four still at the fire.

"What's up," John called.

Al glanced back to the fire and said, "The fire chief is walking this way."

The four at the fire got up and joined the other three. They couldn't see the chief's face, but they could all tell the news was not good. The chief's walk was slow, and he was studying the flat ground in front of him as if searching for words to say. During his last few steps, he looked up at the group standing in front of him, pausing slightly and looking each person in the eyes. When he reached Paul, he stopped.

"I'm sorry. We found your friend," was all the chief said.

Paul let out a deafening yell and he fell to his knees. After his voice fell away, a labored exhale continued long after there was nothing left in his lungs. When he finally took a breath, his face was turning from red to purple. His next sound was pure sobbing. After Sandy recovered from the initial shock, she walked over, knelt next to Paul, and wrapped her arms around his shoulders.

The other three guys just stood in silence, staring at the chief. Their jaws hung open and their faces showed no sign of processing what they just heard. They were used to gathering at the mat's edge to greet the individual just finishing their match. The 'high-fives' celebrated victory or the simple pat on the back consoling a loss was the extent of emotion the wrestlers showed. This was completely different. There was nothing in their training that prepared them for what they felt.

Anne and her mom saw the shock in Tom, Al, and John. They walked over to embrace and console them but were met with what seemed to be cold rejection. Tom flung an arm up and walked back to the fire. John walked away toward the woods and stood facing away from the group with his hands on his hips. He just stared at the ground and shook his head. Al didn't move. Even with Anne and her mom standing on each side embracing him, he showed no reaction.

"Why don't all of you gather around the fire?" said the fire chief, breaking the tension. "We need to pack away our gear, and the sheriff will stop up and talk with you." Knowing there was nothing more he could say to the group, the chief turned and walked back toward the river.

Anne broke away from Al and walked over to John. "Let's go back over to the fire, John. The fire chief said the sheriff will come and talk to us. They will probably have questions about what happened."

John reached up and put his arm around Anne. She returned the gesture by wrapping both arms around his waist as they turned toward the campsite. Sandy helped Paul off his knees and walked beside him. She stopped behind his chair as he circled to the fireside and sat down, wiping his eyes after settling in. Al and Anne's mom were right behind Paul and Sandy. They sat down at the picnic table and faced the fire.

Tom had been stomping about the campsite and throwing rocks and sticks off into the woods. Now that the whole group was around the fire, they could hear him mumbling and sighing as he paced about.

"Why don't you come over and join us, Tom?" Anne's mom called to him.

As Tom came into the fire's light, they could see moisture in his red eyes. His face showed more anger than sadness, and he slapped a water bottle off the picnic table as he walked by toward his chair.

"Why did it have to happen?" Tom screamed as he plopped into his chair. "We spent days fighting fast current, downed trees, and rapids, then on one of the quietest parts of the river, this happens."

"I don't know why accidents happen, but getting mad at a water bottle won't help," John responded.

Tom was rocking in his camp chair. "I'm just so frustrated. I need an outlet to take the edge off, but there's nothing to do around here."

Al reached over to the already full wood pile and pulled the hatchet off the ground. He stretched his arm out with the hatchet and forcefully said, "Here Tom, go cut a tree down!"

Tom took him seriously and got up. Even though it was almost midnight, he was determined to vent his anger. As he grabbed the hatchet and began to leave, a loud voice came from the road.

"Hold on. Can we have a few words?" It was the sheriff. He was walking toward the campfire with a deputy at his side. "I know it's late, but we'd really like to go over incident details while they are still fresh in people's minds. Can we join you at the campfire?" Tom stowed his frustration and sat back in his chair.

The sheriff asked about the canoe trip's starting place and how long the five guys were on the river. He almost couldn't believe how quickly the three canoes had traveled the 122 miles. The group described how Bob and Paul steered their canoe close to the dike's tip and how the undertow grabbed it, capsized it, and sucked it under. The details about how the three women had saved Paul impressed the officers. They complimented them on their quick thinking and action. It was almost an hour before the sheriff and his deputy were satisfied with the details everyone provided. When they stood to leave, the sheriff asked, "Would you like a ride back to your vehicle in St. Croix Falls?"

The whole group looked back and forth at each other, not knowing exactly what to do. Then John spoke up, "What do we do with all of our gear? We'd have to risk leaving it and come back when it's light. Besides, I'm beat. There's no way I could drive up to get the truck and trailer."

"It will be light in a couple of hours," Al said. "Why don't we all get some sleep and do it in the morning?"

"I think we need to finish this trip in Bob's memory," Paul said as he stood. "It will help us deal with what just happened."

The five guys had formed solid friendships they knew would continue after graduation. They planned the trip to remember that bond, and now one of them was gone. They needed time to process what happened and they needed to do it together. Tom, Al, and John all spoke up and said, "Yes. I agree."

Then John turned his head to the three women and asked Anne, "I know you came on the trip to take photos and the accident probably changes how you feel about being here, but you're still welcome to finish the trip."

Anne spoke up without hesitation. "I'd like that. Thanks. Sandy?"

Sandy smiled and said, "I wouldn't miss it for the world."

"Alright then, we'll let you turn in," the sheriff said as he closed his notepad. "You'll need some sleep to handle the next couple of days. I'll call Bob's parents. They will probably want to talk with you tomorrow. Try to get back as soon as you can."

Anne's mom could see how a bond developed between everyone because of the accident. The guys were already close, but now Anne and Sandy had shared a life event with the group. Events, good or bad, were often the kindling for lifelong friendships. She knew her presence would change its growth, so she said, "I called my husband earlier— told him what was going on and that I'd come home after everything settled down." She stood and looked at the other two women. "If you're okay, Anne and Sandy, I'll see you tomorrow?"

"Yes Mom. Thanks."

After Anne's mom left, the group's adrenaline levels dropped and exhaustion set in. The crew headed for their tents one by one until only John and Anne were left at the fire. It was after one in the morning, and the sunrise was coming in a few short hours, but John still couldn't sleep. He was sitting close to the dying fire, poking it with a stick, barely hearing the others' tent zippers closing. He could still remember the first day Bob came to school their freshman year. He met him coming out of the vice principal's office with Paul. They sat next to each other in history class and their friendship slowly grew. John really got to know Bob during the winter's wrestling season. Bob wasn't very good that first year, but after Tom and Paul coached him off season, he eventually became one of the best wrestlers on the team. He pictured Bob in his Air Force ROTC uniform. The guys would rib him on the days he had to wear it, but he looked sharp and he took the playful jabs well. There were so many memories that he could almost see Bob's face in the hypnotic orange flames.

John's trance was broken by a voice from across the fire pit. "You already miss your friend, don't you?" Anne was sitting in her camp chair watching John play with the coals. When he looked up, Anne stood, walked over, and sat next to him on the log bench. She put her arm around him and laid her head against his shoulder.

Wow, John thought. *Bob's dying sucks, but Anne really cares how I feel, and Paul wouldn't be here if she hadn't saved him. I'm so glad she's here.* The two of them just sat watching the flames. With Anne's warm body next to him, John could feel his mind relax and tiredness creep in. After about ten minutes, his eyes slid shut and Anne squeezed him a little tighter when he almost fell off the bench. "I should go to bed," John said as he stood.

"Yah, me too."

When Anne stood and faced John, he slipped his arms around her waist. "Thanks for coming." He leaned in and kissed her on the cheek. Their eyes locked when he pulled away slightly, and she wrapped both arms around the back of his neck. John leaned in again and gave Anne a long goodnight kiss on the lips.

Anne looked up at him and smiled. "Good night, John." She let go of him, turned, and went to her tent. John just stood and watched her until the tent zipped shut. The coals shifted in the fire pit and brought him out of his trance. It reminded him to douse the flames before turning in.

19

Remembering

When John poked his head out of his tent the next morning, he saw Paul at the picnic table with a knife, carving something into a thick branch. Tom was stuffing paper scraps into the fire pit and stacking kindling on top for a fire. Behind John in the tent, Al sat up in his sleeping bag and asked, "Is everyone else already up?"

"It looks like Anne and Sandy are still asleep." John felt a little better after a few hours' sleep but couldn't shake a sense of emptiness. "The camp feels different this morning. You know, kind of weird."

Al unzipped his bag and thought for a moment. "I know what you mean. It feels like some of the energy is gone, almost as if the river swallowed it up."

"It kind of did, literally. Today is going to be tough."

John put on his shoes and crawled out of the tent. He walked over to the picnic table, where Tom had placed the food pack after retrieving it from where they hung it the night before. He pulled out a prebreakfast snack and sat down next to Paul. The three-foot branch Paul had in his lap had a 'B' carved into it. He was working on a curved second letter and John realized what he was doing.

"Have you found a post for the memorial yet?"

"Not yet," Paul replied. "I saw this piece of wood while I was gathering firewood and the idea just came to me. I need to find the vertical piece and lash it to this branch."

"Where do you want to put it?"

"I thought we could dig a hole at the end of the dike and face it toward the river."

"I think that's a great idea, Paul." It was Anne. She was just crawling out of her tent with her camera hanging around her neck. "I'm going to take lots of pictures of this camp and you guys on the river today. A photo of you on the dike at a memorial will be a great memory. The pictures will be something you can look back on to remember Bob years from now." She walked over to the picnic table to admire Paul's work and then snapped a few pictures.

"Thanks Anne," Paul said. "We need to have everyone in the photo at the dike. Can you do that?"

"You bet. I brought a tripod, and my camera has a timer. Let's do it after breakfast."

Paul continued to work on his carving while Tom and John made breakfast. Bob was Paul's closest friend, and everybody knew that he was taking his death really hard. Tom, John, and Anne contently left Paul to focus on something that gave meaning to the hole left in his life. While they worked about camp, they occasionally checked in on his carving. They could tell the piece was developing into a beautiful, rugged memorial.

After Al and Sandy climbed out of their tents, they were introduced to Paul's memorial to Bob. By that time, Paul had almost finished the name on the left side of the log.

"You're going to need a post," Al said as he reached down for the camp saw. "Come on, Sandy. These guys have breakfast figured out. Let's hunt for a solid piece of wood."

"Thanks, Al." Paul didn't even look up as Al and his sister left camp.

Tom and John set six plates out on the picnic table. Paul sat on the bench at the end with his back to his breakfast spot. He barely noticed the meal preparation behind him.

Paul had shaved away the bark where he carved the letters. This created a darker textured frame around a hand-hewed white pine detail. On the wrestling team, Paul was known for his inescapable grip. If he grabbed your wrist or arm, you weren't getting away until Paul let go. When he did, he already set you up for his first attack. Now those strong hands patiently worked fine detail into the wood. The lines for Bob's name formed a perfectly beveled 'V,' leaving islands of wood in the center of both the 'O' and 'B's. Small curls of pine lay on the ground between his feet, and Paul leaned in close to the log across his lap to compensate for his poor vision. The date was nearly complete.

Al and Sandy returned from the woods with a six-foot-long red oak branch. They cut both ends flat and notched the branch so that Paul's carved white pine would seat perfectly. They laid it on the ground next to Paul and joined the others at the table for breakfast.

Paul began whittling the ends of the white pine branch. At the table with him, everyone else was eating breakfast. They could hear the *scrape-scrape-tick* of his work while they ate. There was the occasional comment about the memorial's rustic beauty and how the blunt tips added a nice accent.

"Paul, do you want some of the fruit we brought?" Sandy asked as she pushed the bowl of cut watermelon, pineapple, and strawberries toward Paul's plate. Paul continued whittling.

John, sitting beside him at the table, poked his elbow into Paul's side. "Hey, Sandy offered you some fruit."

"Huh, what?" Paul sat up and turned his head around to see Sandy slide the bowl a little closer to him. "I'm sorry, no. I want to finish this. I'll eat later."

After breakfast, Al and Sandy helped Paul lash the branch to the crosspiece with the sturdy rope used to hang the food pack. When they finished tying off the knot, the three of them picked up the cross and grabbed a camp shovel. They headed for the dike while the others took down camp.

Paul stopped at the trail's end and surveyed the narrow dike. The water jug and paracord still lay on the ground where the women had pulled Paul from the river. His eyes followed the bank down to the water and out into the channel. He could see the line where the backflow met the open river's current.

"That must be what caused us to capsize," Paul commented. He pointed and followed the line in the water with his finger.

Sandy stepped up beside Paul and gazed down at the water. "Yes. It really doesn't give you any clue how dangerous the undertow is. Is this where you'd like to dig the hole?"

"Yah, it's perfect."

The three of them took turns digging over the next hour. A camp shovel wasn't exactly the right tool to dig a post hole, especially since the ground was hard and filled with rocks. To help support the cross, they also gathered a pile of large stones to surround the post. They stopped digging and lifted the cross into place when the hole was too deep to lift dirt out of with the camp shovel. When they finished filling in the hole and stacking stones around the post, they sat down on the dike to reflect on their friend's absence.

A warm morning breeze whispered in the pines behind them, almost covering a sound Paul had found calming in the past. "Did you hear that?" Paul cupped his hand over his left ear. "There it is again. On so many of these canoe trips, I've lain awake in my tent and heard the water speaking to me. It's always calmed me, calling me to enjoy the wilderness."

"I hear the gurgle," Al said. "Is that the river speaking to you now?"

"No, this sound is different. It's menacing, almost like it's warning me to respect Mother Nature's power. One day everything is fine. The next day, life's path is bent. Today, our path is bent in a completely different direction. In Bob's case, it ended completely."

Al wanted to tell Paul that the sound was just turbulence where the backflow meets the main river's current, but the sound of footsteps stopped him.

Tom walked up behind them, stopped, and took in the view in front of him. With his hands on his hips, he nodded his head and said, "That looks fantastic, Paul. It's set at the dike's high point with the river and the far shore in the background. It's peaceful. The cross makes this a sacred place for Bob's memory."

Anne and John came up the trail side-by-side, holding hands. They stopped beside Tom and admired the same beautiful scene. Tom stepped away toward the cross and Anne set up the tripod where he had stood. By the time she mounted the camera and started its video mode, the other five were on one knee in a semicircle in front of the memorial. She joined them, bending to one knee next to John.

After a silent moment, Paul lifted his head, and with tears running down his face, he said, "This is for Bob, the new guy, our teammate, and best friend. You were just starting life, graduating from high school, and going off to protect our country. You were the reason we started this trip. It was your first real river adventure with us, and it was a perfect trip until it became your last. Now you've left us on an adventure of your own, someplace where your teammates and friends can't join you. When you get there, wait for us. Remember everything you experience while we are apart. When we meet again we will want to hear the stories. May God rest your soul."

Paul lifted the bottom of his shirt, wiped his eyes, then stood. Without another word, he turned and walked down the trail. Anne went over, stopped the video, and packed her camera. She followed the others down the trail and was the last one to reach the boat launch. When she arrived, Paul was already in the back seat of his canoe with a paddle in his hand. The others were loading the last of the gear that she, John, and Tom had brought to the river's edge.

As Tom went over to push off Paul's canoe and crawl into the front seat, Anne pulled out her camera for one last photo at Nevers Dam. She lifted her camera as Paul and Tom pulled away, towing an empty canoe behind them.

Epilogue

John turned the last page to show Robby the two photographs inside the back cover. The first photo showed a picture of six campers in front of a rugged wooden cross. The other showed two paddlers towing an empty canoe. "That's the story, Robby. What do you think?"

"Bob didn't go to the Air Force because he died on the trip?"

"That's right. We planned to say goodbye to him at the airport when he left for the Air Force Academy that next week, but we never had the chance."

"Is that you and Mom in front of the cross? You look different."

John laughed as he thought about how time had changed him. "Yes, that's Mom and me. She took this his picture before you were born and before she went off to college. In fact, this book helped her get into the school she wanted to attend."

"But you said Bob took the first picture in the book. How did Mom put it in the book?"

"We gave her all of the photos we took while we were on the river. She created another memorial for Bob to help us remember him and remind us why he was such a good friend."

Robby's face looked puzzled. He sat silently for a few seconds and then said, "I still don't understand why you go camping every year."

"You still remember Mom's dog Molly, right?" It was hard bringing up the memory of a pet, but it was the only way John could think how to relate Bob's accident.

Robby turned and looked up at his dad. "Yah, and I miss her."

"When does the memory of her come back to you?"

"When I go into the backyard and see the big bush we planted for her."

"Me too. That's why we planted that dogwood shrub. You see, people get really busy with everything happening in life, and memories hide away until we see something that reminds us about them. The dogwood brings back Molly's memory for you. This trip does the same thing for us with Bob."

"But I'm really sad when I see the bush in the yard. I don't like that." Robby jumped down from John's lap and took a few steps away. He stared at the floor, clenching his fists.

John leaned forward in the chair and rested his elbows on his knees. "I feel the same way when we are on the river, but some good things happen because we take these trips. I see my friends more and you get to know them better every year. That's important, and if you think about it, Mom and I got together because of the first trip. Good things do come from sad events."

Robby turned and smiled at his dad and then said, "I do like the flowers on the bush in the spring. They smell really good."

"John, the others are here. Are you finished packing yet?" It was Anne calling him from outside the house.

John glanced over his shoulder and out the window. Two cars pulled into the driveway and parked behind the old pickup trailer that would carry the canoes. He closed the book and stood up. "Come on, Robby. Help me pack. It'll be good practice for when you're old enough to join us."

Robby's face lit up as he walked to the couch to stuff the sleeping bag into the Duluth pack.

CPSIA information can be obtained
at www.ICGtesting.com
Printed in the USA
BVHW070820130423
662287BV00001B/24